IT WAS A DELICAT

Betsy knew she needed to choose her words with care. But she was tired and terribly disheartened. They could spend hours going around and around on this issue, and nothing would ever change.

"We only have one real problem, Spence," she admitted sadly. "And it seems to me that there's only one solution."

Slowly Spence turned around, his biceps rigid as he waited for her next words.

When he finally met her eyes, Betsy bluntly told him, "You're afraid to marry me unless you're armed with a prenuptial agreement that's as cold and hard as steel. But if you don't have enough faith in me to get married without one—" she swallowed hard before she whispered the awesome truth "—then I don't think I really want to be your wife."

ABOUT THE AUTHOR

By now, Suzanne Ellison needs no introduction to
Superromance readers. This devoted wife and
mother is a regular contributor to the
Superromance line. Fans look to Suzanne for her
emotional and spiritual insight, a trait inherited
from her minister father, perhaps, and her precise
and pleasing prose. (What else can we expect from
a lover of the English language and a former
teacher?) And now readers may look to Suzanne
for humor! Her latest book represents a departure
in that its tone is relatively light. Suzanne reports
that she's had more fun writing this novel than
any of her previous ones—and the results shine
through!

Books by Suzanne Ellison

HARLEQUIN SUPERROMANCE

HARLEQUIN INTRIGUE

Don't miss any of our special offers. Write to us at the
following address for information on our newest releases.

Harlequin Reader Service
901 Fuhrmann Blvd., P.O. Box 1397, Buffalo, NY 14240
Canadian address: P.O. Box 603,
Fort Erie, Ont. L2A 5X3

Suzanne Ellison
FAIR PLAY

Harlequin Books

TORONTO • NEW YORK • LONDON
AMSTERDAM • PARIS • SYDNEY • HAMBURG
STOCKHOLM • ATHENS • TOKYO • MILAN

Published July 1988

First printing May 1988

ISBN 0-373-70315-5

For my sister Betsy,
with one red rose.

to keep a had found that, upon it first seen together.

because I knew he'd loved it now and that

CHAPTER ONE

SQUINTING IN THE uncertain twilight of the Muskingum High School gym, Betsy Hanover pulled the tattered text of *Romeo and Juliet* a little closer to her deep blue eyes, trying to block out the three dozen adults and teenagers who were perched haphazardly on the wooden bleachers before her. Some of them looked bored, but a few looked amused, as though they already knew the punch line to a joke they'd heard Betsy tell before. At the moment they were all staring at her rather expectantly, possibly because she was dressed up as a very sexy Juliet, or perhaps because they found it easier to look at thirty-three-year-old Betsy than at hunched and wrinkled Mrs. MacGillicuddy, the only other person near the microphone. Before the meeting Oma Potter had told Betsy that Mrs. MacGillicuddy, who was built like a bird but armed with a voice like a bull moose, had been teaching English in Muskingum since the dawn of time. After ten minutes under "Mrs. Mac's" stern tutelage, Betsy didn't doubt it.

She still couldn't figure out just how she'd gotten roped into publicly reciting Shakespeare on this cool spring evening in Ohio. Granted, she had foolishly "volunteered" to help with the costumes for the small rural community's "First Annual" Renaissance Faire, partly to keep Oma from harping on it day and night and partly because Betsy dearly loved to sew and had a passion for design. Still, nobody had mentioned playing the role of Juliet this evening, let alone dressing for the part, until Mrs. MacGillicuddy had arrived wringing her hands and wailing about Janet Spencer dawdling at her law firm till all hours when she *knew* nothing would hold the youngsters' attention like star-crossed teenage lovers. Oma, whom Betsy had hired to help her run her new fabric shop, had quickly pointed out that Betsy was Janet's size, more or less, and could slip on the dress and make a surprise entrance. Unfortunately Betsy had been unable to think of a good reason to refuse.

"They're waiting, young woman!" Mrs. MacGillicuddy boomed into the expectant silence of the gym.

Betsy gathered her thoughts and thanked her lucky stars she wasn't painfully shy. " 'Thou know'st the mask of night is on my face,' " she read slowly into the microphone, feeling as though her mouth were full of cotton candy. " 'Else would a maiden blush bepaint my cheek for that which thou hast heard me speak tonight.' "

How appropriate, Betsy thought, groaning inwardly. She was hardly the blushing type, but she suspected that by the time she was done wading through the ancient words of love in front of the crowd of strangers, her cheeks would be flaming. She tried to think positive thoughts. Though her costume had clearly been designed with a flat-chested schoolgirl in mind, Betsy decided she could take comfort from the fact that the Elizabethan-style bodice—what there was of it—could not have been more flattering to a woman of her generous curves. And the full skirt accentuated her graceful movements. Unfortunately the tomato-red velvet was not even remotely flattering to her fair complexion and blond hair. One quick glance in the mirror had told Betsy that the vibrant shade made her look fragile and fatigued, and the harsh gym lights completed the washed-out look, which was the antithesis of the crisp, cheerful image Betsy usually presented.

A group of new arrivals drifted in from the football field, clattering up the bleachers with sufficient noise to require a break in Betsy's recitation. Taking advantage of the diversion, she quietly clicked off the mike. "Mrs. MacGillicuddy," she declared as assertively as courtesy would allow, "I really think that somebody else could do a better job with this. I'm not very familiar with Shakespeare and—"

"Not familiar with Shakespeare?" Mrs. MacGillicuddy repeated incredulously, as though Betsy had just confessed to an ax murder or two. "My dear young woman, if that appalling condition should be an accurate description of your pathetic literary fate—and may the good Lord forbid it—that's all the more reason to rectify your situation at once!" Betsy found herself wincing as the old woman thumped the yellowed pages of her favorite dog-eared textbook. "'Fain would I dwell on form!'" Mrs. MacGillicuddy quoted indignantly, without so much as a glimpse at the words on the page. "'Fain, fain deny what—'"

"What does 'fain' mean?" Betsy asked, certain she'd end up stuttering like a two-year-old if she tried to render the same words theatrically. "And what does it have to do with sewing Elizabethan costumes for the Renaissance Faire?"

She didn't mean to sound rude, but the simple truth was that she was feeling a little used. She was new to the tiny town—new to Ohio, for that matter—and had a fledgling fabric store to get off the ground. Her spare time was worth pure gold. Unfortunately her job left Betsy with little time for her first love—sewing—and only

a worthy cause could justify the hours she'd spend away
from the costumers of Ye Olde Fabric Shoppe. Oma had
told her that the profits from the Faire—assuming there
were any—would be spent to refurbish the city park on
the south end of town, which was sadly in need of new
playground equipment and landscaping.

Betsy didn't think Mrs. MacGillicuddy had volunteered to help train participants in the faire because of her
passion for public parks. It was obvious that the old
biddy was tickled pink to have an excuse to command
people to master Shakespearean English.

Oma Potter had informed Betsy at the outset that Mrs.
MacGillicuddy had single-handedly inculcated a love—or
dread—of Shakespeare in every person who'd grown up
in town. "Every semester we all had to memorize a scene
or a soliloquy from Master Will, and our senior class play
was always one of Shakespeare's. That's why we think we
can handle a Renaissance faire here in Muskingum,"
Oma had informed her proudly. "We may be a small
town, but by golly, we know our Shakespeare."

Because white-haired, spunky Oma was such a sweetie,
not to mention a crackerjack assistant at the shop, Betsy
had merely smiled. At the moment, Oma was sitting in
the bleachers with her pretty redheaded granddaughter,
Laurie, chuckling right along with the rest of them. On
Laurie's left was a gangly, black-haired boy of fifteen or
sixteen. He was surreptitiously holding her hand. On his
other side was a man who bore an amazing resemblance
to the boy, but was probably twice his age. The elder
version looked so appealing that Betsy wanted to hold *his*
hand.

He was a big man, not heavy but solid as a rock. Clad
in faded jeans and a blue plaid shirt, he looked like a pro
linebacker or the driver of a big rig. He was leaning for-

ward, his arms sprawled over his solid knees, and his dark gray eyes were resting intently on Betsy. He didn't look particularly pleased with her appearance or amused by her predicament.

To Betsy's dismay, Mrs. MacGillicuddy clicked the mike back on. "My dear, I do believe you may be missing the forest for the trees," she chided her new "pupil" in front of the audience, somehow giving the impression she was looking down at Betsy, even though Betsy, at five foot nine, was a good six inches taller than the elderly teacher. "The costumes for this faire are merely window dressing, as food, music and the customs of the rich and the poor are merely background details." She sniffed, snatching the book from Betsy's hand. "The true heart of any culture is the *language* of the people. And the best example we have of Elizabethan speech—" she shook the raggedy book at Betsy "—lies in the literature of the greatest playwright in the history of mankind!"

She beat the subject into the ground for several minutes after that, but Betsy shut out the voice long before the old woman pointed a bony finger at the black-haired man in the bleachers. "Geoffrey," she commanded, "you come down here and help out Juliet!" It was obvious she had every expectation of being obeyed, and Betsy would have bet her last dollar that "Geoffrey" had once been one of Mrs. MacGillicuddy's hapless students.

The big man opened his mouth—in protest or surprise—then closed it prudently. He stared at the old woman—and she stared right back—for what must have been a full minute. Finally he sputtered, "Mrs. MacGillicuddy, I'm sorry, but it's just been too long. I don't think I remember."

By the look on her face it was obvious Mrs. Mac-
Gillicuddy thought that Geoffrey, like Betsy, was guilty
of felonious literary taste, but she tried another tack with
him. "Geoffrey Spencer, what did I tell you on the very
first day you walked into my class? What did I say about
every scene I ever asked you to memorize?"

At this point a communal snicker swept through the
audience, and Betsy belatedly realized that this crowd
expected old Mrs. MacGillicuddy to put on exactly this
kind of a show, and they all would have been disappointed if she'd shown the slightest bit of diplomacy or
tact. It was only Betsy, the newcomer, who hadn't realized this was an ongoing joke. Betsy also suspected she
was the only one there who didn't know whether the ab-
sent Janet Spencer was related to Geoffrey or whether
their identical last names were pure coincidence. On the
afternoon that Oma had introduced Betsy to Janet, Betsy
had learned that Janet's husband had died in a wreck
three years earlier, but aside from that personal revela-
tion, most of their brief conversation had centered on the
faire.

"Come on, Spence!" a man in the back shouted.
"Give her the MacGillicuddy Mastery!"

"Yeah, Spence, go for it!"

As the big man smiled, tiny crow's-feet framed his kind
gray eyes, giving Betsy the impression either he was older
than he looked or he'd been through a lot. For some reason, though, the lines didn't make him look worn so
much as mellow and understanding—as though he'd
conquered most of life's trials and had learned to accept
the rest. "Could we all do it together?" he asked, actually winking at his former teacher. Though he spoke
with grave respect, his grin revealed that the roles they

played were part of the game. The time had long since passed when he'd cowered before her.

Mrs. MacGillicuddy looked more stern than ever, but Betsy had the distinct impression she was trying to hold in her laughter. "You have exactly thirty seconds, Geoffrey!" she commanded.

The group hooted. One or two howled. The man they called Spence rose slowly to his feet, looking bigger than life as he stood up in the bleachers. He was grinning now, but he scratched his head like a little boy who was embarrassed. He started once, smothered a chuckle, then tried again, making a great effort to keep a straight face while he galloped artlessly through the ridiculous poem:

The words of Master Will
are the words I'll remember still,
when I'm old and gray and fading away
and eager to drink my fill....

Of life's great poet—
oh, boy, don't I know it—
when I look back, I'll see Mrs. Mac,
and say, "Thank you for making me quote it!"

"Way to go, Dad!" the handsome boy next to him called out, releasing Laurie's hand long enough to applaud.

"Let's hear it for Spence!" a pretty young woman cried.

"Spen-*cer*, Spen-*cer*, Spen-*cer*!" a group of men in one corner began to chant. Somebody else whistled when two girls in the front row jumped up and did an impromptu cheer with imaginary pom-poms: "Give me a *G*, give me an *E*, give me an *O*, *F*, *F*, give me an *R*, give me an *E*, give me a *Y*, *S*, *P*, give me an *E*, give me an *N*, give me a *C*, *E*, *R*. What's that spell? What's that spell? What's that—''

"Let's come to order now," Mrs. MacGillicuddy commanded the group, causing the crowd to burst into giggles again. "I hope you remember your lines in Act II as well as you remember my poetry, Geoffrey. Now come up here and read with—" she glanced at Betsy and finished sternly "—Lady Elizabeth."

"Oooh, Spence, *Lady* Elizabeth!"

"Go for it, Dad!"

"Maybe she'll let you kiss her hand!"

"His name is 'Sir Geoffrey,' if you please," Mrs. MacGillicuddy corrected everyone. By now even *she* was grinning.

"That's tellin' them young whippersnappers, Mrs. Mac!" an elderly man crowed. He was seconded by several similar calls.

Why, they love her! Betsy realized with surprise. They had probably all moaned and groaned about her when they were in school, but it was obvious this old lady had a very special rapport with her ex-students. It made Betsy wish she'd been more cooperative. In the beginning, she had considered Mrs. MacGillicuddy pushy and unreasonable. Now Betsy felt as though she, not the older woman, had been the poor sport.

Geoffrey Spencer clambered over the bleachers and joined Betsy on the gym floor amid the cheerful catcalls and good-natured backslapping. As he moved it was easy to see that he was remarkably graceful for such a big man. His hips were lean and his gait was easy. The closer he got to her, the better he looked, she decided. The brush of curly black hair that sprang forth from the vee front of his blue plaid shirt made Betsy curious about the rest of his broad chest, which was hidden from her view. His grin for the crowd was so casual, so relaxed, that she was surprised to read discomfort in his gray eyes when he reached the foot of the bleachers. Up close, his smile looked less confident, and Betsy realized that his earlier resistance to reciting Shakespeare with her had been genuine.

"Hi. I'm Spence Spencer," he greeted her politely, holding out his hand. It was a big hand, clean but callused, a hand that looked gentle yet firm.

Betsy was about to reach for it, when Mrs. MacGillicuddy's drill sergeant tone stopped her cold. "You are not Spence Spencer!" she informed the man. "You are not even Romeo! You are the knight, 'Sir Geoffrey,' playing this part for the court!"

She turned to the audience, really hitting her stride now. "This is not Muskingum, Ohio! This is Chipping-under-Oakwood in the year of our Lord 1588! We do not talk about what *they* did *then*. We live as *we* do *now*. And by *now*, what year do I mean?"

"Fifteen eighty-eight!" the group called out in unison, as though they'd practiced choral speaking many times before.

"Thank you," Mrs. MacGillicuddy replied sedately. "I'll be preparing a handout to help you memorize some appropriate phrases. In the meantime—" she turned back to Spence "—you were about to introduce yourself to this young lady."

This time he looked at Betsy, really looked at her, and she saw something in his eyes that surprised her. It was an apology. But for what? His old teacher's behavior? That of his friends? Or the way he took her hand—even before Mrs. Mac commanded him—and kissed it as he knelt, in parody of a chivalrous knight?

If the touch of his lips on her hand had any impact on Spence, he concealed it well. But Betsy wasn't sure she managed to hide her own reaction. The instant his fingertips grazed hers she felt a flip-flop in her stomach that had nothing to do with Shakespeare. It was a little scary, considering the circumstances; they had an intent audience, for one thing, and worse yet, a fierce chaperon. And although Betsy wasn't afraid of what the knights of old held sacred—loyalty, honor and selfless love—she hadn't come to Muskingum looking for any of those things. While she didn't really expect to find them in Spence Spencer, the possibility was intriguing, and worth the ghost of a spontaneous smile.

Her smile, however, was not returned. When Spence's gray eyes met Betsy's blue ones, his face darkened with the same frown she'd noticed when he'd first spied her from the bleachers. The sense of "Hey, at least we're in this together" seemed to vanish as he stared at her now. "Lady Elizabeth," he intoned coolly, "I am Sir Geoffrey, of Chipping-under-Oakwood, humbly at your service."

Deciding it was possible that he simply felt Sir Geoffrey would behave in a grave and distant fashion, Betsy mimicked his stiff demeanor. "I am Lady Elizabeth," she answered in what she hoped was a haughty royal tone. "My father owns this castle and all three hundred leagues of this noble kingdom. Only with his permission will I deign to signal the guards to lower the drawbridge so that you can cross the moat."

The crowd whooped its approbation; Spence's eyes widened with respect. Mrs. MacGillicuddy took advantage of the slightly more serious tone of their exchange to amplify her earlier assertion that it was vital for Renaissance faire participants to speak, act, think and *feel* like sixteenth century English citizens of Chipping-under-Oakwood. Since Shakespeare's characters were already cast in this mold, aping their language and their ways would be a crucial part of the group's training. The crowd remained quiet during the five minute speech, but the minute she placed *Romeo and Juliet* back in Betsy's hands, the catcalls started up again.

"'Dost thou love me?'" Mrs. MacGillicuddy prompted when Betsy was slow to pick up where she left off.

"Answer that one, Spence!" somebody hollered.

"Does this mean we'll have to give up batching it, Dad?" the dark-haired boy next to Laurie called out.

Spence turned to give the boy a mock glare but ended up breaking into laughter. So did his son. Betsy couldn't help but be warmed by the obvious camaraderie between the two of them. But when she took her cue and repeated, "'Dost thou love me?'" the joy in Spence's eyes faded again. Betsy had a long part to stumble through before Romeo had to answer, and to her surprise, Spence came in at the right time with a remarkably close paraphrase of his single line, which proclaimed his undying love for her.

"'I have no joy of this contract tonight'" was Betsy's all-too-honest reply. "'It is too rash, too unadvis'd, too sudden.'"

"That's telling him, Lady E!" somebody called out.

"You're not gonna score tonight, Spence!"

Without looking at Betsy, Spence chuckled again, playing along with the crowd. Betsy liked the sound of his laughter—rich and hearty, like the feel of sunbeams on a long, lazy afternoon on the beach. But his smiles did not seem to include her, and he did not meet her eyes when she quoted, "'This bud of love, by summer's ripening breath, may prove a beauteous flower when next we meet.' ''

"Summer's just around the corner, Spence!"

"Pick that flower when it blooms!"

This time when his eyes met hers, she read the same note of apology she'd imagined once before. What was going on behind those thick black lashes? Why was he all smiles for his friends and so prudently discreet with her? Why did he heave a slight sigh of relief when Mrs. MacGillicuddy said, "You may join the court for a moment while I address the throne, Sir Geoffrey. Do find a seat for your lady."

By now Betsy was immune to the crowd's response. With dignity she allowed Spence to lead her to the nearest wooden bleacher. He held her hand high in the air, his palm up, hers down on top of it, and once again she felt a tremor pass through her fingertips as she warmed to his touch. It was moist where their palms were joined, but Betsy couldn't tell whether it was her hand or his that was sweating. Either way, she told herself, the wetness was due only to the mugginess of the gym on the warm spring night, and the fact that neither one of them was accustomed to being onstage.

"Now as you can see," Mrs. MacGillicuddy told the assembled group as Spence and Betsy sat down, "this Renaissance faire is going to be a great deal of fun. Every person who is involved—whether he or she plays the part of a noble, a tradesperson or a peasant—must master the type of speech and behavior that is appropriate. Miss Betsy Hanover here—" she actually winked at Betsy "—has only lived in Muskingum for a short time, but she has graciously consented to serve on our core faire committee and take charge of all costuming for the faire. She is an expert in this field, and I, of course, have some small

knowledge of the language of the period—" she stopped
as the crowd erupted into appreciative guffaws "—so we
can cross off two crucial areas of concern."

Betsy stared at the woman, mouth gaping, as she realized how her offer to "help with the sewing" had been
portrayed. Had Oma overstated Betsy's willingness to
help out? Or had Mrs. MacGillicuddy taken it upon herself to enlarge Betsy's role? She felt herself whiten as she
contemplated the long hours that were bound to be involved. For several moments she didn't hear anything else
the woman said.

"Betsy," a calm voice beside her whispered, "don't
panic. She won't make you do it by yourself."

Betsy turned, startled, to look into Spence's eyes. They
were kind eyes, compassionate eyes, that looked too old
for his handsome, rugged face.

"People in this town are eager to help, but afraid to
take charge. By putting your name at the top of the list
Mrs. Mac has just guaranteed that everybody else will be
eager to sign up. As long as you pretend to know something, you can delegate all the work."

Betsy appreciated his effort to soothe her, but she still
felt uncomfortable as she spelled out the truth. "I know
nothing about Renaissance costumes," she confessed. "I
know fabrics and design, and how to sew. That's the only
reason I let Oma rope me into this."

He grinned, a wide-eyed, friendly grin. She noticed
that his mouth was a shade too wide, but for that reason, it was all the more beguiling. "Lady, you need help
with more than sewing if you haven't learned your way
around Oma yet. She'd give you the shirt off your back,
but she'll also turn your life upside down when you're not
looking."

Betsy would have defended her friend if she'd felt that Oma was under attack, but it was obvious that Spence was fond of the older lady... and had pegged her perfectly. "What do you suggest?" she asked, delighted that he seemed to be loosening up with her. "All I did was agree to help out, and by the time she was done I had *chairperson* written next to my name."

Spence grinned, and this time the grin was just for Betsy. "Next time don't agree to anything. Whatever it is, just say no."

That was the motto of most of the people in the gym that night, Betsy soon realized. Mrs. MacGillicuddy explained in detail that volunteers would be needed for planning parades, acting out skits, selling "Renaissance" food and running activity booths. She also added that it was the unfortunate custom to include medieval activities at these faires, so they would have to put together a first-class jousting arena. Spence and another man offered to build sets for the booths, and Mrs. MacGillicuddy promptly made both of them committee chairs. Spence was put in charge of the omnibus Booths committee, and the other man was told he'd head up the jousting arena crew.

"You ought to practice what you preach," Betsy whispered.

He grinned, then confessed, "There's a method to my madness. My sister-in-law, Janet, is going to be up to her eyeballs in this faire, which means that sooner or later I'll have to help. By getting in on the ground floor, I come out looking like the best thing since popcorn. And best of all, by volunteering for something mundane I can't get drafted into doing something worse later on."

"You're a very clever man," Betsy observed with just the right hint of cynicism, making note of the fact that Janet's husband must have been his brother.

He shook his head. "Actually, I'm a very slow learner when it comes to people. I've just got the edge because I've lived here all my life."

After that Betsy found it easy to talk to Spence. Hunching forward casually, he imparted tidbits about various people in the town as they volunteered or were volunteered by their friends. Despite her quiet awareness of his straightforward virility, Betsy soon felt remarkably comfortable with Spence, and was grateful, in hindsight, to Mrs. MacGillicuddy for putting her on display. Despite her initial embarrassment, playing Juliet had been fun, and meeting Spence had been . . . well, intriguing.

"I know that many of you have gone to the Renaissance faire in Pittsburgh," Mrs. MacGillicuddy declared, switching gears as the volunteering came to an untimely end. "My Uncle Fred used to teach history with the gentleman in charge of the faire there, and he tells me that Paul Hardison was already sixty-nine years old when he founded it twenty years ago, and he still participates as Master of the Guild. We are deeply honored by his offer to let two of our people, Janet and Betsy, attend the regular Tuesday night meeting of his faire group next week. They'll get a chance to view his nationally acclaimed collection of Renaissance and medieval artifacts, coins and costumes, and hopefully will come back with some pointers about our own training program and faire preparations."

The group remained courteous during Mrs. MacGillicuddy's extended lecture on the fascinating activities at the Pittsburgh faire. Volunteers included jewelers, blacksmiths, horseback riders, and even a fencing instructor who conducted mock duels. An hour later the venerable teacher concluded, "I'm sure there will be a job for everyone."

"The question," Spence whispered to Betsy, "is whether there will be a person for every job."

"What happens if there isn't?" Betsy asked him. To her surprise, her interest in the faire had grown a great deal this evening. Once Mrs. MacGillicuddy warmed up to her subject, she really did have a way with words.

Spence shrugged. "I suspect that the same few loyal subjects will end up carrying the load for everybody else. It always seems to work out that way."

"But Spence, this is a huge undertaking for such a tiny town. It's probably not a good idea to go ahead with it if only a handful of people are interested."

He glanced at Betsy, then at Mrs. MacGillicuddy, then back at Betsy again. His gray eyes were sober. "I know that, and you know that. But who's going to tell Mrs. Mac?"

They shared a smile, and Betsy had the most delicious sensation of finding a new friend. Side by side on the bleachers, they'd departed from their theatrical roles. Spence didn't even seem to remember she was in costume. Despite the low neckline, he'd studiously kept his eyes off her cleavage. Was he inherently courteous, she wondered, or hadn't he noticed her attractive shape?

Before she could ponder the question, Mrs. MacGillicuddy suddenly turned back to the two actors. "Sir Geoffrey, will you please bring your lady forward once again?" She made "again" rhyme with "rain" in a tone that made it clear she would brook no opposition. Despite the lateness of the hour, the crowd carried out its assumed obligation of teasing Spence as soon as he stood up, gave Betsy a courtly bow and offered her his hand.

When she smiled up at him, Spence met her eyes with the same reserved, noncommittal expression he'd worn when she'd first noticed him sitting up in the bleachers. He'd been so friendly for the past hour, so casual and at ease! Was it just this dramatic recitation that made him so uncomfortable? Was it something about her he didn't like? Or was it something else that had nothing to do with the faire or the crowd or the new owner of Ye Olde Fabric Shoppe?

They started up again, on command, tripping over "thees" and "thous" and "dosts." The crowd loved it, but Spence did not. Most of the time he didn't really look at Betsy, and when he did, his expression was tense and dour. It was hard for Betsy to continue to play the love-struck young girl opposite such an unwilling partner, but she did her best, all the time wondering why it was so easy for Spence to be friendly when he sat beside her, out of the limelight, and so hard for him to act passionate in front of the crowd.

Maybe he's just shy, she tried to console herself. *Maybe this harassment bothers him more than he's willing to admit.*

But his tone was urgent, not bashful, when he finally said to Betsy, "'O, wilt though leave me so unsatisfied?'"

For a moment she went absolutely blank, because his eyes, so distant just moments before, suddenly met hers with an aching confusion that made no sense at all. The only thing she was sure of was that Romeo wasn't the only man who would leave the gym tonight aching for something more from the lady decked out in the vermillion velvet dress.

Spence Spencer wanted something from her, also.

CHAPTER TWO

JUST MINUTES AFTER the meeting broke up, Spence hopped into his truck and slammed the side door emblazoned with the words Black Gold Supply. Randy still lagged several yards behind him. It hadn't been easy dragging his smitten son away from Laurie, but Spence had wanted to pull out of the parking lot before every matchmaking busybody in Muskingum had time to descend upon him.

"*Please*, Dad, can't I drive?" Randy begged beside the open window. He'd had his learner's permit for a month now and could hardly endure another moment of his young life as a lowly passenger.

"Not at night," Spence reminded him, wondering how many dozens of times he'd end up repeating those words before Randy turned sixteen in the fall. "Tomorrrow's Saturday. If you help me deliver some things in the morning, we can work on your driving later in the day."

Randy beamed. "I'm spending most of the day with Laurie, but I'll try to work it in."

"That's big of you. Want to fill your old man in on your plans?"

Randy, who knew perfectly well he had to clear everything with his father, hopped in the truck and promptly gave a rundown of his Saturday schedule, which consisted mainly of meeting Laurie at various places before and after his three-thirty baseball game. The only surprise was his announcement that he was taking Laurie to a movie on Saturday night.

Ever since Spence had gained custody of Randy, the two of them had gone downtown to see a movie on Saturday unless there was a football game at Muskingum High. It was a ritual that had special value for father and son because it was the one time of the week they reserved exclusively for each other. On these nights they tried to make up for all the Saturday nights they'd had to spend apart.

"You're going to see *American Graffiti* with Laurie?" Spence asked in some surprise. Since the film depicted the era during which Spence had been Randy's age, he'd really been looking forward to seeing it with his son. "Can't you take her some other night after you go with me?"

Randy shook his head emphatically. "No way. I'm having dinner at Laurie's house, and then we're going to the theater with her sister and Bob Henry."

Spence knew it was time for Randy to spread his wings, and he liked the idea of the two kids doubling with Iris Potter, a levelheaded twenty-two-year-old, and her solid-as-a-rock fiancé. Still, it felt odd to be abandoned on Saturday night, and odder still to be told, "Dad, I'll go back and see the movie with you some other night if you want, but you can't show up there on Saturday!"

"Why not?"

"Remember what happened the day we ran into you when I was buying Laurie a chocolate shake? I've never been more humiliated in my life!"

Spence vaguely recalled the incident, after which Randy had told him that his comment to Laurie—something "dorky" about how pretty she looked now that her braces were off—was the sort of thing a man said to a child, not a *woman* of fifteen! "Look, pal, I did okay at the meeting, didn't I? Did I say anything to embarrass you tonight?"

"Well, no," Randy conceded. "But that was different."

Mystified, Spence said, "Give me a hint."

Randy shook himself like a sheepdog escaping from a bath. "Tonight wasn't a *date*, Dad. There were a lot of other parents around. If you show up at the theater, it'll look like you don't trust us!"

"It'll look like I want to see the movie," he countered, surprised that such a thought would cross Randy's mind. *My little boy is growing up,* he realized with a jolt, turning back his mental clock to the things he'd done at fifteen that he wouldn't have wanted his father to watch. The memory made him a little uneasy, but he'd never done anything in his teen years to seriously betray his father's trust in him—unless he counted marrying Tiffany Atkinson—and he didn't think Randy would, either.

"Okay," he relented. "You can go with me on Monday."

"Uh, how about Tuesday?" Randy suggested, having the grace to appear embarrassed.

This time Spence quelled his son with a look of fatherly impatience. "I don't like you out so much on weeknights, Randy. Whatever you and Laurie have cooked up can wait until—"

"It's not a date, Dad. It's for school."

"School?" He raised one eyebrow skeptically.

Randy blushed. "It was Mrs. Mac's idea. She wants to start a poetry club. We'll start with Shakespeare's sonnets and—"

"Poetry?" Spence guffawed, knowing that Randy had even less interest in literature than he had in cleaning up his room. "You've taken an interest in sixteenth century poetry?"

This time his son turned crimson. "Well, not exactly, Dad. I mean, Laurie says—"

"I get the picture," Spence cut him off. "I just hope that Laurie's extracurricular interests remain so noble. What are you going to do if she decides to start running guns for some commando unit in Central America or parading down the streets of Washington, D.C., in some political protest?"

"Dad!" Randy was shocked. "Laurie would never do anything like that. She's so sweet and nice and quiet and..." He went on cataloging his girlfriend's virtues for several saccharine paragraphs, but Spence stopped listening as he turned on the engine.

"So what am I supposed to do while you're at this poetry club on Monday night?" he asked when Randy had finished his romantic recitation. "It's too far to drive home and back for just a couple of hours." They lived on the family farm, fifteen miles from town, and trips to and from Muskingum were still planned as carefully as Spence's grandfather had planned the trip in the buckboard wagon. His Uncle Clay, who owned most of the land and still farmed it, rarely went into town at all if he could help it.

"You can drop me off, go to the movie and pick me up by eleven," Randy suggested, remembering his weeknight curfew. "That'll give me some time to walk Laurie over to Charley's Café for an ice-cream float."

"And what am I supposed to do between the time the movie ends and the time I'm supposed to pick you up?"

Spence asked. "Can I join you and Laurie for an ice-cream float?"

"Dad, you wouldn't!" Randy flushed again, and this time Spence took pity on him.

"All right. I'll go visit somebody," he promised, then headed for the street. "But just this week. After that, we'll have to arrange some regular transportation for you with somebody else who'll be going to this poetry gig."

He reached the stop sign just as a red Datsun 280ZX pulled around the corner, stopping opposite him—so close that he and the driver were almost face-to-face.

"You're not leaving already, are you, Spence?" the pretty brunette called out to him. "I didn't think I was that late."

"Janet, you are not only late, you're exceedingly lucky," he teased his sister-in-law. "We drew the short straw tonight."

"Oh, no! Mrs. Mac didn't warn me."

"She never warns anybody. If I'd known my number was coming up this evening, I would have stayed home."

Janet laughed. "Which scene?"

"Act II from *Romeo and Juliet*," he replied with a groan.

"Ah, I'm sorry I missed that! I still remember how grand you looked in those purple tights when you played Romeo in high school! It's a wonder I didn't fall in love with you there and then."

Randy's eyes widened. "You mean you were in love with Dad before you married Uncle Bill?"

"I was never in love with anybody but your Uncle Bill, honey," Janet softly informed her nephew. "But when I moved to town he was only thirteen. He had buckteeth and horn-rimmed glasses and pimples all over his face.

Your dad was three years older, you know, and he'd out-grown all that by the time he played Romeo."

"I spent most of my senior year playing football," Spence reminded Janet quickly, uncomfortable with the memory of the purple tights Mrs. Mac had commanded him to wear onstage. He'd forgotten them until now. What he remembered more acutely was that tomato-red dress with the neckline that almost wasn't—at least, it seemed that way on Betsy Hanover, who had the most exquisitely shaped breasts he'd ever seen. His last Juliet had sported small, selfish breasts that had teased and tantalized him for years, as the girl herself had. There was a time when he would have sold his soul for the privilege of slipping his hands under Tiffany Atkinson's blouse. In the long run, he mused uneasily, that was exactly what he'd done.

"You should have seen Dad tonight, Aunt Janet!" Randy exclaimed, his excited voice wavering between the high pitch of youth and the unaccustomed tones of manhood. "He got all moony eyed and even kissed Juliet's hand! It was great!"

Spence tried to look stern but failed. "Remember who pays your allowance, kid," he reminded his son.

Janet laughed. "I'm really sorry I missed it. Who'd she draft to fill in for me?"

"She suckered that new gal in town into playing the part." He sought to conceal the intensity of his reaction to his leading lady with a casual tone. After all, he didn't even know the woman, and didn't plan to get acquainted, even though he knew his resentment toward her was unjustified and unfair. It had far more to do with Tiffany Atkinson and Mrs. Mac's blatant attempt at matchmaking than it had to do with her.

"You mean Betsy Hanover?" Janet asked.

"'Lady Elizabeth,'" Randy corrected, grinning ear to ear. "She was wearing that old red Juliet dress Sally McCormack wore when she played the part last May. The one that comes to about here." He slapped one hand on his chest just a few inches above his belt. "But Sally's flat as a pancake, and this new—"

He stopped as his father squeezed his arm. Spence had taught his son that there were certain things a man did not say about a lady, and he was about to cross the line.

"Miss Hanover looked just fine in the Juliet dress, Aunt Janet, though not quite as pretty as you probably do," Randy corrected himself quickly.

Janet chuckled. "We're not in competition, Randy. I've met Betsy Hanover and I think she's very nice. Single, too. I asked."

Spence rolled his eyes. "Come on, Janet. I thought I could count on you." Janet was one of the few people in Muskingum who didn't consider it her God-given duty to find Spence a wife, and one of the few who hadn't contributed to the gross misunderstanding he'd had with the last hapless female who'd come to town. Poor Carole Elliot had been an inexperienced gal who'd taken Muskingum's communal matchmaking seriously. When Spence had failed to show any overt romantic interest in her, she'd convinced herself that he was just shy, and by the time he'd realized she had misinterpreted his casual friendliness, she'd learned to care for him so much that she'd been badly hurt. The memory still made Spence angry. He'd been damaged too much by unrequited love himself ever to want another human being to be subjected to the same sort of misery.

"I'm sorry, Spence. I'm not pushing. I just . . . well, I like Betsy. And I think if you'd ignore the town and her, well, familiar appearance, you might find you have a lot in common."

"Sounds to me like she's pushing, Dad," Randy chirped helpfully. "What's it sound like to you?"

Spence studied his son, who was glowing with the vigor of youth and the hopefulness of first love. It was hard sometimes to smother his cynicism around Randy, but he did his best. He believed that everybody had the right to enjoy the delirium of teenage passion at least once before he fell flat on his face. He just hoped he'd be able to cushion Randy's inevitable fall.

"It sounds like we need to go home." He reached out through the open window to squeeze Janet's hand, as he often did when they parted. Then he asked, "You don't need anything, do you, honey?"

She shook her head. "I'm fine. You know I'd tell you if I did."

He nodded, satisfied. He knew there were times when his brother's death still haunted Janet, crippled her with grief. On those occasions she'd call Spence, and he'd lock the door to his precarious business for as long as it took— sometimes an hour, sometimes a day—until she'd released the latest batch of stored-up tears. Unless Randy needed him, he never took time off work for anything else.

As he released her hand, Janet said, "Come to think of it, Spence, there is something I need."

"Name it."

She grinned so delightedly that he knew he'd been had. "The faire committee is desperately in need of activity booths. We've made a list of ideas and local people with various talents, and—"

"And I've already volunteered to help build booths," Spence declared smugly, proud of his clever foresight.

"Randy and I will donate a weekend or two near the end. Won't we, Squire Randall?"

Randy grimaced. "Aw, Dad, I don't have time for—"

"Laurie will be there," Janet reminded him. "She can watch you swinging a hammer, all bare chested and sweaty. No woman can resist a man whose muscles are rippling with hard work."

Somehow Janet managed to keep a straight face, but Spence could not stifle a hoot of laughter.

"Dad!" Randy protested indignantly. "You promised not to laugh at me!"

Spence couldn't deny he'd vowed to cease reminding his son of the ephemeral quality of teenage love, but he couldn't recall swearing to take Janet's teasing seriously. "I'm not laughing at you. I'm laughing at her," he assured his son.

"Scout's honor?"

Spence held up the appropriate three fingers, then turned back to his sister-in-law. "Just give us the date, honey."

"Will do." Then Janet licked her lips and leaned out the window so that she was a little closer to the truck. "Uh, actually, Spence, I, uh, had something special in mind for you."

His eyes narrowed. He knew he was about to fall into some sort of female trap. "Yes?"

She looked slightly embarrassed. "We were thinking of a fencing booth like the one they run in Pittsburgh. The visitors could have a minilesson and then challenge the—"

"Oh, no! Get that idea right out of your head!"

"Dad, come on!" Randy crowed. "It sounds great!"

"Janet, I haven't picked up a foil in fifteen years, and I have no desire to."

"But Spence, you were so proud of yourself when you got an A in that fencing class you took in college!"

"I wasn't proud, Janet. I was relieved!" he corrected her.

Janet grinned beguilingly. "You were proud of that grade, Spence. I remember. You can't deny it."

"I can and I will," he insisted. "I felt stupid every time I put on a face mask. And if I did it for the Renaissance faire, you'd probably make me wear one of those ridiculous velvet-and-satin getups with puffy shoulders and those damn purple tights!"

"You told me I should be proud to wear one of those outfits, Dad!" Randy cried out indignantly. "You said I would be a living model of history!"

He sneaked a quick glance at Randy to make sure he was just feigning outrage and wasn't genuinely hurt. After all, Randy's sole motivation for participating in the faire was that he wanted to spend time with Laurie, and she was excited about the whole event. Certain that their till-death-do-us-part affair, now in its second or third week, would fold long before the faire got off the ground, Spence didn't expect Randy to keep coming to the training sessions for the next six months, but he'd encouraged his son's interest in the event, anyway, just because he figured that a few lessons on living history were more valuable than none.

"Randy, I've got a business to run. I don't have time to saddle up my white charger and defend a lady with a sword and shield." He turned back to Janet. "Besides," he admitted a trifle sadly, "I think my armor's rusted over."

"Nonsense," Janet insisted. "It just needs a little polishing."

He was certain she wasn't talking about fencing anymore, but he was even less willing to converse about marriage. He'd been single for twelve years now, and had only had custody of Randy for the past seven. The years before that were a nightmare he didn't want to remember... a nightmare he never intended to repeat.

He didn't care how pretty Betsy Hanover was; he didn't dare care how confused she'd been by the brusque way he'd treated her. When they'd been sitting side by side in the bleachers, he'd almost managed to forget her appearance. But whenever he'd really looked at her, it was somebody else he'd seen. With that heart-shaped face, blue eyes and blond hair, Betsy looked appallingly similar to Tiffany—sweet, helpless and inescapably feminine—which was reason enough to run right there.

At one time Spence had sworn he'd never remarry, and he'd avoided dating for years. But time had mellowed the wound enough that he was willing to admit by now that eventually he might take an interest in a woman again. But if he did—and he was in no hurry—he'd reach out for a sturdy, practical woman with common sense and financial acumen. She could be a partner to him as the business grew, a friend to share quiet suppers and walks in the country with as his son reached manhood and took flight from the family aerie. She would *not* be a delicate princess like "Lady Elizabeth" Hanover, and she would not be a woman who filled him with restless need on first sight.

"Janet, I'll try to spare the time to help you build some sets, but seriously, the fencing gig is out."

"Okay." She looked disappointed, but she did not push him. Her glance shifted to Randy's face as she said, "I'll try to make it to the game tomorrow."

"You'd better, Aunt Janet," Randy insisted, grinning. "I'm pitching, you know."

After they'd all exchanged good-nights, Spence leisurely turned the truck toward home. Beside him, Randy was humming a love song from one of his father's twenty-year-old albums, reminding Spence of how passionately he'd once believed that true love conquered all.

"Dad, when Aunt Janet said not to let Lady Elizabeth's appearance bother you, what did she mean? I was just kidding about that costume, you know. I like the way that lady's built, but there's nothing indecent about a little bit of cleavage."

Spence couldn't stifle a grin. Up close he'd seen a lot of cleavage, not a little, and he'd bet his last dollar that Betsy Hanover was not accustomed to revealing so much of herself in public. She struck him as—well, not shy, but certainly not aggressive. Just...reserved. Self-contained. Content with her life, whatever it might be. For some reason that realization made him jealous. He hadn't been particularly dissatisfied with his current situation until he'd gazed at Betsy, felt the softness of her skin when he'd kissed her hand.

"I thought she looked great," he admitted to his son, trying to convince himself his reaction to the pretty woman had been natural. Of course, her delicate coloring and fragile features had been overwhelmed by the vibrant color of the dress, but that had done little to detract from her beauty. "In fact, I must have seen a dozen women in that dress over the years, and I've never seen one who looked better in it." *Not even Tiffany,* he might have added.

"So?" Randy pressed. "Why did you and Aunt Janet talk about Betsy's looks as though she were ugly or scarred or something?"

This time Spence took a good look at his son, and he knew what Randy was really asking. *Why do you still resent any woman who looks like my mother? Will you ever stop hating her?*

He pulled into the gravel driveway of the old Spencer farmhouse, but did not get out of the truck right away. "Randy," he said softly, "I try not to run down your mom in front of you. And I do a pretty good job of it, don't I?"

Randy shrugged. "Most of the time."

Spence winced, wishing he'd done a better job of acting. "Your mother is a very attractive woman, Randy. She was even prettier as a girl. The only reason I let Mrs. MacGillicuddy talk me into playing Romeo when I was a senior was that she'd chosen Tiffany as Juliet. We'd been going together about six months by then, and we practiced every word of that play like two besotted fools. What a great excuse to whisper sweet nothings into each other's ear! We rehearsed on top of picnic tables at the park, on the hood of my old Chevy, on the roof of her dad's store. It was a blissfully happy time." His grim expression was anything but blissful. "Looking at Betsy Hanover in that red dress and mouthing all those silly, meaningless lines brought it all back to me. I don't *like* thinking about your mother. Even the good times remind me of the bad." He didn't need to specify the bad times for his son; poor Randy had lived through most of them. Tiffany had nearly destroyed Spence's peace of mind and had almost cost him the family business as he'd doggedly spared no expense in his struggle to bring his beloved son home after the divorce. Despite Tiffany's inept parenting, the courts had awarded her custody of Randy for years. Even now, each contact Spence had with Tiffany, though mercifully brief, was still a thorn in his side.

Fortunately he'd developed an ironclad immunity to Tiffany's wiles, but Betsy Hanover's sweet face, framed by that romantic velvet dress, reminded him of how vulnerable he'd once been and could be again if he were ever to be foolish enough to let another woman steal his heart. It was a possibility he'd vowed to guard against, and he itched with the uneasy feeling that he ought to start building a stone-wall fortress tonight.

"Look, Randy, all I'm saying is that no man likes to dwell on his mistakes," he blurted out truthfully. "And just thinking about your mother reminds me of what an idiot I used to be."

Suddenly Randy's sunny smile vanished, and he looked lost and frightened in the dark. Like a little child he mumbled, "I didn't realize you thought of me as a mistake."

Spence lifted his son's chin with a gentle, manly fist, remembering that even though Randy knew how much his father loved him, he was still at an awkward, vulnerable age. "Son," he told the boy he'd give his life for, "in spite of everything, you know I'd do it all again."

Randy took a quick look around the yard to make sure no one could see him, before he slid across the seat to give his dad a quick, embarrassed hug. "I know you would, Dad," he whispered.

In the old days they'd often shared such moments, but now that adolescent interests tugged Randy out into the world more and more—as Spence knew they should—it was rare that Randy dared to reveal his feelings so openly. Spence held the boy tightly, savoring the rare moment, but Randy was quick to pull away.

"There's a doubleheader on TV tonight," he told his dad, grinning once more. "If we hurry, we might catch the end of the second game."

Spence had two hours of paperwork to finish by morning, but he took an hour to make some popcorn and cheer on the Reds with Randy. By the time the game was over, he could barely remember Lady Elizabeth's real name.

Betsy Something-or-other, wasn't it?

WHEN OMA POTTER arrived at the shop the next morning, Betsy was happily perusing a library book on Elizabethan costuming. On the opening pages were drawings of three ornate dresses—one black, one red, and one deep blue velvet gown with a straight, square neckline shrouded by lace. The sleeves were generous and the skirt was full and billowing.

"Well, what do you think?" Oma asked. She was wearing a pair of trim white pants and a matching boat-necked cotton top, both of which looked very smart on her petite frame.

"That one." Betsy pointed to the blue gown. "Although I don't know how on earth we're going to be able to afford velvet for very many costumes."

Oma gave her an exasperated grin. "I wasn't talking about the dress, dear, though it will look positively sensational on you." She closed the book meaningfully. "What do you think of Spence?"

Betsy looked her right in the eye and said truthfully, "I think he's a good sport."

Oma frowned. "That's all?"

"Isn't that enough?" Belatedly remembering that Oma's granddaughter was dating Randy, Betsy added, "I like his son. My brothers didn't have much use for my parents when they were that age. It's kind of nice to see a father and son so close."

The diversion worked for a moment. "Yes, Randy's a jewel, and in a few years, I don't think he'd be a bad match for Laurie. I just hope they don't get too serious at this age, though. When I was a girl, getting married was the thing to do by the time you graduated from high school, but nowadays I think that a girl should go off to school first."

"And then she should get married?" Betsy teased, knowing that Oma considered a single woman's life sadly incomplete.

"Don't play games with me, Betsy," the older woman warned. "I don't believe all that stuff about how happy you are by yourself. You need a good man to make you happy. A man like Spence."

Betsy sighed as she walked over to the bolts of velvet to see what she had on hand. She was disappointed to find that she'd sold almost none of the lush fabric. The wall of calicoes and quilting cotton was sorely depleted, but her profit margin on cotton was so tiny that so far Ye Olde Fabric Shoppe wasn't even paying for itself. Fortunately the other stores in her chain were long established and doing a brisk business.

Oma followed right behind her, like a trained dog in the obedience ring. "Now, Betsy Hanover, you listen to me. I've known Spence Spencer since he was knee-high to a grasshopper, so if there's anything you want to know about him, you just go ahead and ask me." She waited expectantly while Betsy picked up a bolt of royal-blue velvet and counted out the number of yards she'd need for the dress. "Well? You must be curious about something!"

Betsy considered telling Oma to back off, but when she saw the expectant look on the white-haired woman's face she didn't have the heart. Instead she asked the most innocuous question she could think of. "Why do they call him 'Spence' when he's got a perfectly good name like 'Geoff'?"

Oma beamed. "His grandfather went by 'Geoff.' His father went by 'Junior.' We called Spence 'Geoffrey' when he was little, but it always seemed a little stuffy. In sixth grade another Geoffrey with a 'G' showed up, and there was already a Jeffrey with a 'J', so old Miss Fritz started calling him 'Mr. Spencer,' kind of like a joke, and over time—" She stopped and glared at Betsy, who was now rummaging through the plastic frames of lace and braided trimming. "Betsy Hanover, you aren't listening to me!"

"I'm listening, I'm listening!" She flashed Oma a dutiful smile. "Three Geoffs. Three Spencers. One Spence." Determined to keep the discussion light, she asked, "Why isn't Randy named 'Geoffrey IV?'"

To her surprise, Oma's face instantly went dark. "Because *she* wouldn't hear of it. Tiffany said she had a father, too, and since he'd never had a son, his grandchild was going to be his namesake." Oma clucked disapprovingly. "Tiffany's still her daddy's little girl. Even though she's remarried now and lives over in Bremer—that's an hour from here—she still runs home every time anything goes wrong."

Betsy was about to ask why Randy didn't live with his mother, when a new customer arrived...then another and another in a steady stream. In fact, it was the busiest morning she'd had since she'd opened Ye Olde Fabric Shoppe, and by lunchtime she was feeling downright ragged.

"What is this? Did I put an advertisement in the paper?"

"Better," Oma said. "You made a public appearance last night. Word gets around fast."

"You mean they want to see how I look when I'm not Juliet?"

Oma chuckled. "It's not Juliet they came to see. It's the woman they think will end up with Spence Spencer."

Betsy rolled her eyes in exasperation. She didn't find the idea of ending up with Spence Spencer untenable, but it was certainly premature. "Oma, what is this?" she demanded. "I've been in Muskingum for six whole weeks, and the shop's only been open the past three. I spent a minute and a half on the gym floor with this fellow, and to listen to you, we're already engaged. Does this happen every time a new woman comes to town?"

That stopped Oma cold. She actually blushed. "Well, not every time."

Betsy laughed out loud. "Just usually?"

"Now, Betsy!" Oma stammered. "When Irwin Elliot's niece came to visit last summer, there was just a little talk—"

Betsy shook her head. "From her? From him? Or just from this ingrown community?"

"Please, Betsy, I don't think that's fair. We love Spence. He's been alone too long. He deserves a good woman to make him happy."

"And what about me?" Betsy snapped back, feeling like a cut of meat on a butcher's block. "Don't I deserve to decide whether I have any interest in this man?"

When Oma fell silent, Betsy was sorry she'd lost her temper, but she decided to state her case once and for all. "I am a businesswoman, Oma. This is the seventh store in a lucrative little chain that I built with my own two hands and my own nimble sewing fingers. I enjoy men, when I've got the time for them, but getting married is not my ultimate goal.''

All that was the truth, but there was more she could have added. While marriage was not a *goal* of Betsy's, it *was* one of her secret dreams. Yet she was in no hurry to get caught up in a short-term romance, because she was sure that the man she was meant to be with would cross her path when the time was right. In the meantime, she was enjoying the challenge of expanding her business and was quite contented with her life.

While Spence Spencer didn't strike Betsy as her long-awaited white knight, she could have told Oma three things she liked about him very much: his laughter, his eyes and the way he treated his son. She was hopeful that in time Spence might also find a few things to admire about her, but if he didn't, that was okay, too.

At least it seemed okay until Randy burst into the shop after lunch with Laurie in tow. The first thing Betsy noticed was how much he *looked* like his dad. The second thing she noticed was how much he *smiled* like his dad.

"Hi, Mrs. Potter," Randy greeted Oma politely, leading Betsy to notice how much he *talked* like—

"Hi, Randy. Have you met Miss Hanover?"

"Call me 'Betsy,' please," Betsy told the boy, intuitively feeling that "Miss Hanover" stressed a difference in their ages that Randy, who probably thought of himself as a man, might prefer to overlook.

"This is my girlfriend, Laurie," Randy announced with reverence, placing one arm possessively around the pretty redhead, who was wearing an oversize sweatshirt and a denim miniskirt.

Betsy smiled, remembering her high school boyfriend fondly. Though he was happily married now, she still thought of him as a good friend and had pleasant memories of a love that was special . . . just not quite special enough. "It's nice to meet both of you," she said warmly. "Are you excited about the Renaissance faire?"

"You bet!" Laurie squealed. "I'm going to be an abigail at the horse tournament. You know—the special maidens who serve the knights and their ladies?" She batted her eyes at Randy. "Janet said that Randy could be a page at the arena, so we'll be together all the time."

Randy's eyes glowed with the majesty of it all, and Betsy struggled to keep her composure. "That sounds like a lot of fun," she managed to say.

"It'll be *won*derful!" Randy exclaimed. For a moment he and Laurie gazed at each other with youthful adoration, then Randy turned his attention back to Oma and said, "Laurie said you found a coin for me, Mrs. Potter."

"Yes, indeed. It's an old silver dime. I hope it's not a year you already have." She bent down to pull a small envelope out from under the cutting counter. Betsy hadn't noticed it before. All it said on the front was "Randy."

Gray eyes shining, Randy ripped open the envelope and seized the silver dime. "Nineteen fifty-four!" he shouted. "Somebody just walked in here with this?"

"I guess so," Oma told him. "I always check the coins for you as they come in, so a customer must have given it to Betsy. I almost gave it to Hattie Marshall for change on Tuesday."

Betsy strolled over to gaze at the coin. To her it looked singularly unremarkable, but it was obviously a source of great excitement for Randy.

"I take it you have a coin collection, Randy?" she asked, trying to show some friendly interest in the boy.

"You bet. The best one in town." He couldn't mask his pride. "U.S. dimes were made with ninety percent silver until 1965, but now they're mainly made of nickel and copper. I've already got a dime for twelve of the years between 1950, when my dad was born, and 1965. With this one—" he grinned at Oma "—I'll only need two more!"

"My goodness," Betsy answered, wishing she could think of something more meaningful to say. "I guess you've been collecting for a long time."

"All my life. Actually *before* my life. My dad and my Uncle Bill started this collection when they were kids, and they passed it on to me."

"He got a head start," Laurie added, as though she felt the need to contribute something to the conversation.

Apparently Oma felt the same urge, because almost instantaneously she chimed in, "Oh, I remember your dad when he was your age, Randy! You're the image of him, and just as nice a boy as he was, too. Why, I remember once when—"

Betsy sailed off gratefully in the direction of a customer who'd just drifted in the front door. She was a frail, elderly lady who needed to talk to somebody about her arthritis as much as she needed to shop. Betsy spent fifteen minutes helping her select a seven-inch zipper, and she was glad to see that the woman left with an added buoyancy to her uncertain step.

She wondered why some women grew fragile as they aged, and some, like Mrs. MacGillicuddy, seemed to grow feistier with each passing year. Gazing at Randy, she also wondered why some children looked just like their parents and some bore no resemblance whatsoever to their folks. And then, as her concentration drifted, she stopped seeing Randy as a younger version of Spence and just let Spence fill her mind altogether. He was a curious blend of rugged manliness and gentle sensitivity, a big man who moved like a cat but alternately smiled like a clown, a prince and the boy next door as the spirit moved him. He was also a man she wouldn't at all mind seeing again, she decided—a possibility that was more than likely in a town this size. Granted, she'd gotten some mixed messages from Spence—he certainly hadn't been happy sharing the stage with her—but when they'd parted, something in his puzzled gray eyes had confessed a spark of some deep feeling.

Betsy let the breeze of pleasure sweep over her, acknowledging the flutter of anticipation in her heart. She didn't luxuriate in the vision of her next encounter with Spence Spencer more than a second before she headed back to the counter. Oma, Laurie and Randy were studying her intently when she got there.

"What?" she demanded playfully, hoping her thoughts didn't show on her face. "Do I have green hair or something?"

Laurie giggled.

Oma blushed.

Randy said, "My dad says you look just like my mother, Miss Hanover. But I don't think so." He turned to Oma for confirmation. "What do you think, Mrs. Potter?"

Oma glanced at Betsy, then quickly jerked her gaze away. "I think they're both very pretty," she stalled.

"That doesn't mean much to Dad," Randy answered artlessly. "He still thinks Mom's a beautiful woman, you know, but he can't stand the sight of her most of the time."

Laurie gasped, "Randy!" and Oma cringed.

Poor Randy's ears grew red, and Betsy couldn't help but feel sorry for him. He was at such an awkward, gangly stage, so easily embarrassed. She knew he hadn't meant to hurt her.

In a squeaky voice he blurted out, "I'm real sorry, Miss Hanover...er, Betsy. I guess that wasn't a very courteous thing to say."

Betsy had to agree with him. It wasn't very courteous, but it certainly explained a lot. And for some reason, it seemed to sap the joy from the rest of the day.

CHAPTER THREE

THREE DAYS AFTER Spence met Betsy Hanover, he strolled into the Muskingum Movie House at 7:25. He hadn't called or checked a newspaper to determine the time the film would start; since his boyhood, the theater schedule had remained unchanged—7:30 every night but Wednesday, and on that night the theater was closed because Hal and Hattie Marshall, the owners, went to choir practice at the Good Shepherd Church.

"Howdy, Spence!" Hal greeted him heartily as he stopped at the front booth to buy a ticket. "Missed you on Saturday night."

"Yeah, sorry I couldn't make it." Remembering his promise not to make fun of Randy, who'd returned from his date in a state of euphoria, he finished stoutly, "I had other plans."

Hal winked. "Yes, sir, I gathered that. And your 'other plans' are waiting for you over on the left-hand side."

"Run that by me again?" Spence asked, wishing he'd been listening more intently.

Old Hal grinned and winked again, more dramatically this time. "Betsy Hanover," he whispered, then gestured with his thumb toward the left side of the theater as he greeted the next patron in line.

Spence stifled a frown as he entered the theater, which was poorly lit but not darkened yet. He'd planned to stop and get some popcorn, but the movie was about to start and it was important that he get the awkward meeting with Betsy out of the way. He was tempted simply to ignore her, but since there was a good chance Hal had told her that "her date" would be coming along later, there was a good chance she was expecting to see him...or somebody. Better to just lay things straight out on the table and get the whole matter out of the way. After all, his resistance to the woman was nothing personal.

He found himself looking for a swirl of red velvet, a great deal of appealing cleavage and a cascade of golden hair. He found three teenage friends of Randy's in the center of the theater and four adults on the right, but to his surprise the only person on the left-hand side was a shapely young woman in blue jeans and a plain pink T-shirt. Her hair was wrapped tightly in an artless bun. He tried to remember what Betsy looked like, but all he could recall was Tiffany's delicate heart-shaped face. Yet when Spence ambled down the aisle to say hello, the minute Betsy turned to face him, he realized that she couldn't have looked less like his frilly ex-wife.

"Sir Geoffrey?" she greeted him cheerfully. "I've been waiting for you."

"You have?" It was not at all what he had expected her to say. What on earth had Hal Marshall told her?

"Well, not waiting as in holding my breath or expecting you to ride up on a white charger, but I did think we might need to talk."

"We do?" Actually, he'd been thinking the same thing, but *he'd* planned to explain his indifference to that pretty, helpless photocopy of Tiffany he'd met on Friday night. The woman he faced now was just as attractive as the one he'd met, but there was nothing helpless about her. She exuded calm and confidence.

"Yes, indeed." She turned to face him, tucking one foot under her legs as she twisted casually in the sagging red theater chair. "While Muskingum's enthusiasm for our 'budding romance—'" she held up her fingers to make quotation marks "—is improving my business by leaps and bounds, I don't believe in deceptive advertising. Since I imagine you've been through this many times before, I thought you might have some ideas. If you don't, I do."

"You do what?" he asked, baffled but already admiring her style.

"I have some ideas about how to quell the rabble so we can carry on peacefully with our private, and very separate lives. I take it that in all the time you've been divorced, nothing has really worked before?"

He shrugged, feeling the way he had when he'd been ten and John Harwood's pony had run off with him gripping the saddle horn for dear life. Spence hadn't fallen off, but he'd bounced up and down in the saddle for several minutes, falling from one side to the other as he'd tugged on the reins. He hadn't been *too* frightened, but he'd felt like a fool. "Uh, actually, they usually run out of breath about the time the young lady in question comes to realize that I don't return her interest. Sometimes it's comparatively painless, and sometimes... well, someone gets hurt."

Betsy seemed to take his warning in her stride. "Are you telling me that every single woman who comes to this town falls head over heels in love with you?"

He didn't like the way she said it—as though a woman would have to be crazy to find him appealing. Somewhat defensively he countered, "There isn't anybody else for a young woman to fall for. Oma Potter's crowd has already married off every other bachelor in town."

To his surprise, Betsy laughed. "Now *that* I can believe. But it might hearten you to know that I grew up with an aunt just like her, and I've become quite proficient at outwitting that sort of crafty mind. In fact, Aunt Alma managed to marry off four daughters and six nieces, including my two sisters, but I eluded her." Her tone was triumphant. "Time after time."

Breathless by now, Spence said, "Congratulations."

"Thank you. But I'm really not tooting my own horn, Spence. My point is that I have, over the years, developed a nearly foolproof method of nipping gossipmongers in the bud, and should you be agreeable, I think we might want to give it a try."

Spence was dumbfounded. How on earth had he ever thought this woman was anything like Tiffany? Tiffany might be as pretty, but was nowhere near as clever, as forthright. For some reason he wasn't at all comfortable with Betsy's eagerness to dispose of him, as though he were as undesirable as ring around the collar or a case of summer fleas.

"What exactly did you have in mind?" he asked cautiously.

"Aha!" She smiled at him—a beautiful, radiant, self-sufficient smile that eclipsed the image of Tiffany's perfect pout. Tiffany was the most helpless person he knew, and she rarely smiled unless somebody else had just promised to take care of her.

"As you know," Betsy continued breezily, "they won't be satisfied unless and until you and I have a head-over-heals, stars-falling-out-of-the-sky affair. So we do exactly that, as publicly as possible." Her tone implied that she'd consider anything they did without an audience a waste of time. "You'll have to decide how long we need to carry on with the farce—a week or two at the least, I imagine—before we have the world's worst fight at the best attended public gathering coming up in the near future. Which is?''

"Uh, the Memorial Day picnic."

"Muskingum has a Memorial Day picnic?" Betsy crowed in delight. "Perfect. Four-and-a-half weeks from now. We ought to be able to fall in and out of love by then, don't you think?"

He had to laugh. She looked so capable, yet so lovely, as she grinned at him from her crumpled-up position in that big red chair! "Where's that dear little Juliet I used to know?" he teased her, still not certain whether she was pulling his leg.

"Fain I would tell thee but didst I know," she misquoted with a grin. "I looked it up. 'Fain.' It means 'eagerly.' I bet you knew that already."

He tried to come up with a witty reply, but Betsy was moving too fast for him. He was used to running his own show, but with this perplexing female he didn't have any idea what approach he ought to take. Swallowed up in those lovely blue eyes, he was temporarily paralyzed.

Spence leaned against the back of the upholstered chair next to hers and studied her delicate heart-shaped face, crowned by a determined but very graceful widow's peak. He tried not to think about the feel of her hand in his during those brief public seconds in the gym, but the memory came back to him, right along with the hungry sensation of sitting beside her in the bleachers, and feeling the cascading folds of her red velvet dress spill onto his thigh as if in invitation for some intimate caress. There was no rhyme or reason to his fantasy, and certainly no rhyme or reason to the fact that he was now stifling a reckless urge to undo the stiff schoolmarm's hairdo that made her look so unapproachable, so immune to his presence or his power as a man.

Betsy spoke again, interrupting his reverie. "Spence, I didn't come to Muskingum to find a husband," she said very seriously, her gaze now penetrating, "but on the other hand I'm not allergic to decent men. I haven't the slightest idea whether you and I would have anything in common—" he couldn't tell by her tone whether she hoped they might "—but I'd hate to have you avoid me just because of the gossipmongers in this town."

Spence was surprised and humbled by her insight. Ashamed of the way he'd misjudged her, he sputtered lamely, "Betsy, I don't know if I was planning to avoid you, exactly," aware that his words stopped a bit short of the truth.

What had been his true intentions? To let her know he wasn't interested in being anything but friends? It sounded logical, but at the moment, Spence wasn't feeling logical. He had the strangest sensation that somebody had just slipped a blindfold over his head and was twirling him around. Awkwardly he finished, "I just didn't want you to... well, to misread any friendly signals you might pick up from me."

"Fair enough," she agreed, her blank tone revealing nothing. "I had the feeling the other night that you were... well, resentful of me, even though we hadn't really met. Maybe I was just feeling a little sensitive. That whole scene with Mrs. MacGillicuddy was interesting, but... a little bit embarrassing, to tell you the truth. I'm not in the habit of making a fool of myself in public."

He nodded in sympathy. "It was all in good fun, and people will stop treating you like an outsider now that you've been initiated. Still, it would have been nice if somebody had warned you."

To her credit, Betsy grinned. "If somebody had, I wouldn't have come. And the kick-off night for the faire wouldn't have been nearly so successful. Janet tells me her phone's been ringing off the hook since then!" Before Spence could reply, Betsy changed the subject again. "You'd better hurry if you want some popcorn, Spence. I'd offer you some of mine, except I try to keep my girlish figure by eating it dry, without butter or salt."

He recognized the casual brush-off—if one could call it that—as her way of offering him a diplomatic out. Obviously she didn't want him to sit with her just because there was no courteous way to avoid it, and he liked her tact. What bothered him was that she'd left him with no way to settle down beside her inconspicuously. He'd either have to go sit somewhere else or bluntly invite himself to stay. And for some reason, he was no longer in the mood to watch *American Graffiti* by himself.

As Spence's options clattered through his mind, the lights began to dim, and Betsy, having dismissed him, turned to face the screen. The only logical thing for him to do was march back to the snack bar to arm himself with popcorn, a large Coke and a bag of the tiny sweet candies he'd been buying at the Muskingum Movie House since he was ten. At the candy counter, Hal's wife didn't badger him about Betsy because she knew the movie had already started. Relieved, he slipped back into the theater before the opening credits had ended. After his eyes adjusted to the darkness, he picked out a spot in the center aisle near Randy's friends and started toward it at a steady pace.

Yet a moment later he found himself over on the left side of the theater, his big knee barely grazing Betsy's smaller one. He hadn't the slightest idea how he'd ended up there, or how he was going to find an excuse to get up and leave.

But when Betsy's soap-clean scent wafted over to him, he abandoned the struggle to think of one.

WHEN THE HOUSELIGHTS rudely flashed on in the theater two hours later, Betsy blinked and tried to think of something to say to Spence Spencer that wasn't totally inane. After their earlier brief conversation, she hadn't expected to see him again this evening, and she'd been surprised by his decision to return to her side with a huge tub of popcorn, which he silently offered to share with her during the show. Except for a mumbled "Thank you" and the camaraderie of mutual laughter during the most outrageous scenes in the nostalgic comedy, they'd sat together like strangers, courteously avoiding bumping elbows and shoulders in the dark. Despite that, the initial awkwardness of their meeting at the theater had abated simply by virtue of their having shared a pleasant experience. Now, for no reason that Betsy could put her finger on, she was reluctant to go.

"Welcome to Muskingum, Betsy," Spence said with a grin when she met his gaze. The tiny lines around his gray eyes fanned out with native friendliness, warming her in a way that his earlier wariness had prevented him from doing. "Now you know the full extent of cultural opportunities available to you in this charming little town."

Betsy laughed as she recalled the moment when the film had broken and a man had hollered out, "Hey, Hal! When are you going to replace that old clunker?" The other highlight had come when Hattie Marshall had prowled up and down the aisle with a flashlight, making sure that all the teenagers were behaving in accordance with their parents' expectations, despite the cover of darkness in the theater. "And here I thought that Mrs. MacGillicuddy was the cultural center of Muskingum," Betsy mused.

"She'd like to be." Spence grinned beguilingly as he picked up Betsy's watery Coke, then carefully brushed a pair of uncooked kernels off his seat into the empty popcorn tub. "As a matter of fact, I guess she is. My boy's with her tonight, you know."

Betsy tried to mask her surprise. "Working on the faire already?"

Spence shook his head. "Not exactly. Mrs. Mac has started a poetry reading club for the kids. Randy, mind you, wouldn't recognize a metaphor if it bit him on the kneecap, but as long as Laurie Potter wants to listen to rhymes on Monday nights, I suspect that his passion for love sonnets will remain intense." His tone made it clear that love sonnets weren't at the top of his evening reading list.

"Have they been dating long?" Betsy asked, trying to keep the conversation light as she picked up her canvas purse and sauntered toward the door, pausing while Spence stuffed their trash in the appropriate container.

"Yes, indeed." He grinned. "Two or three weeks now, seems to me. Randy could probably tell you right to the hour."

"I suppose you never went through a mushy puppy love stage at fifteen?"

"If I know Oma Potter, you've already heard everything about my puppy love stage at fifteen . . . and sixteen and seventeen and even at twenty," he answered dryly, then tugged the conversation back to his son. "I do my best not to tease Randy about his girlfriends, but it's not easy. He trades them the way he changes socks."

"Every two or three weeks?" Betsy teased.

This time Spence laughed out loud. "I guess you've lived with a teenage boy before!"

"Well, I grew up with two brothers."

"They live near here?"

"No, unfortunately. One's in the army and moves around a lot. The other one is a Chevrolet dealer based in Detroit. We get together every now and then." They were standing in front of the theater now, inches from the curb, but Spence didn't seem to be in a hurry to go.

"Where are you from originally?" he asked. "I don't mean to be nosy, but I'm curious. I've known most of the people in this town all my life. We have young people leave Muskingum all the time, but it's not often that somebody chooses to move here."

Betsy still couldn't tell whether he was glad she'd decided to set up shop in his hometown; she wasn't even sure whether she wanted him to be. But it was a lovely night—a crisp but gentle breeze was fanning the two of them—and she couldn't think of a single good reason to rush home to enjoy her customary evening solitude.

"I've lived in Pennsylvania and Michigan, mainly in suburbs and big cities, and I guess I was looking for a change of pace. Last fall I was on my way to Columbus to visit a friend, and stopped in Zanesville for lunch. Somebody had left a newspaper on my table, open to the classified section. I was just reading to pass the time until my order came, when lo and behold, a tiny ad for a floundering fabric shop caught my eye." She grinned. "So here I am."

It was the logical moment for Spence to say, "And I'm glad you are," but he didn't. In fact, he didn't say much of anything until Hal and Hattie Marshall strolled out of the theater a moment later and turned to the two of them after Hal had locked the front door.

"Fine night, ain't it, Spence? Miss Hanover?" Hal said, while Hattie favored them with a romantic smile.

"Sterling, Hal. Just a sterling evening." Spence said the words with feeling, as though the simple pleasure of enjoying a beautiful spring evening meant a great deal to him. After the older couple had started down the street, Spence turned to Betsy and recited melodramatically, "'The moon shines bright: on such a night as this, when the sweet wind did gently kiss the trees and they did no noise make....'"

Betsy stared at him blankly, certain that he was quoting Shakespeare or some other distinguished Renaissance poet, but she'd been spared the trial of Mrs. MacGillicuddy in high school, so her knowledge of early English literature was meager compared to his. "If I'm supposed to answer, Spence, you'll have to cue me."

He chuckled, reaching out to touch her arm with what felt, disappointingly, like sympathy. "It's a scene from Shakespeare's *Merchant of Venice*. Two young lovers are taking a stroll and trying to one-up each other with lines about the beauty of the evening. My brother had to memorize it when he was a junior. I just remember a couple of lines."

"Your brother?" Betsy asked. "The one who was married to Janet?"

"Yes. Bill was my only brother."

Betsy regretted her question as she watched his face darken with lingering grief. Struggling for a lighter tone, she said gently, "I haven't had a chance to spend much time with Janet, but I hope to get better acquainted when we go to Pittsburgh tomorrow night. She seems like a very special person."

His eyes warmed hers gratefully. "Yes, she is." He braved a forced smile. "We used to live together, you know. All three of us—then four when I got Randy back. After Bill died, Janet just couldn't bear to stay in the house or even drive the old Chevy I'd passed on to Bill when they were dating. Randy and I miss her a lot, but I suspect she did the right thing to get her own place when she opened up her law firm. She's starting to bounce back now, a little bit at a time.'' Before Betsy could reply, Spence gestured across the street toward a sleepy café. Betsy guessed that the eight blinking letters on the sign probably spelled Charley's when they were all working. "Look, I live just far enough out of town that it's not worth my time to drive out there and come back for Randy at eleven," he said abruptly. "I've got another hour or so to kill. Would you like to join me for some coffee?''

It wasn't the most enthusiastic invitation Betsy had ever received, but she understood the logic behind Spence's determined nonchalance. With the whole town shoving the two of them together, he wanted to make absolutely sure she didn't misinterpret his friendliness as budding romance. She had the feeling he liked her a little bit—at least as a friend. If he didn't, he wouldn't have come back to sit beside her with his popcorn. Still, that didn't change the fact that his invitation had been less than gracious.

Apparently Spence wasn't too happy with his wording, either, because before Betsy could answer, he said, "I don't think that came out quite right, Betsy. I'd really like to buy you a cup of coffee so we can talk." This time his smile was genuine, if reserved, and his friendly gray eyes made her feel more welcome.

It wasn't the first time that a Muskingum man had asked her to join him in the evening, and it wasn't the first time she'd decided to say yes. But Betsy realized, as she nodded once in acceptance of his invitation, that she didn't feel quite the same way about this man as she did the other friendly locals who'd shown interest in her. She wasn't sure whether it was his cautious smile, his hidden grief, his love for his son or his determination not to break a newcomer's heart that made him different. But whatever it was, it caused her heartbeat to speed up just a bit, and it nudged a wide smile on to her face.

As they crossed the street, Spence rested one hand lightly on the small of Betsy's back. Old-fashioned chivalry seemed to come to him naturally, she mused. The casual gesture touched her, and the gentle touch aroused a flicker of need in Betsy, a need for the feel of his whole massive hand spread out enticingly across her spine.

Spence opened the door of Charley's Café for her, but before Betsy could take a single step inside, he clutched her arm and pulled her back. "About-face, Betsy," he whispered. His warm breath fanned the sensitive curl of her inner ear, and for an instant she imagined that he'd gotten close enough to brush his lips across her skin. "Randy and Laurie dead ahead. Mission aborted."

Betsy glanced up, startled, as Spence tightened his grip on her arm and spun her around. He led her quickly down the block until they were beyond the view afforded by the dusty café windows, then he released her with a grin. "Sorry about the subterfuge. He told me they'd be coming here tonight, but I forgot. Last week I made the mistake of dropping by the drugstore for an ice-cream cone while Randy happened to be buying a shake for Laurie. I tried to be sociable and even gave her what *I* thought was a compliment, but when I got home that night Randy was so mad he'd barely speak to me. I had embarrassed him beyond all measure." He shrugged with a grin that was part sympathy, part frustration. "It's a hell of a trial, being a fifteen-year-old boy. Almost as hard as living with one.''

Betsy was surprised at his willingness to honor Randy's adolescent sensitivity; most men she knew would have plowed into Charley's, anyway, either joining the boy or taking a nearby booth. Now she said hopefully, ''Well, you know this town better than I do. What else is open this late?'' It was only a little after nine-thirty, but after eight, the town pretty much closed up for the night.

A look of genuine regret shadowed Spence's craggy features. ''I'm sorry, Betsy, but there isn't anything else open on Monday nights. I know it seems silly—'' he glanced at Charley's, as if reconsidering his decision ''—but that's life in Muskingum. Maybe we can make it another time.''

Betsy was surprised at the sharp stab of disappointment rendered by his words. She realized that his suggestion had been strictly off-the-cuff and he wasn't likely to ask her out again. He'd already made it crystal clear he wasn't interested in pursuing a romantic relationship with her, a message she'd do well to remember. Two hours ago, Betsy hadn't been the least bit alarmed about the prospect of going home alone after the movie. But now, for some reason, she felt an urgency to spend some time with somebody.

Somebody? the voice of honesty challenged her. *You want to spend some time with Spence.*

Instinctively she blurted out, ''My shop's only a block away, Spence, and I always keep instant coffee and cookies on hand. I've got a comfortable couch in my office—'' she gulped as she considered the misinterpretation she'd left herself open to ''—if you're in the mood to talk.''

Quickly his eyes found hers, pinning Betsy to her tiny square patch of concrete. She wasn't sure what he was thinking, but she had no doubt that he was weighing every possible ramification of her invitation—what she wanted, what *he* wanted and what the town would decide they both wanted if anybody ever found it.

This is crazy, she told herself. *Don't lie to yourself. He couldn't make his feelings any plainer. Why do you keep pretending that he might change his mind?*

Before the silence grew painfully awkward, Betsy said, "Come to think of it, I've had a pretty long day. I think I should just call it a night." Her tone was overly bright, almost brittle. "Thanks for the popcorn, Spence. I'll see you around."

If she'd glanced away an instant sooner, she would never have seen the momentary flash of regret in his eyes, the confession of shock that *she* was the one who had willingly called it a night.

Does he want to come with me? Her heart pounded with the question. *Was there more to his casual invitation than I know?*

Forgetting momentarily that most men had little interest in fabric or the exquisite items women created with them, Betsy licked her lips and tacked on hurriedly, "Maybe sometime you'd like to see what I've done with the shop."

Spence raised his eyebrows. "I'd like that, Betsy." His tone was even, but a husky burr gave him away.

Betsy tried to smile, but she was uneasy and sure that her discomfort showed. "Well, feel free to drop by anytime."

His eyes caressed her slowly, and this time Betsy had no doubt he was studying her the way a man looked at a woman he'd really rather touch. He didn't reach for her, though—didn't move an inch in her direction. Yet she started trembling as though he'd crossed the uneven crack in the sidewalk between them and had taken her in his arms.

"How about tonight?" he said simply.

And Betsy answered, "Follow me."

CHAPTER FOUR

WHEN BETSY UNLOCKED the front door of Ye Olde Fabric Shoppe, dark and empty at this hour of night, Spence remembered how he'd felt as a teenager when Tiffany had pulled him into the storage room of her father's grocery store next door. Moonlight cast an eerie glow across the floor of the shop, and for just a moment, he wasn't quite sure what was expected of him.

He was alone with a lovely young woman. She didn't have Tiffany's ethereal beauty, although she'd certainly conveyed the same kind of exotic frailty in the high school's old red Juliet dress. Tonight she looked like somebody's sister in blue jeans and a ponytail. Of course her hair was in a bun, not a ponytail, but it was starting to spill out around her face in delicate, lacy tendrils.

Abruptly, it seemed to Spence, Betsy flicked on the overhead lights, and the glare was as intrusive as the sudden brilliance that had invaded their privacy a few minutes earlier in the theater. He knew he should have been grateful for this unspoken reaffirmation that they really were just two friends meeting for a late-night snack. But for some reason, he resented the brightness—perhaps because it was less threatening to study her face in the dark.

"Well, here it is," Betsy said brightly, gesturing to the colorful bolts of fabric artistically arranged along the walls.

Displays of buttons framed the wide wooden counter-tops, and racks of ornamental trim, thread and zippers hung behind them. The shop looked very spiffy and well organized, but beyond that Spence, who knew nothing at all about sewing but remembered that he'd shown an interest in her business, could only say, "It looks...well stocked."

Betsy laughed as she started toward the back. "That it is. Shall we have some coffee now?"

Grateful for her patience with his masculine blunder, he protested lamely, "Really, Betsy, even I can tell that it's well organized and maintained. I mean, all the thick stuff—"

"The velvet and brocade?"

"Exactly. The velvet and brocade are all together, and the stuff that looks like little girls' dresses is all over here." He pointed toward the far wall, noting that one pink print bore a striking resemblance to the fabric on the dress Laurie Potter was wearing tonight.

Betsy took Spence's arm and tugged him toward the back of the shop. "It's a great store. You've convinced me. I'll try to sound equally informed if I ever see the place where you work." The warmth of her strong fingers burned through his chambray shirt for just a moment, and as she released him, he was astonished at the realization that he ached to feel her touch once more.

Whoa, fella, he cautioned himself sharply. *You've been alone for a long while, that's all. Don't forget the rules of the game just because you're alone with a woman after dark.*

"Spence?" She sounded perplexed, as though she'd already repeated herself. "I said, where do you work?"

"Uh, I own my own place. Oil supply business. It belonged to my dad." He met her eyes, those honest blue circles of friendliness and truth, and remembered to add, "And to my grandad before him."

"Oil?" she asked, plugging in a self-contained burner on a small counter near the back wall. "I thought all the American oil was in California and Texas these days."

He grimaced. "I'm afraid most of it is. But it wasn't always that way. The first well ever dug in this country was just over the Pennsylvania state line about a hundred miles from here. When my grandad was young, the southeast corner of Ohio and most of Pennsylvania were dotted with oil wells. And not the crude black gold they've got in the southwest. It was so pure that he'd pour it straight into his engine and his truck would purr like a kitty."

Betsy gestured toward the couch, and he perched uneasily on the far end of it. Her office was very small, and she stood only a few feet from him, her nicely curved hips swaying temptingly an arm's length away. She shook some cookies out of a box and dumped them on a tiny paper plate, then pulled a couple of mugs out of a cabinet near the opposite corner of the couch.

"So what happened?" she asked. "Isn't it pure anymore?"

"Oh, it's pure, what there is of it. Still used for lubrication, never for gasoline. The trouble is, there isn't as much as there used to be, and the big supply companies service most of the oil patch. After you've been in business for a while you'll realize that it's very hard for the little guy to compete."

Betsy turned to face him, startled, as she asked, "How long do you think I've been in business, Spence? A day and a half?"

He swallowed uncomfortably. "I . . . well, I got the impression that you'd just set up shop."

She smiled kindly, but he had the distinct feeling that he'd made another major miscalculation about Betsy Hanover. In fact, it occurred to him, as another curly lock of blond hair spilled down across her delicate neck, that he really didn't know her at all.

"I've just set up shop in Muskingum," she informed him. "But Ye Olde Fabric Shoppe isn't my first store. It's the seventh in a fairly successful chain."

"Oh, really?" Spence was surprised. Betsy Hanover might look as frail as Tiffany, but she was obviously a capable, efficient woman. Tiffany couldn't have run a business to save her life. "How did you get started?"

"About twelve years ago I rented a tiny hole-in-the-wall in Pittsburgh and made every mistake a beginner could. Fortunately I'm the type of a person who learns from my mistakes and doesn't repeat them often."

Before he could respond to that, she handed him a steaming mug of coffee and said, "Sugar? Cream?"

"Cream," he answered, accepting a spoonful of the nondairy white grains that came in a jar.

A moment later she joined him on the small couch, tucking one foot underneath her in the same cozy fashion she'd adopted at the theater, and suddenly the tiny office began to shrink until they were only inches apart.

"So tell me about your business," Betsy suggested. "Exactly how does an oil supply business work?"

It was an innocent, courteous question, but for some reason he didn't want to think about the business tonight. Whenever he thought of Tiffany and the family business at the same time, he felt weak and ashamed. His grandfather had worked too hard—as had his father and his brother, as well—to risk losing Black Gold Supply in an endless squabble about court costs triggered only by Spence's inability to see past a woman's pretty face. How many thousands of dollars had gone into lawyers' fees in his struggle to regain his son? How many times had the business perched on the edge of oblivion as a result? Even now, was it really strong enough to sustain any unexpected emergency?

Betsy sipped at her coffee and pretended not to notice Spence's delay in answering her question.

"I deliver equipment to oil drilling sites," he replied belatedly. "There are all kinds of pipes and valves needed by various workers, and when somebody needs them, he needs them *right now*."

"So you drive out to these places?"

"Instantly."

Betsy relaxed slightly against the couch, oblivious to the fact that most of her golden hair was now cascading down her back. "Somehow it seems it would be more efficient to have your customers come to you."

"In the fabric business, maybe. When it comes to oil, time is money. Besides, delivery itself can be a problem. And the guy ordering the part has to know what he needs without looking at it, and so do I. It's not like picking out a dress from a catalog."

"I guess not."

"Actually, I enjoy the challenge most of the time. The only real problem the business gives me these days is that I'm on call twenty-four hours a day and have to wear a pager all the time." He patted the silver case that hung on his belt. "That can be a hassle when I'm sick or out of town. In a pinch my Uncle Clay fills in for me, but at heart he's never been an oilman. His life is the family farm."

Betsy's mouth curved into a beguiling smile. "Have you ever considered going into some other line of work?"

"Never," he replied without hesitation. "This isn't just any business I'm running. It's my grandpa's pride and joy. My dad inherited it from him when Grandpa died, and I took over later. Bill—" his lips tightened as he said his brother's name "—Bill helped me for a while. I probably would have lost the business altogether during my darker days if I hadn't had Bill to buck me up and give me a heady dose of common sense now and then."

Betsy could have asked him what he'd meant by that bald statement; any other woman surely would have. But her quiet eyes revealed that she knew he'd made an inadvertent blunder and didn't want to dwell on his shortcomings with a stranger. Artfully she left the topic, earning another dozen points of Spence's respect.

"I'm not sure I showed much more common sense than those kids in *American Graffiti* when I was young," Betsy confessed with a mischievous grin. "For a while there tonight, I was thinking that if somebody could have turned back the clock twenty years, I could have climbed right on to the screen."

Grateful for Betsy's deliberate attempt to lighten his admission of poor adolescent judgment, Spence was happy to swap stories about the youthful hi-jinks he and Betsy had indulged in with countless other teenagers. After a while the conversation drifted toward other aspects of their background—their childhoods, their biggest failures and achievements, their still-unfulfilled dreams. Spence was open about most of his background, but deliberately avoided revealing any details about his marriage or divorce. When he asked Betsy if she'd ever been married, she replied airily, "Nope. But I imagine I will be, sooner or later. I just haven't met the right fellow yet."

Spence admired her sunny disposition; she seemed to take everything in her stride. According to Betsy, her failures had been mercifully few and she'd already accomplished her greatest dream. "I always wanted to run my own shop," she told him. "I didn't care if I made a lot of money. I just wanted to be in charge of my life."

Unconsciously he edged a little closer to her. "Then I guess you've achieved all your goals."

She sobered then, eyes wide as she studied his face. She put down her mug and edged almost imperceptibly in his direction. "Some of them," she confessed, her voice dropping a note. "But I think that life is like a daily walk down a country road. Every time you go out, you see something new, and you always wonder what exciting possibilities will be waiting for you tomorrow."

Put like that, all he could see was the wonder of Betsy Hanover's arrival in Muskingum. The town hadn't changed one iota in his thirty-seven years there, but suddenly, Muskingum was spring-morning fresh and new. He felt himself sliding ever so slightly toward her, wondering why, and then wondering, why not?

The sudden flicker of desire that darted through his body surprised Spence, and he wondered if Betsy could sense the sudden upsurge of tension that had gripped him. When he'd set out for the theater tonight, a romantic moment with Betsy Hanover had been the last thing on his mind. Now he couldn't seem to think of anything but the winsome sprite before him.

The banter between them seemed to die as Spence stared at Betsy. She licked her lips as she stared right back. He suddenly longed to explore her mouth with his own, but years of self-control caused him to stifle the need instinctively. He didn't dare reach out for her, yet he couldn't quite bring himself to back away.

And then, once again, Betsy made the decision for him.

"So what else has Mrs. MacGillicuddy roped you into doing for the faire, Spence?" she asked abruptly, standing up to dump another handful of chocolate chip cookies onto the empty paper plate.

Spence stiffened, pressing back against the couch as he feigned great interest in his tepid coffee. "Well, nothing yet," he managed to say. "I told Janet I'd volunteered to nail a few sets together. I think I convinced her I don't have the time or the inclination to do much else."

"I think you ought to be one of the players, Spence." Betsy was back beside him now, looking happy and relaxed. Her eyes twinkled as she teased, "I mean, you have such a knack for Renaissance drama."

Her dry tone did not escape him, and this time they shared a chuckle. The tense moment had passed, leaving a compelling sense of giddiness in its wake. "I can't help it if I still remember those old lines," he protested playfully. "Mrs. Mac drilled the words into me at a vulnerable age. But I'm not about to start parading around in public in a pair of tights. I'd be ruined if word got out around the oil patch."

Betsy grinned, a twinkling, pixie grin, before she said, "It's a waste not to take advantage of your expertise."

"Oh, no!" he protested quickly. "I suppose Janet told you all about my fencing class."

"Your what?"

Her genuine bewilderment convinced him that he should have left well enough alone, but he'd gone too far to leave the comment dangling. "Fencing class in my senior year in college. I was a physical education major who'd lost a whole semester with a dislocated shoulder and knee trouble." His eyes met hers conspiratorially as he added, "You guessed it—football. Anyway, I simply had to scarf up another three units to graduate on time, and even though my knee was doing better, my left arm just wasn't healing right. In desperation I signed up for fencing, because you have to keep your left arm behind you and out of the way." He demonstrated by hopping up to assume the first position, holding his left arm above his head as he grabbed a yardstick from Betsy's desk and pointed it dramatically in her direction. "You score each time you touch your opponent—" he tapped her shoulder gently "—and if you don't keep your left arm out of the way, points are subtracted from your score."

Betsy rubbed her shoulder as though he'd mortally wounded her, and gave him a knowing grin. "I can see that you don't recall a thing about it."

He dropped the yardstick and returned to the couch, embarrassed at his inadvertent confession that he still remembered a great deal about the sport. Betsy was still smiling—laughing?—at him with the spunky, upturned corners of her small and perfect mouth, and for some reason that he couldn't fathom he wanted to kiss that smile right off her face.

Instead he smiled back, unable to help himself. And then, for no reason at all, Betsy was laughing, and Spence was laughing with her, feeling like a little kid on Christmas Eve. If anybody had shown up in that instant and asked what was so funny, he would have been at a loss for words, and he suspected that Betsy would have been equally dumbfounded. Spence suspected that his odd exhilaration had something to do with the wave of desire he was struggling to suppress, but Betsy was acting just as silly, and he wondered if she might be trying to cope with a similar feeling. Or maybe, he admitted more realistically, she was still feeling giggly from the nostalgic absurdity of the movie they'd just seen. All Spence was sure of was that it had been a long time since he'd felt so uncontrolled, so alive, with a woman. For no logical reason he suggested suddenly, "Do you want to go up on the roof, Betsy? The view of the stars is just incredible up there this time of year."

She stared at him mutely.

"I said, do you want to go up on the roof?" he repeated, unable to stifle his ever widening grin. For emphasis, he hummed a couple of bars of an old tune by The Drifters with a title that echoed his words, and Betsy immediately chimed in, as though they'd sung the same song together dozens of times. It was a song from Spence's teenage years, the *American Graffiti* part of his life, and for some reason the notion of roof climbing seemed perfectly appropriate on this nostalgic, off-the-wall evening.

"I used to go up there with my girlfriend when I was Randy's age," Spence explained. "Her dad owned the grocery store next door, so we felt as though we owned the whole block. One time Officer Marvin Oates and his partner caught us up there, though."

"What were you doing that you got in trouble with the police?" Betsy asked, eyes shining.

"Well, nothing, actually. The problem was that we were supposed to be at the library, and we'd gone there first, of course. But I always kept an old blanket in the back of my Chevy, and we'd carted it up to the roof on our way home to—"

"I get it." Her tone was so straightforward that Spence wasn't even embarrassed.

"Anyway, when Marvin was making his rounds and heard us up there, he thought we were burglars, I guess.

When he called out for us to identify ourselves and we didn't—well, there was hell to pay."

Betsy laughed. "And here I thought nothing ever happened in this town."

He was glad he could laugh about it now. At the time, facing Marvin Oates with his jeans half off had not been a laughing matter.

"Actually, the roof is the best place to see anything going on in Muskingum. We always have a parade on Memorial Day—"

"After the picnic?"

"Before," he said with a grin. "And when we were little, Bill and I would climb up on the roof and perch on the edge with our feet hanging down as we threatened to jump on the folks below."

Again she laughed—sincerely—despite the fact that his comments were only moderately funny. It was infectious now; they were both getting punchy. "But you never did."

"Of course not! If I'd done even half the things I threatened to do as a kid, I never would have reached my eighteenth birthday."

"Remind yourself of that the next time Randy suggests something absurd."

"Like tonight, tomorrow, or the day after?"

"Exactly."

He grinned, feeling refreshed and keenly excited, as though he were Randy's age himself. Abruptly he took Betsy's mug out of her hand, his fingers lightly grazing her smooth white ones. Again he was struck by a bolt of desire, but he struggled to ignore it as he pulled her to her feet. "Come on. This way you'll know what to do on Memorial Day."

To his delight, his spunky companion offered no resistance to his suggestion for nocturnal fun. He grabbed an old newspaper off her desk for them to sit on, then led her out the back door of Ye Olde Fabric Shoppe and up the cement blocks that served as steps to the roof of the store next door. Only then did Betsy ask, "We're not trespassing or anything, are we? I've met the owner of this market and he seems nice enough, but—"

"We're going to sit on *your* roof, not his, and besides, he's—" Spence paused as he considered explaining the relationship and decided to avoid it "—sort of a relative of mine."

"Sort of?" she asked, giggling now as the night air intensified their mutual spirit of playfulness.

Spence steadied Betsy with both hands, astounded by the realization that every time he touched her, he felt hot and weak in the knees. Somehow, he didn't think this was the time to tell her that Randall Atkinson had once been his father-in-law and hadn't spoken to him in over eight years. In fact, he refused even to think about it.

The roof was flat and level, but terribly dirty, and Spence was glad they were both wearing old and washable jeans. He led Betsy to the street side of the building, stopping several feet from the ledge to spread out the newspapers he'd taken off Betsy's desk, then he sat down cross-legged and waited while she did likewise. They were close enough to see the street, but not close enough to be plagued with vertigo. "You sort of have to warm up to the idea of sitting on the edge," he remarked with a whimsical smile. "You can come up here every night and sit a foot or two closer until you're ready to dangle your tootsies over on Memorial Day."

"I'll look down when it's time for the parade, Spence," she promised. "In the meantime, I think I'll just enjoy the aerial view."

Spence followed her gaze, struggling to identify the nighttime stars. "It's easier to see the sky out in the country where we live," he pointed out. "Randy can name them all. Here the light interferes a little bit."

"A likely story," Betsy teased him. "I bet you can't even find the North Star."

"Can, too!" he asserted in a deliberately childish tone.

"Cannot!" she retorted in the same way.

"Can, too!"

"Cannot! I dare you." She grinned, her pixie smile underlining the tender teasing of her bright blue eyes. "I *double*-dare you."

He leaned toward her—she was sitting to the north of him—and pointed toward the sky. He tried to look where he was pointing, but it wasn't easy when he was drawn so intently to a sight that was just as heavenly and so much closer. Betsy's face was just inches from his, her cheeks pink in the crisp evening air, her eyes alive with joie de vivre. He sucked in his breath and whispered, "You could see it better if you'd turn around."

For the first time that evening, a quick blush stole across her face. He was amazed, alarmed...and secretly very pleased. She'd been so cool, so casual, so determined to convince him that Muskingum's rumors of romance between them meant nothing to her! But now, in that single shy glance, she'd given herself away.

Betsy turned around to look where he was pointing, and in so doing inadvertently nestled against his chest. He could have shifted into another position; he could have dropped the arm that pointed skyward and enfolded her in his arms. The fact that he even considered doing so alarmed him beyond measure.

There's no time for this folly, Spence, he reminded himself. *No room in your life to get bulldozed by a pretty face and a laughing smile.* Deliberately he reminded himself of the last time he'd sat on this very roof—twenty years ago?—on a night just this full of stars. He hadn't asked Randy's mother to marry him that evening, but the words were already in his teenage heart. That boy—so sweet, so innocent, so certain that his love for Tiffany and hers for him would last through all eternity—could have traveled through a time machine into the future and watched each thread of his life unravel, and he would not have believed it even then. How could he have imagined how pathetic a mother she'd turn out to be, or how much he'd grow to love his only son? How could he have believed that the sweet and helpless child-woman who had been his first love could be manipulated to such vengeance by another man, the one who had stolen his young wife even as she'd continued to assure him of her undying love? And how could he have foreseen that his passion for an angel's smile and a Siren's ripe breasts would all but sound the death knell to the family business, let alone his masculine pride?

His thoughts chastened him as he pointed toward the North Star, then shifted position—away from Betsy—as he outlined the Big Dipper. "Do you see the shape of the saucepan?" he asked as coolly as he could. "It's actually not a constellation, though it's a very well-known asterism. Astronomically it's more important as a part of Ursa Major, the Great Bear." Again he shifted position, trying to move farther away from Betsy but somehow finding her almost in his lap... and, to his discomfiture, relishing the sensation. "If you follow my hand to the right, you'll see the bear's nose. His feet are directly below the bottom rim of the saucepan.''

Still leaning against him, Betsy said, "I guess I was wrong about you."

He could feel her warm breath against his bare arm, but her tone was noncommittal. "How do you mean?" he asked uncertainly.

She met his eyes with a bright, mischievous expression, then sobered as she read his ill-concealed tension. For a moment he ached to pull her close, but he knew he'd regret it if he did. If he'd learned anything from his ill-fated marriage, it was to listen to the voice of caution when it thundered in his head.

Again Betsy read his hesitance and subtly shifted away from him. "I mean, you do know something about stars," she finally admitted, though Spence was sure that that was not what she'd originally intended to say. She smiled again, but this time her smile was thin and uncertain, and Spence felt a wash of confusion. When she looked strong and capable, she only vaguely resembled Randy's mother. But when her heart-shaped face took on a vulnerable cast, she could actually have passed for Tiffany.

It wasn't a particularly comforting notion. Spence reminded himself that he had no intentions toward this woman other than simply friendship, so her resemblance to his ex-wife surely didn't matter.

Did it?

"Do you really think Muskingum can pull off this Renaissance faire?" Betsy asked almost bluntly, as though she realized that the conversation was about to lag. "I know that everybody in town can quote Shakespeare, but the organization involved is going to be staggering."

"Don't sell Mrs. Mac short," Spence replied, glad to be on sturdy ground again. He struggled to toss out a few more safe comments, but he only came up with "And Janet is a whiz at organization," before his mind went numb.

For no reason that he could explain, Spence found himself staring into Betsy's truthful blue eyes again, wanting to go on staring into them forever. She didn't look hopeful, or worried, or even particularly hurt. She just looked as though she found his face as fascinating as he found hers, and she looked as though she, too, wanted the moment to go on forever.

Against his will, against his own best judgment, Spence trailed his right hand along her jaw. His fingers were grimy from the rooftop dirt, but he didn't apologize for the streak he tracked across her chin; it seemed to fit her quiet courage. She didn't move as his fingertips slipped into her hair and clumsily spilled the remaining loose bobby pins until her blond hair spun around her head like a halo. His palm grew warm as he cradled her jaw...and then, ever so slowly, began to tug her toward him.

It occurred to Spence, in some distant part of his brain, that maybe Betsy didn't want him to kiss her. It occurred to him that he really didn't think it was such a good idea himself. And then it occurred to him that he wanted to kiss her more than he'd wanted to kiss anybody in a very long time, and unless she told him flatly to get his hands off of her, he was going to nuzzle her inviting lips with his own and revel in this reckless, delicious moment of decadence as long as he possibly could.

And then the red light flashed upon them from the street below. It was slowly circling, like a hawk pursuing its prey.

"All right, you kids," an authoritarian voice—a terribly familiar authoritarian voice—boomed up from beneath them. "Come on over here where I can see you. Just edge over nice and slow."

Betsy blanched.

Spence closed his eyes and desperately wished that he lived anywhere but in Muskingum. He dropped his hands from Betsy's face as though her pale skin had burned him, then he raised his voice just slightly to respond to Officer Marvin Oates, who was doing one of the jobs he got paid for—supervising the unofficial evening curfew of the local kids.

"It's okay, Marvin," he called out. "We're just up here enjoying the view."

He crawled over to the edge of the roof and looked down just as Marvin said, "Geoffrey Spencer? Is that you?"

"It's me, Marvin. Sorry to have troubled you."

By this time Betsy had crawled over beside him, whispering, "Should I tell him that I lease this place?"

Spence shook his head, comforting her with an embarrassed grin. Instantly she started to chuckle at their predicament, but she couldn't laugh out loud, so she covered her mouth and shook silently. In an instant, Spence was shaking in silence, too.

"Geoffrey, you feeling all right?" Marvin asked again, as though he thought a breathalizer test was in order. "Do you want me to come up there and help you down?"

It took all of Spence's willpower not to go into hysterics now. Randy would simply die when he heard about this. And since Charley's was just closing up for the night and a half a dozen people were now gathered across the street, staring, there was no doubt that Randy *would* find out.

"No, Marvin. We're just fine. Fortunately overindulgence is not one of my shortcomings. It's a lovely night, lovely moon, lovely girl. Just thought I'd enjoy them all."

He was feeling good again. He didn't care what the town thought of his interest in Betsy; when Marvin left, by golly, he just might try to kiss her again. He felt silly and young and full of life. When Randy told him he was the laughingstock of the town, he'd just grin and say, "That's the breaks, kid. That's the breaks."

And then Betsy crawled into Marvin's view, and the old policeman's face turned positively white.

"As I live and breathe, Geoffrey Spencer, the things I see on this beat never cease to amaze me. Are you really up there again with *Tiffany*?"

Spence heard the sharp intake of his own breath, a near gasp as he considered the meaning of Marvin's words. Tiffany, Betsy: wasn't it all the same? Was the similarity only in their looks? Was it in their hearts, as well? Or just in his? Did it matter? A love-besotted fool was an idiot at any age. Thank God he wasn't smitten with Betsy Hanover yet, just drunk on the cool spring air and a rare playful mood. It had been great fun, but he'd enjoyed Tiffany, too, on this roof and in dozens of other places. And he'd paid for his folly—oh, God, how he'd paid for it!—and if he continued down the path he'd picked this evening, it was just a matter of time before he paid for this rerun, as well.

"Fortunately I'm the type of person who learns from my mistakes and doesn't repeat them often," Betsy had said this evening. *So am I,* Spence vowed, challenging her with eyes that were suddenly cold and wary. He ignored the sudden flash of hurt and confusion that shadowed her calm expression as he said to the policeman, "Just a trick of the light tonight, Marvin. This woman only looks like Tiffany. You'll never see me up here with *her* again.''

He realized that Mrs. MacGillicuddy wouldn't approve of his last sentence; he could have been referring to either woman when he'd vowed to keep his distance from ''her.'' But Spence knew that the grammatical question was a moot one, because it didn't matter whether he was speaking of Betsy Hanover or his traitorous ex-wife. He'd never let either one of them uproot his life again.

CHAPTER FIVE

BY EIGHT O'CLOCK the next evening, when Janet's red Datsun 280ZX pulled into the long blacktop driveway that led to Paul Hardison's stately Pittsburgh mansion, Betsy was feeling the strain of her long day and beginning to regret that she'd agreed to attend this meeting. Mrs. Mac had insisted that Betsy's expertise in costumes made her presence mandatory, but she suspected that Spence's former teacher simply didn't want Janet to go alone, and was just too proud to admit that the long trip, which would conclude with their return to Muskingum in the wee hours of the night, would be too much for an elderly gal. Betsy just hoped it wouldn't be too much for Janet or her, either. Both women had put in a full day's work before starting off for Pennsylvania, stopping not only for dinner but also for a brief check on Betsy's Pittsburgh store. She had been a little disconcerted to find her manager, Wilma Cox, in an obvious state of exhaustion after working twelve-hour days for the past week while two of her part-time employees struggled with the flu. Betsy had called a former employee who was an old friend to fill in for Wilma, who she'd sent home with orders to spread out overtime among other employees in the future no matter what it cost.

"I can't say I expected anything quite like this," Janet commented as she parked her car in a small clearing across the street from a wooden sign that said Hardison in Gothic script. "This looks more like a castle than a home for real people."

It was an accurate description. The isolated house was so big it was anybody's guess how many rooms it contained. The ones that faced the road had obviously been attached over the years: the outside walls were a jumble of odd angles. Turrets and balconies abounded, and one could almost imagine a tower lurking somewhere above the pointed rooftop. And Mrs. Mac had said that the Hardison property included one hundred oak-studded acres—behind the mansion—which served as the grounds for the Renaissance faire.

"I thought you said Paul Hardison lived alone," Betsy said to her companion. "This doesn't look like a single man's abode."

"From what I hear, it's more like a museum. Mrs. Mac says he thinks of himself as the caretaker," Janet replied. "He's incredibly wealthy and has no heirs. He treats all of his collections like children."

Betsy pulled on her trim blue coat and followed Janet toward the locked wrought-iron gate, where they were greeted by a cacophony of growls and barks—awesome in the darkness. Instinctively she and Janet huddled together as two snapping, snarling Dobermans hurled themselves at the heavy fence with a vengeance.

"I can't imagine why anybody would be foolish enough to ignore *that* warning," Janet declared, shivering as she pointed toward the bright silver sign that told all would-be burglars the premises were also guarded by an electronic alarm system. "I'm normally very fond of dogs, but *I* certainly wouldn't take any chances with one of them!"

"My sentiments exactly," Betsy replied with feeling. "Let's push the buzzer and just wait for Paul."

It turned out to be a long wait. Nearly two minutes passed before they heard a creaky voice on the intercom asking them to identify themselves, and they waited that long again before they heard the same faint voice calling off the dogs.

"I'm so glad you were free to come along with me tonight, Betsy," Janet confessed as they stood in the darkness, waiting. "Spence really didn't want me to drive back so late alone."

Betsy was touched by Spence's solicitude. Her own brothers had stopped worrying about her when she was in college, and neither one of her brothers-in-law had ever expressed the slightest interest in her comings and goings. "Is he always so protective of you?" she asked.

Janet smiled. "Yes, he is, and I love him for it. When Bill was still alive, Spence only stepped in when Bill was gone, but even then I always knew I could count on him in a pinch. He was so used to being Bill's big brother that I think it was natural for Spence to take Bill's wife under his wing."

"He mentioned that you all used to live together," Betsy said.

"Yes, we did. For nearly five years." Her nostalgic tone made it clear that the experiment had been a great success. "When I married Bill, we were both in college and nearly broke. Bill's dad was helping us out, and when he died so suddenly—he had a heart attack—Spence took over paying the bills. By then Tiffany had left him and he was fighting for custody of Randy, so every penny counted. I had a long commute to law school, but I'm glad we came back when we did because it meant so much to Bill to be able to help Spence with the family business." Briefly she met Betsy's eyes in the light of the streetlamp. "I don't mean that Spence couldn't have managed it on his own, but the two of them had always wanted to run the business together, and with their father gone, it just didn't seem right for Spence to be taking care of everything by himself."

Hating to sound nosy but too curious not to ask, Betsy questioned, "Where was Mrs. Spencer during all this time?"

"Bill's mom? She died when the boys were in grade school. I think that's part of what made them even closer than most brothers, and especially close to their dad. It's also what made Spence so sure he could raise his son without a woman. Don't get me wrong—both boys adored their mother and so did their dad. I think the family kind of lost its breath for a while after she died, but eventually they all put the pieces back together and found a way to make things work." Suddenly she was blinking back tears. "And that's just what Spence had to do all over again. Not just when Tiffany left him, but again when his dad died, and then his brother, too."

Instinctively Betsy reached out a hand to rub Janet's shoulder. It was the second time this evening that the mention of Bill had produced tears, and Betsy knew by now that she didn't have to speak; Janet was working through her grief in her own way, deliberately teaching herself to get used to talking about her husband again.

There was hardly a subject that the two women hadn't discussed on the long drive from Muskingum. Janet had chatted openly about the joys and frustrations of getting a fledgling law practice off the ground. She'd also revealed a thousand tiny things about Spence that Betsy would never have asked but was delighted to know. He had a sweet tooth, a fondness for cats and a great weakness where babies were concerned. He hated housework and he wasn't much of a cook, but he resisted the idea of making a woman do the chores he detested, even for a good wage, so he did them all himself. He'd had a rough time letting Randy outgrow his need to spend all his spare time with his father, but he was determined not to hold on too tight. Though he never said so outright, Janet suspected that Spence would have liked to have another three or four kids if he could have found a way to do it without taking on the burden of a wife.

"He's still allergic to marriage after all this time?" Betsy had asked.

"Not exactly. I think it would be more accurate to say that Spence is allergic to *divorce*. If the right woman could ever convince him that she'd never be unfaithful, walk off with his child or drain the coffers of Black Gold Supply, I think he'd like the idea of sharing his life with somebody again. He's far too sociable to be happy as a hermit."

Betsy had struggled to smile. "Marriage doesn't come with any guarantees," she'd pointed out. "And I'm not sure it should. Some things you just need to take on faith. Without trust, I don't think any relationship has much meaning. And what relationship could be more important than marriage?"

"You don't have to convince me," Janet agreed. "Bill and I never wanted any guarantees. We just loved each other, and that was enough. My only regret is that we didn't have another fifty years."

It seemed nearly that long before Paul Hardison managed to lock up the dogs in their pen and unlock the front gate. By then the two women would have been glad to see anybody, but the grinning octogenarian who greeted them was an extraordinary delight.

He couldn't have been more than five foot five or six. He wore a padded brocade doublet and slops of a vibrant kelly green, with glimmers of red satin showing through the deep, rounded pleats. A red velvet cape was draped around his shoulders, a heavy lace ruff encircled his neck and an ornate black cap perched jauntily on his head. With his long curly beard and flyaway white hair, shaggy where it met his shoulders, he bore a passing resemblance to one of Santa's elves.

"By the faith, Mistress Janet!" he greeted them exuberantly. "Thou wast to have been up betimes!"

Betsy stared at him blankly, but Janet would have done Mrs. Mac proud. "Aye, even so, Gaffer Paul," she replied with a deep curtsy that lost none of its panache despite the fact that she was wearing black gabardine slacks. "But my good gray mare threw a shoe upon the road. Naught could I do but lead her to the smithy."

"By Saint Christopher, 'tis ill luck!" he replied sympathetically, brandishing an enormous collection of keys that hung near his velvet belt between a dangling tin cup and an orange dotted with whole cloves.

While he fussed with the gate for an incredibly awkward period of time, Betsy whispered to Janet, "What was that all about?"

"He asked why we were late, even though we aren't, and I told him the car broke down, so to speak, even though it didn't, because that's the kind of answer Mrs. Mac taught me to give. Either he's crazy or he's really into this faire thing!"

"Let's hope it's the second," Betsy said. "Why did you call him 'Gaffer'?"

"It means grandfather. It's a mark of respect for an older person, and I just remembered that Mrs. Mac's uncle told her that Mr. Hardison prefers to be called 'Gaffer Paul.'"

A moment later they were inside the gate and "Gaffer Paul" was saying, "And who might this be, Mistress Janet?" His gaze fell warmly on Betsy's face. "An angel! Aye, or if not, an earthly paragon."

Any reservations about the old man that Betsy had harbored melted in that instant, and she dropped a curtsy herself. "They call me 'Lady Elizabeth,' Gaffer Paul," she introduced herself. Sweeping one hand graciously toward the mansion, she intoned melodramatically, "Never did I think to meet heaven while still on this earthly place, but I have surely crossed through Saint Peter's pearly gates." Betsy was sure that her lame rendition of Elizabethan English was a poor imitation of Janet's, and she wished she'd spent more time reading the list of phrases Mrs. Mac had given her.

But apparently Gaffer Paul was pleased with her effort; he gave Betsy a wink as he crossed his arms over his chest, letting his ring-laden hands clank against four rows of heavy gold chains. "Oh, sweet princess! Thou couldst sing the savageness out of a bear!" he murmured with a heartfelt sigh.

Betsy and Janet exchanged enchanted grins, struggling to respond in equally lofty terms as they followed the old man into his extravagant house. The living room had high sculpted ceilings and wall hangings of Renaissance design. A full suit of armor stood like a statue in the main hallway, and a brace of sabers crowned one wall. He offered them "mead and ale" while he quizzed them about their own plans for the faire—in twentieth century English, fortunately—showing a great deal of interest in Betsy's background in fabric and design.

"Let me show you my costume collection," Gaffer Paul suggested after she'd shared her preliminary ideas. "Now we'll be using these at the faire in June, but after

that I'd be happy to loan them to you. Most of our people have been doing this so long they have costumes of
their own, so I really don't keep that many here. But I
think you'll find enough samples of each type to give you
something to model your own on."

He led them through the house to another large room
near the back, which he had to unlock. An enormous
portrait of Queen Elizabeth I dominated one wall and an
antique tapestry of a pastoral scene owned another. Underneath the tapestry was a row of plush-lined glass cases
that cushioned hundreds of artistically displayed coins.
On a nearby table sat a clear Lucite box, a stained piece
of velvet, a bottle of olive oil and number of odd-size
coins.

"Here they are," he announced, opening a walk-in
closet that housed at least a dozen exotic costumes.
"You'll find them all arranged by sex and social class—
women on the right, men on the left, noble, merchant
and peasant. All the men's clothes are in my size, I'm
afraid. I pick something different to wear every year."
Before Betsy could ooh and ah over the beauty and di-
versity of the clothes, Gaffer Paul seized a fringed leather
vest and matching chaps and stared at the vest in wonder. "Now what's this doing in here? I remember some
young whippersnapper brought it to a meeting because
it was leather and he thought it would work as a jerkin,
but of course this fringed look was never used in Elizabethan times. It's totally unsuitable for a Renaissance
faire, but I must have left it here because I couldn't remember who it belongs to." He paused for a moment, his
eyes glazing over, and Betsy had the distinct feeling that
the name of the owner of the cowboy outfit wasn't the
only memory that eluded him.

He was still trying to remember the "young whipper-snapper's" name, when a loud buzzer rang inside the house.

"Ah! The rest of my guests. You young ladies go ahead and study the costumes while I let everybody in. I should have left the gates unlocked."

On that note he hobbled off toward the front door at a speed that clarified why Janet and Betsy had had to wait so long to enter his estate.

Janet jabbed Betsy's rib cage with her elbow the minute he was out of earshot. "Isn't he something?" she whispered excitedly. "Mrs. Mac will go crazy when she meets him!"

"He's too sweet for her," Betsy replied without thinking. "It would be like tossing a rosebud under the wheels of a Mack truck."

"Betsy!" Janet admonished her. "You've got to look past the mask of a prickly person and see what's in her heart. I agree that Gaffer Paul is a sweetie, but underneath all those puffy feathers, so is Mrs. Mac."

Betsy was saved from a reply by the slow return of Gaffer Paul and his debonair companion, who turned out to be called John Percy. John was a tall man—at least six foot three or four—with jet-black hair, radiant blue eyes and a bushy black mustache. He was agile on his feet and lithe, and the smile of greeting he gave Betsy was obviously designed to make her glad she'd been born a woman on his side of the continental divide.

The fact that it was identical to the winking grin he gave Janet didn't bother Betsy in the least. She told herself she didn't care because she liked Janet and honestly believed she'd been in mourning too long. But the voice of honesty prodded her to admit that there was another reason, a reason she could run from but never quite escape. A reason that bore the name of Geoffrey Spencer.

She'd gotten his message loud and clear on Monday night. He desired her as a woman and liked her as a friend, but he was serious about keeping his distance from any single female in Muskingum, and he never would have spent the evening with her, let alone nearly kissed her, if her bold greeting in the theater hadn't taken him off guard. Even before she'd heard Janet's summation of her brother-in-law's ill-fated marriage, Betsy had realized that if she ever wanted to get to know Spence better, she'd need to back off and give him lots of room. Intellectually, that was easy to do. All she had to do was act friendly but casual when she ran into him again. And it took no genius to see that she was only going to see Spence by accident; he wasn't likely to call her up for a date. And considering everything that had happened so far—and everything that hadn't—calling him up herself would be the worst thing she could possibly do.

It all sounded very logical, very rational. But for some reason Betsy felt restless with the notion of letting her fledgling relationship with Spence coast along unattended. It could end up anywhere . . . or get lost forever at sea.

"So you two ladies are from Ohio?" the Tom Selleck look-alike greeted them warmly.

"Muskingum," Janet told him. "Just over the state line. It's a very small community, but a close one with a lot of interest in Shakespeare. We may be biting off more than we can chew, but we're willing to give it our best shot."

"Who can ask for more than that?" He gave Janet another appreciative grin, then went on to ask her what sort of booths she was planning to set up at the faire.

Betsy listened to the conversation with one ear, her mind still on the costumes, while Gaffer Paul hobbled over to the coin case shaking his head.

"Is something wrong?" Betsy asked when she heard him moan.

"I'm missing some of my English monarch coins," he declared in a ragged voice, turning desperate, blurry blue eyes on Betsy as she hurried toward him. "They go right here." He pointed to a hole in the middle of a case that Betsy quickly guessed was meant to hold a single Lucite box...a box just the size of the one on the worktable.

Instantly Betsy touched his arm and tugged him lightly in that direction. "There are some coins out over here, Gaffer Paul. Is there any chance that—"

"Oh, they're all right!" he burst out with a sigh, running his thin fingers through his salt-and-pepper beard in keen relief. "I thought...I thought..." He stared at Betsy, clearly disoriented, and for a moment she was sure he was going to say he'd never seen her before. Then he said slowly, "I must have been cleaning them. Yes, that's right. I was cleaning them this morning. Or was it yesterday?" He debated the two possibilities for a moment or two, then gave up the riddle as insurmountable. "Coins have to be cleaned quite often, you know," he cautioned Betsy. "Like children. They never play in the dirt, but they get dirty just the same."

He dragged himself over to the worktable just as John and Janet, who'd been interrupted by the commotion, gave up on their conversation and joined him. As Betsy trailed the old man, she met John's eyes, and he shook his head in a gesture that seemed to imply such episodes of forgetfulness on Gaffer Paul's part were not uncommon.

But to his host he said only, "They're nice and clean now, Gaffer Paul," as he knelt down to study the coins with a professional eye. "Do you want me to put them away for you?"

Paul laid one frail hand on John's shoulder and nodded gratefully as the buzzer went off again. Looking like a blind puppy in search of his mother, Paul wobbled out the door again as Betsy, eager to help, plucked the first giant coin from the table, securely pressing it between her thumb and fingers to make sure she didn't drop it.

"No!" John Percy burst out so suddenly that she almost dropped the coin, anyway. "Don't ever touch a coin like that!"

Horrified, Betsy laid the coin back on its temporary velvet bed. John had been so amiable a moment before that his sudden vehemence had taken her totally by surprise. But when his eyes met hers he looked shamefaced and apologetic.

"I'm sorry, Betsy, I didn't mean to shout," he told her, his voice low and quiet now. "But some of these coins are worth thousands of dollars, and their faces should *never* come into contact with the human hand."

"Why not?" she asked humbly.

"Because the moisture and oil on even the cleanest skin can stain them. Worse yet, their value is determined by how close they are to mint condition, and mint condition means a coin didn't even spend one afternoon in a woman's purse or a man's pocket. Extremely fine condition means they've been handled but still look nearly new, and each gradation after that can mean hundreds of dollars to the seller or buyer."

Betsy found it hard to believe she'd just cost Gaffer Paul a few hundred dollars by picking up one scuzzy old coin, which clearly had spent a lot more than one afternoon in somebody's pocket. She made a mental note to ask Spence about it the next time they met. "I'm sorry, John. I certainly didn't mean to hurt the coin," she said truthfully. "But this one is obviously pretty old, and—"

"It certainly is. It was minted about the time of the Revolution."

"The American Revolution?" Betsy asked. "I thought these were English coins."

"They are. But this cartwheel—they call it that because it's so big—came out during the reign of King George III. It's not nearly as valuable as some of the rare, earlier coins Paul has, but it's hardly something to play games with."

"I wasn't playing with it, John," Betsy felt compelled to say in her own defense. After all, he might have known Paul longer than she had, but they were both guests in his house and neither one was in a position to act possessive about coins. "I was just trying to help."

"I know," he replied with a hint of his earlier warmth. His cultivated smiles sought to whisk away his earlier hard words. "So was I."

"Well, then," said Janet, who bravely picked up the coin in question by surrounding its rim with two fingers, as she'd no doubt been taught by one of the male Spencers, "let's put these lovely things away."

Betsy gingerly followed suit, and her handling of the coins seemed to meet with John's approval. But it occurred to her, as he lovingly tucked the box of monarch coins back into the glass case, that if he'd really wanted to help the tired old man who was so easily befuddled, John would have let Gaffer Paul put away his own precious coins while *he* volunteered to answer the front door.

FOR A GOOD SOLID WEEK after Marvin Oates caught him on the roof with Betsy Hanover, Spence asked himself over and over again, *What the hell was I thinking of? Ten minutes alone with that woman and I promptly lose my head.*

He didn't mind all that much that Marvin had had a good laugh at his expense. He didn't even mind that Randy had razzed him about the incident for days. What troubled him was what had gone on *before* the flashing red light of Marvin's squad car had broken up their rooftop tête-à-tête. Betsy had been nestled in Spence's arms, and there was no way he could look himself in the mirror and deny that he'd been about to kiss her.

Idiot! Fool! he reproached himself. He didn't have time for such nonsense. Neither his role as a father nor his personal values allowed for meaningless sex in his life, and the scars he still bore from his marriage tended to make him leery of any other kind. His situation left him in a quandary; he was neither a misogynist nor a celibate man at heart. Fortunately, during the difficult years immediately following his divorce, he'd had too many other things weighing on his mind—securing his son, holding on to the family business, coping with his brother's tragic death—to worry much about women. But now that his life was on a pretty even keel, he had time to take note of all the joys of manhood he'd been missing. Betsy Hanover, he told himself, was just the first unattached female to catch his eye.

Ignore her, he warned himself on Thursday night when he walked into the gym for the second Renaissance faire meeting and found her perched on the bleachers near the mike. She was wearing a casual oxford shirt, rolled up at the wrists, and a well-worn pair of jeans that lovingly caressed every one of her perfect curves when she stood

up a few minutes later and helped Janet give the group a
summary of their trip to Pittsburgh.

She didn't seem to notice Spence until the meeting
broke up a few hours later, when she flashed the most
casual of friendly smiles in his direction. To Spence's relief and uncomfortable consternation, she did not make
a beeline for him even then. In fact, if his path to the exit
door hadn't taken him within a few feet of her position
at the foot of the bleachers, he didn't think she would
have spoken to him at all.

"Good evening, Spence. Hi, Randy," she greeted his
son.

Randy, who was trying to hop from bleacher to
bleacher on one foot and hold on to Laurie with both
arms at the same time, disentangled himself when his father lightly slapped his shoulder. He somehow managed
to say hello.

"Did your Aunt Janet tell you about the coin collection we saw in Pittsburgh?" Betsy asked, her eyes focused not on Spence but on the gangly, younger version
of him. "It was really quite spectacular. The elderly
gentleman we met there has at least a half-dozen coins
from the reign of every English monarch."

Randy actually released his octopus grip on Laurie, his
eyes riveted on Betsy's face. "You mean he's got coins
from the Renaissance? They must be five hundred years
old!"

"He's got coins predating the Norman conquest in
1066, Randy!" Betsy went on, apparently sharing Randy's enthusiasm. "Each one is specially displayed in a
glass case lined with velvet and he's got burglar alarms set
round the clock. His collection must be worth a fortune."

"I wish *I* had a fortune," Randy lamented. "All I've got is a bunch of cardboard penny cases full of American coins that anybody could buy. It would be so neat to have a medieval collection. Even one single coin! Dad—"

"Forget it," Spence answered more bluntly than he might have if they'd been alone. "Betsy's right. They're worth a fortune. Even more than I spent on those running shoes."

Randy promptly tugged off one of his spanking new shoes and handed it to his father with a grin. "Do you suppose we could trade it in for a Queen Anne shilling?"

"Gee, I don't know," Spence replied with a wink, then tossed the shoe to Laurie. "Why don't you ask George about a trade-in next time you're downtown?"

Laurie giggled, then said good-night as she tugged Randy toward the parking lot. He followed eagerly, hopping along on one foot as he pleaded for his shoe. As the two young lovers disappeared in the darkness, Spence found himself unable to dodge Betsy's thoughtful gaze.

Despite the ongoing hubbub in the gym, the tiny circle of awareness surrounding Spence and the ash-blond woman who stood beside him seemed infinitely silent and intense. He tried to divine what she was thinking—what she expected from him after Monday night—but after a fleeting awkward moment, her face quickly brightened as she began to talk about the faire.

"We met the man in charge of the fencing booth in Pittsburgh, Spence, and he gave Janet all the details. It really doesn't sound all that difficult for somebody who knows how to fence."

He smiled but shook his head. "Sorry. You ladies are out of luck. I'm not into spectacular displays. I'm strictly a behind-the-scenes player."

He expected her to argue with him just a little, at least feed his ego in hopes of getting him to change his mind. But she quickly dismissed him as Oma Potter caught her eye. "Looks like my behind-the-scenes work is just beginning, Spence," she informed him cheerfully, with no hint that she regretted cutting their conversation short. "Oma's signaling me that she needs some help with measurements for the queen." She flashed him the quickest of farewell smiles before she disappeared.

Well, good, Spence told himself. *She knows that moment on the roof was just a fluke and doesn't mean a thing.* Convinced that he'd have no trouble with Betsy Hanover viewing him as a likely lover, he strolled slowly out of the gym into the clear, star-spangled night.

The air was unusually crisp, and he tried to tell himself he found it refreshing. But for some reason, as he spied Randy and Laurie huddled beside the truck giving each other the feverish, I-can-hardly-wait-till-tomorrow kisses of puppy love, he felt nostalgic for the innocence of his youth. Would he ever dare give himself so freely to a woman again? *I doubt it,* he admitted, surprised that the notion troubled him.

And then he glanced back at the gym, where he caught the slightest glimpse of Betsy's tousled hair and carefree smile as she trotted past the bleachers. The sharp lurch in his stomach took him by surprise, and he realized in an instant that he'd been lying to himself all evening. He'd come here planning to make it clear to Betsy that there was no hope whatsoever that the romantic moment they'd shared on the rooftop would ever be repeated, no matter what feminine wiles she might cleverly employ to entice him. It didn't do much for his ego to realize that while he was still struggling to come to grips with everything that had happened Monday night after they'd left the movie, Betsy Hanover had apparently washed the entire episode from her mind.

CHAPTER SIX

BETSY SAW SPENCE three times in the next week. The first
time he was picking out ripe peaches in Shuley's Meat
and Produce Mart, and they talked about the relative
merits of clings and Babcocks. The second time he was
driving east on Main Street while she was driving west,
and he pulled up to talk to her in the middle of the street.
Sitting in their respective cars, motors idling, they chatted elbow to elbow about the record-breaking heat. The
third time he was leaving Charley's just as she dropped
in for lunch, and he mentioned, just in passing, that he'd
heard *Grease* was the current feature at the Muskingum
Movie House.

It was, Betsy told herself, sheer coincidence that she
and Spence happened to drift into the theater about the
same time the following Monday evening, and chance,
nothing more, that caused him to join her at the shop
again for a late-night snack. There was nothing remarkable about their discussion, nothing unique about the
way they sat on opposite ends of her tiny office couch.
Certainly nobody mentioned getting together at the theater a third time, but the following week, Betsy decided
that the new movie listed on the marquee was one worth
viewing, and she chose to go on Monday because the
"crowds" of downtown Muskingum were lighter on the
first night of the week. Spence showed up, too, but he
was quick to remind Betsy that he'd only come to the

theater because he had absolutely nothing else to do while
his son attended Mrs. Mac's poetry club.

It was a scene they repeated for three consecutive weeks
before Betsy said one Monday evening, "You know,
Spence, I had a yen for peach pie over the weekend so I
did some baking. I put one in the freezer, but I'll never
be able to eat all of the one that I sampled last night. Any
chance you'd like to try a piece?"

Spence stared at her blankly for a moment, caught off
guard. She could see the resistance in his eyes, the questions about where such an invitation might lead and what
the town would make of it. But ultimately his sweet tooth
won the battle. "Peach, you say? It's been a long, long
time since I've eaten homemade pie. If it's really going to
go to waste, I imagine I could be persuaded to help you
polish it off."

Despite the casual words, the smile on Spence's face
revealed that it wasn't just the pie that drew him to Betsy's little house. And though he didn't touch her as he fell
into step beside her, it seemed to Betsy that he strolled
along a lot closer to her than was absolutely necessary,
and he didn't pull away when their elbows brushed.

The air was warm and still and the tangy scent of
orange blossoms permeated several square blocks of the
town. They didn't chat much as they walked together, but
each felt a comfortable sense of camaraderie. Betsy noticed that Spence was steering her unerringly toward 238
Scarlet Elm Street, even though he'd never asked her
where she lived, and as he followed her through the front
door he told her the history of the quaint little red house
as though it were an old friend.

"Milton Jeffries put it up in 1916 for his youngest son
and his bride. Their only daughter, Sara Jane, never
married, and she stayed on here for some thirty years af-

ter her father's death. Her mother died when she was a baby,'' he added parenthetically as he perched comfortably on Betsy's brightly flowered couch.

She'd made the cover for the couch herself in a dozen hues of mauve and blue that harmonized well with her favorite navy recliner. The house was rented, and her furnishings weren't perfectly matched to the beige drapes and carpets, but at least they were bright and cheerful. Betsy had also dressed up her double bed with a green-and-white tree of life quilt and had transformed the second bedroom into a sewing workshop. She'd hung copper kettles all over the kitchen, as well. After having been in the tiny house a couple of months, she was starting to feel at home.

"A few years later, one of her nephews moved in with his wife and kids, but they up and moved to Nebraska last winter and that's when Carl Jeffries decided he'd rent it out.'' Spence grinned, pleased with his recital. "Carl is—''

"My landlord,'' Betsy supplied, suddenly aware that Spence was chattering because he was nervous. She was nervous, too. There was something...well, *intimate* about sharing her tiny living room with him. It felt as though the two of them were the only man and woman in the world.

"I guess you know who your own landlord is by now,'' he admitted sheepishly. "I was just going to point out that Carl is old Milton's grandson. That makes him a first cousin to Sarah Jane, the last single woman to reside in this house.''

Betsy chuckled, determined to mask her own jitters. "Is that indicative of something?''

"Not to me. But you'd be surprised how many folks have drawn that parallel while bringing me up-to-date on the history of this place."

"They've done that a lot, have they?"

"They certainly have. They've also pointed out that Carl's really too old to take care of the plumbing, the electrical work, things like that. They figure you'll need a younger man to look after you."

"I'm getting the picture."

They shared a laugh, but it was an uneasy one. Betsy had no doubt that Spence was trying to emphasize his interest in her was strictly platonic. Ironically, just the sight of him comfortably slouched on her couch was a poignant reminder of how many nights she'd dreamed of this very moment. She wasn't sure she could keep her joy—or her cautious hope about their future—from shining in her eyes.

Betsy's knees weren't more than six inches from his as she stood awkwardly in the middle of the room, and she had to suppress an almost overwhelming urge to curl up on his lap. She wished she could have said, "Spence, I don't particularly need a man to look after me, but you're one man I'd be delighted to have as a *very* special friend." But she knew that if she did—if she even took the liberty of sitting down beside him on the couch—he'd never come home with her again.

Instead she excused herself to go cut the pie in the kitchen, plopping down in the recliner adjacent to the sofa when she returned with a piece for each of them.

Spence said thank-you before he took his first apprehensive bite, but a moment later a sunbeam smile broke out on his face. "Betsy Hanover," he proclaimed, "this is, without question, the finest peach pie I have ever tasted in my life. If you ever get tired of running a fabric store, you could go into the bakery business.''

"I'm glad you like it," Betsy replied, a bit surprised by the force of his response. Granted, she did consider herself a good cook, and desserts were her specialty, but she was hardly a world-class baker. "I almost didn't make peach this time. Lately I've had a yen for my grandma's pineapple cream pie."

"Pineapple cream?" he repeated hungrily after he'd swallowed another bite. "I don't think I've ever eaten a pineapple cream pie."

"My grandma always made us one for Christmas. Maybe I'll carry on the tradition."

When his eyes met hers they were full of surprise and hope, but Betsy suspected that his enthusiasm was due largely to the prospect of sampling her grandma's recipe. She still wasn't sure what was on his mind when he asked her quietly, "Do you really expect to be here until Christmas, Betsy? Oma says you've only got a six-month lease because you'll be leaving her in charge while you go start another store in the fall."

Betsy's eyes grew wide. "Oma talks too much. Those are just plans on the drawing board. Nothing's been confirmed."

A quick blur of emotion—regret? relief—crossed Spence's face before he said, "I guess I'm the one who's guilty of spilling a confidence. It's hard for me to think of you as Oma's boss."

For some reason his words caused Betsy's heart to lurch and quicken. It didn't help any when she met Spence's gaze and saw the sudden surge of hunger in his dark, vibrant eyes. She held her stiff position in the upright recliner, but bravely she asked him, "Exactly how *do* you think of me, Spence?"

For a moment all of Scarlet Elm Street seemed swallowed up in silence while Spence stared hard at the tines of his fork. Then, very slowly, he took a deep breath and said, "I think of you as a friend, of course. You're my age, after all, not Oma's. It seems odd that she should be working for you instead of the other way around."

It wasn't the answer she'd hoped for, but Betsy realized that it was the answer she should have expected. "Well, experience isn't always a function of age, Spence," she pointed out in a deliberately offhand manner. "Quite frankly, I'm not at all certain I'll be able to leave Oma in charge of Ye Olde Fabric Shoppe in six months. The last time I did that—in Tennessee—my manager had owned a fabric store before. She has far more business skills than Oma does. Though, in all fairness—" she softened her words with a grin "—Oma has a bigger heart."

Her prosaic words seemed to mollify Spence. "She's really very fond of you, Bets," he informed her. "I don't know how she feels about running the store by herself, but I think that on a personal basis, she'd really like it if you found some reason to stick around in Muskingum."

And what about you, Spence? she longed to ask him. *Do you really like me? Do you want me to stay?* After all the time they'd spent together—always by "accident"— she still didn't know. Not once since that night on the roof had he ever touched her on purpose, let alone caressed her face or warmed her lips with a kiss. There were times when she was sure his eyes burned with barely restrained passion, but she had no proof to back up that suspicion, which could have been no more than wishful thinking.

Spence met Betsy's eyes for a long, quiet moment, but he said nothing as the almost palpable need between them throbbed. Betsy waited tensely for Spence to reach out for her hand, to touch her face, to say anything at all that she could translate into a message of desire, but once again he disappointed her.

The last few bites of Spence's pie suddenly seemed to require his utmost attention, and he didn't glance at Betsy until his plate was clean. When he set it on the end table and glanced conspicuously at his watch, Betsy declared as brightly as she could, "Well, I'm very fond of Oma, too, Spence. She's very efficient and she has a special knack with people. She always makes sure that all my customers leave happy and eager to return. She's convinced a number of them to join our sewing classes, even though they probably sew as well as I do. And besides that—" her smile was genuine as she thought of her white-haired older friend "—she has the most wonderful way of bucking me up when I'm feeling down."

Spence studied her carefully, as though she'd just presented him with a new idea. "I've never thought of you as feeling down, Betsy. You always seem so cheerful."

She shrugged. "I generally am. But I've got the same problems as anybody else."

He leaned forward, elbows on his knees, absorbing her words with care. "What sort of problems? I mean, if it's all right to ask."

Betsy waved away his concern. "Oh, nothing particularly traumatic. With a business expanding as fast as mine, there are bound to be headaches along the way. Not that I'm complaining, mind you."

Spence nodded sympathetically. "Boy, I've had *my* share of business problems in the past. When I was shelling out thousands of dollars every year for court costs, just keeping the doors open from one day to the next was a challenge."

Not certain whether this was the right time to lead him into a discussion of his custody battles with his ex-wife, Betsy suggested cautiously, "I imagine that was a very difficult time for you."

For just a moment, a bitter grimace streaked across his craggy face. "'Difficult' is an understatement. I wasn't just worried about losing Randy and the business. I thought I was losing my mind."

I wish I could have been here to help you, Betsy longed to say. Instead she reminded him prudently, "But you did hold on to everything, Spence. Randy, Black Gold Supply and your very clever mind." She grinned and was rewarded by a cautious smile from Spence. "How did you do it? Plain hard work, or did a miracle come your way?"

He chortled without mirth. "I'm not sure I'd ever call one of Tiffany's stupid stunts a miracle," he confessed, using his ex-wife's name with Betsy for the first time. "But I guess in a sense that's what it was. Tiffany had done everything imaginable to prove to the court that she was an incompetent mother, but in the days before *Kramer vs. Kramer*, it didn't seem to matter."

He sketched Tiffany's transgressions quickly, and Betsy found it hard to conceal her shock. While Randy's mother loved him in her own immature fashion and had never deliberately abused him, her faulty judgment had resulted in several harrowing experiences for him as a baby and small child, including an evening when she'd tucked her preschooler in bed for the night before going out on a date, assuming he'd stay asleep the whole time. She had neither hired a baby-sitter nor notified her neighbors of her plans, so by the time she got home at 2:00 a.m., the lady next door had called the police to break into the apartment to find out what was wrong with the terrified child who'd been screaming hysterically for over an hour. Yet even this incident had not been enough to persuade the court to award custody of the young boy to his father.

"Well, anyway, one day she fell in love with an Italian she met in New York and followed him back to Milan. On the spur of the moment—which is the way Tiffany makes most crucial decisions—she decided to take Randy with her. So overnight, she pulled up stakes and disappeared."

"She left the country with him?" Betsy gasped. "Without even letting you say goodbye?"

His rugged features darkened, but he swallowed the anger before it could consume him. "In all fairness, I have to say she didn't do it on purpose. She wasn't trying to punish me. In fact, *I* was the last person on her mind. It never occurred to her that I'd go crazy upon showing up for my next weekend visitation and finding that my eight-year-old son had disappeared."

"Oh, Spence!" Betsy burst out, too overwhelmed by sympathy to keep the dignified facade she'd planned. "What did you do? Hire a detective?"

He shook his head. "I didn't need to. She'd made no secret of where she'd gone. She'd proudly blabbed it to at least a dozen people. The irony of the thing is that she hadn't told the one person that the law required her to tell."

"You?"

"Nope. Her lawyer. An officer of the court, as it were. She violated a legal court order of the state of Ohio and forfeited her right to be physical custodian of my son. I'll tell you, Randy was halfway around the world when Janet explained that to me, but I was still jubilant."

Betsy leaned forward tensely, oblivious to how her knees now brushed against his. "So what happened? How did you get him out of Italy?"

He raised both hands in an expansive gesture. "I didn't. Randall Atkinson did."

"Mr. Atkinson who owns the store next door to me?"

"Precisely. Didn't I mention that he was Tiffany's dad?" His tone was innocent, but he couldn't quite meet Betsy's eyes.

Betsy knew perfectly well that he'd avoided clarifying his relationship with Atkinson on the night they'd climbed up on the roof, but she decided that this was not the time to make a federal case out of it. Quietly she answered, "No, I guess it slipped your mind."

Spence's grateful smile made the crow's-feet around his eyes grow deeper, and his apologetic expression tugged at Betsy's heart. "Well, I guess Tiffany slipped from the Italian's mind after a while, which doesn't really surprise me," he acknowledged with a sigh. "She makes a great first impression, but what you see isn't exactly what you get."

Suddenly his gaze pinioned Betsy, as though he were thinking, *Is it the same with you? Here we sit, so friendly, so warm, but in a week or a month or a year, might you turn on me, too?*

But apparently he pushed away his uncertainty, because a moment later he concluded, "When her new lover ran out on her, she called her dad and asked him to send her two plane tickets home. He did, of course, and the Muskingum rumor mill got the word to me by dawn the next day. I met her at Kennedy Airport with a pair of cops and a new court order." He couldn't conceal the pride of his victory, or the fierce determination never to let a woman put him through such hell again. "And seven years after that woman stole my only son, I brought him home to stay."

AN HOUR AFTER Spence left Betsy's, he received a call for an order of four five-gallon drums of pipe dough from Sonny Barnes, the graveyard shift driller at Williams Number Nine. Sonny was a gangly redhead who'd been mooning over the same girl for so long that every man in the oil patch, including Spence, found it necessary to rib him about the deaf ear she turned on his weekly proposals. Spence was surprised when Sonny reversed the tables on him tonight.

"Didn't interrupt nothing *private*, did I, Spence?" he asked with a chuckle in his voice. "Word in the patch has it that it's real hard to get a hold of you on Monday nights."

For a moment words failed Spence. Three or four trips to the theater—just to pass the time—and even the men at the drilling sites had him matched up with Betsy? He expected that from the local ladies, of course, but not from his friends in the oil business.

"Tell the boys to keep their shirts on, Sonny," he ordered firmly. "My son has a cub meeting on Mondays and I've got to kill a few hours somewhere. I don't play games with Cupid anymore. I'm no good with a bow and arrow."

"Yeah, I guess you were always better with a sword. I hear you're going to start fighting duels for this damsel in distress."

"Boy, you fellows must not be spending much time running pipe these days!" Spence quipped with all the humor he could muster, secretly vowing to make Janet pay for this one. Even the *possibility* that he might don those purple tights was enough to mark him in the patch!

"Don't you guys have anything better to do than spread lies about me?"

"Hell, no!" Sonny countered with a laugh. "We've even been laying odds on whether you're going to crack Mike Ralston's jaw when you get ahold of him."

This time Spence really was in the dark. Mike was an old teammate of Spence's, who was now the foreman at the old Wasco site, and though he no longer did business with Spence for various reasons, there was no bad blood between them. "Why would I be gunning for Ralston?"

"Rumor has it that Mike's got the hots for your girl. I hear he's started meeting her for lunch at Charley's."

For a moment Spence was blinded by the piercing vision of Betsy's heart-shaped face smiling into Mike's ugly mug as they chatted at Charley's, then moseyed on over to 238 Scarlet Elm for some peach pie and cozy conversation on that soft blue-and-purple couch. And maybe...after that...a visit to the bedroom, which Spence had glimpsed from the hall?

"No skin off my nose," he insisted, biting off the indifferent reply with terse, hard syllables. "Betsy Hanover's free to see any man she wants." *Why should I care? We're only friends, and I want to keep it that way!* Spence reminded himself fiercely. But sudden panic lurched through his chest all the same.

THEY SAT SIDE BY SIDE *in their regular seats in the theater, but instead of a movie screen they were looking at a Shakespearean stage. The players and the audience alike were dressed in Renaissance costumes, and Betsy's blue velvet gown sparkled with jewels. Even Spence was dressed like a knight, clad in clumsy armor. But one of his hands was uncovered, the hand that slipped around and over her shoulder to smooth a nonexistent wrinkle in the front of her low-cut dress. His warm, callused fingers stroked the deep square corner of her Renaissance neckline, exploring the upper curve of her full breast. Slowly his fingers slipped beneath the sensuous fabric; slowly they found their way inside the chemise. In the darkness they moved over her rigid nipple, back and forth and up and down, seizing it and letting it go, tugging on it ever so gently as the desire within her sparked and crackled and finally burst into flames.*

Just as Betsy felt herself opening up to him, losing all control, Spence noticed that everyone in the theater—Oma, Janet, Randy, even Mrs. Mac—was staring at them, and he abandoned her aching breast.

"Sir Geoffrey!" she pleaded in desperation. "O, wilt thou leave me so unsatisfied?"

"For thee I would do anything, my lady," vowed her shining knight, reading from a photocopied sheet that Mrs. Mac had suddenly thrust into his metal-gloved hand. "Run through fire would I for thy sweet sake, or bare my chest to another man's sword!"

A moment later, like magic, they were in Betsy's room, under the green-and-white quilt, and she saw Spence without his armor for the very first time. His broad chest was a mass of curly dark hair and his eyes were nearly black with desire for her. His strong body loomed above her, and then he lowered it until skin met warm, quivering skin. Two massive palms massaged each of her tingling breasts, while his lips seared her delicate throat with a thousand erotic kisses.

"Oh, Spence!" she cried as his tongue flicked over her upright nipple and his hips slid down to meet her own. "I love you, I love you, I love you!"

She waited for him to moan her name or call out "I love you, too!" but suddenly he started to fade like a

*ghost. She slid her eager palms over his back and below
to try to hold him, but suddenly there was nothing to
hold. Aching to finish the erotic journey she'd just begun, Betsy's legs quivered as she cried out loud, "Spence,
don't leave me like this! Don't leave me! Don't leave me
now!"*

But suddenly Betsy was wide-awake, gasping for
breath, in an empty bedroom that was chilly in the midnight darkness. Her body begged for completion of the
joy Spence had inspired within her, and she realized with
acute dismay that the dream was not an accident, a fleeting wish that daylight would sweep away. She'd been
craving his touch ever since the night they'd met, and
night after night she'd gone to sleep with his face in her
mind.

"Damn you, Spence Spencer!" she moaned into her
pillow, helpless to relieve her agony. "You want me, too.
I know you do! How long do we have to play this game?
Do you think I can wait for you forever?"

As Betsy lay alone in her empty bed, the questions
seemed to echo back and forth from wall to wall, waiting for an answer.

A WEEK AFTER Spence told Betsy how he'd gotten custody of Randy, she invited him home after the movie
again—she'd made cherry tarts—and the week after that
she bribed him with macaroons. They never discussed
their posttheater plans after that; they just headed toward Scarlet Elm Street on Monday evenings as regular
as clockwork. Of course, Spence never mentioned the
word "date," nor did he ever make arrangements to meet
Betsy in advance. He never called her on the phone for
any reason, though he often dropped by the shop to say
hello when he was downtown, occasionally armed with a

boxful of doughnuts, which he invariably left behind for
Betsy and Oma. When he ambled by her store on Memorial Day and saw that she was there even though the
store was officially closed, he went inside. She persuaded him to join her on the rooftop to watch the parade, and later they went to lunch—dutch treat, of
course—at Charley's. There were times when she'd find
him gazing at her with a kind of tender longing that had
little to do with their purportedly platonic friendship, but
every time she got her hopes up—every time she felt a
tremor of desire sweep through her when he accidentally
brushed her thigh or laid a consoling hand on her face—
he quickly filled the silence with talk of Betsy's business
or the Renaissance faire.

They talked a little about Spence's business, too, but
mainly they talked about life. Randy featured prominently in almost every discussion, and it grew increasingly evident how much Spence had sacrificed for the
singular privilege of living with his only son. Some subjects he avoided with determination—notably the details
of his life with Tiffany and his anguish over losing Bill
and his folks. So Betsy was surprised when, on a sweltering, humid Monday evening, as they sat side by side in
her front porch swing, he opened up again about his ex-
wife.

"I really don't know how it happened," he admitted
thoughtfully while he nursed some fresh-squeezed lem-
onade. "I mean, I know how I fell in love with her. A
teenage boy doesn't have a chance of defending himself
against the lethal combination of raging hormones and
an angelic face like that. I can even see how I managed to
miss the fact that her helplessness would turn out to be
more burdensome than enchanting over time. But what
I can't understand—" he finished off his third éclair and

made no protest when Betsy handed him a fourth "—is how she turned so vicious overnight. How she could seem so... well, so gentle, so kind—if ineffectual—and then turn into a..." He swallowed the description, as though he'd decided that Tiffany would suddenly appear on the porch if he let his full hatred of her loose.

"I know, intellectually, that it was just that aspect of her personality—her malleability—that I had enjoyed in my selfish adolescent days. The divorce might not have been so bad if I hadn't gone crazy every time I saw the guy she left me for. I was furious, hostile and possessive, of course, when I really didn't have a right to be anymore. And he decided he was going to prove to me that he was the winner—lock, stock, and barrel—and that's when he got her to start gunning for me in court. In the end, of course, that relationship died, and she flitted on to some other fellow—I've lost track of how many by now—but by then the damage was done. No matter how hard she tries to act pleasant these days, I'll never trust her again."

There was no truly safe reply to his lengthy dissertation, but Betsy felt the need to say something. "Maybe she just was too young to be fully formed as a person when she married you, Spence, and she still had to get the wrinkles out," she suggested, feeling hot and sticky— Tiffany's essence seemed to permeate the still, muggy air. "I don't think I turned into the woman I am today until just a few years ago, and I'm still changing a little all the time."

Spence eyed her carefully as he asked, "How much are you changing?"

"I just mean that nobody stays the same forever," she answered quickly, not certain that she liked his suspicious tone. "We all *grow*, Spence. At least we ought to."

"I'm not sure that growing and *changing* are exactly the same thing," Spence observed with ill-concealed bitterness. "Growing is a natural process of maturation. It ought to refine a person's character, sort of flesh it out. It shouldn't turn a lovely, adoring creature into some demon from the unknown."

The humidity was enough to make anybody testy, but Betsy was sure the weather was the least of what was bothering the virile man beside her. Quietly she asked, "You still hate her, don't you, Spence?"

A dark frown seized his handsome features, but he shook it off with a determined grin. "No. Not really. I'd like to think I've moved past that. But there are things that I learned from my experience with Tiffany that I'll never forget." Suddenly his tone softened as his eyes rested on Betsy's heart-shaped face with a shadowy kind of longing. "No matter how much I'd like to."

It was the first time in weeks he'd left himself open with such an ambiguous comment, and Betsy wasn't quite sure how to respond. They were sitting so close on the porch swing that their knees were almost touching, and they could have shared a kiss without moving an inch, if they'd both been so inclined. But when Betsy turned to study Spence's blunt features, his eyes were trained on some distant sight, and he didn't meet her gaze.

Oh, Spence, why do you keep pushing me away? she wanted to cry out. But somehow she managed to swallow her frustration. She shifted uncomfortably on the porch swing as she asked, "I don't suppose you'd like to expand on that."

He shrugged uneasily, his glance flitting briefly to her face before he looked away. "Well, let's just say that Tiffany's colored the way I look at things—women, for instance. I have trouble trusting them because she lied to me so often."

"I can understand that, Spence," she countered bravely, "but it's sort of an unfair generalization, don't you think?"

"Of course it is," he readily admitted. "I didn't say it was a good idea. It's just an old scar." He scratched one ear, as though the moist, hot air was becoming untenable. "I don't distrust every woman I know. After all, I have complete faith in Janet."

Now or never, Betsy, some voice within her prompted as she asked with quiet courage, "Do you have faith in *me*?"

Betsy counted seven chirps of a nearby cricket before Spence replied, "Of course I do," but not before she had glimpsed the rush of panic on his face. "I mean, my relationship with you is a lot like my relationship with Janet."

Not certain whether to take this observation as a compliment or an insult, Betsy pointed out, "She's practically your sister, Spence." She waited for him to say *So are you*, knowing that she'd asked for it, but also knowing that she'd never forgive him if he did.

But Spence uttered nothing as he met her eyes, did nothing to stop the great swell of longing she read there. For the first time in all the weeks they'd been friends, he gazed at Betsy as a lover looks at his beloved, with no shields to mask his anguish or regret. To her amazement he reached out to touch her face with the back of his hand in a gesture of infinite tenderness. The caress was so loving, so unexpected, that her eyes filled with tears as she savored the warmth of his knuckles.

"I could never trust a woman I allowed myself to fall in love with, Betsy," he answered slowly, as though he were willing to let down the barriers for just a second...long enough to tell her the truth. "She'd have too much power over me."

Betsy closed her eyes, unable to meet the intensity of his gaze as he continued.

"She could bear my babies and take them away from me. She could parade every one of my foibles before a courtroom full of strangers, strip my soul naked until I didn't even know myself. She could steal the business that three generations of Spencers have tried to build, a business that I've got to hold on to for the next three generations." His knuckles lingered on her cheek for only a moment longer before he withdrew his hand quickly, as though he'd just brushed a fingertip through a candle's flame. "If I ever fell for another woman, I'd end up giving her everything in the world that mattered to me."

Bravely Betsy met his eyes, ignoring the sudden chill of her cheek where his touch had so briefly warmed her. "And she might cherish it, Spence. Guard it till the end of time."

He shook his head. Infinite sorrow darkened his ragged features, and his lips tightened with frustration and suppressed desire. "I don't deny that it's a possibility, especially with a woman like . . . Janet. I mean, a woman of her moral fiber." He stood up and rubbed his hands together briskly, as though it were very cold. "What's more likely is that she'd tear me apart. I could protect my business with a premarital contract, but there's no legal procedure that could do much for a broken heart or restore the shredded childhood of my children."

"Premarital contract?" Betsy echoed, belatedly realizing he was talking about far more than a simple love affair; he was talking about marriage now.

"Yes, indeed. If I ever had call to marry again, I'd cover all the angles."

"The angles?" She knew she was starting to sound like a parrot, but she was too stunned for rational thought.

Spence had started to pace restlessly back and forth on the wooden porch, tapping the fuchsias hanging from baskets above him each time he marched by. "Look, Betsy, Randy won't be with me for too much longer. I mean, in August he'll turn sixteen. In two more years he'll leave for college. Now I'm not quite thirty-eight and I'm a sociable soul, and I can't really see living the rest of my life alone. I'd like a companion—" he could have been describing a particularly loyal breed of dog "—to stroll with in the evenings and keep me warm at night. No flibbertigibbet like Tiffany, mind you, but a levelheaded lady who understands how a business runs. I'll need a partner in *life*, not a partner in love." Still he paced back and forth; still he kept his eyes from meeting hers.

Is he just rambling? her pounding heart queried. *Or could he actually be testing the waters?*

"I'd examine the situation from every possible practical angle," he continued stoutly, "then have Janet draw me up a premarital contract that protected the business in case of divorce and gave it to Randy whenever I died. And of course there would have to be some sort of clause granting my physical custody of any more children who might be involved. With that kind of security, I might— hypothetically, you understand—be willing to risk marriage again. Someday."

Betsy was stunned. She could never even consider such an agreement with any man! That wasn't marriage, and it certainly wasn't love! It sounded like a blue-chip investment, a calculated gamble, with a dozen defenses against going bankrupt. And when it came to the chil-

dren—*her* babies—she'd sooner die than sign a paper
guaranteeing that she'd give them up to anyone!

Stiffly she retorted, "Why don't you order this woman
from a catalog, Spence, to make sure she's the right shape
and size? And don't forget to keep the receipt in case you
have to return her!"

He whipped around to face her, dismay coloring his
sweat-beaded face. "Betsy, you're the most practical,
business-minded woman I know. If anybody would understand how it's got to be with me, then—"

"Look again, Spence!" Betsy ordered, rising to face
him with angry eyes. She wished she'd been wearing
something more feminine than jeans and a T-shirt, but
she'd always avoided dressing up on Monday nights for
fear it might alert Spence to how very much she wanted
her appearance to please him. "This practical, business-
minded woman locks up the front door to Ye Olde Fabric Shoppe every night and comes home to an empty
house. She's got as much to risk as you do in the mar-
riage-and-family department, but *she* is not afraid. The
only thing about marriage that would frighten me would
be committing myself to a man who had so little faith in
me! I'd live alone for the rest of my life before I'd sign a
premarital contract of any kind, let alone one with the
kind of one-sided rules you've just spelled out!"

"One-sided?" he thundered back. "Your business is
worth three times what mine is! A premarital contract
could only protect a woman in your position. It would be
in your own best interests, Betsy!"

"I'll decide my own best interests, thank you," she
snapped, not even bothering to point out how unfair his
intended child-custody clause was. "And when it comes
to marriage, or even love, what I need is somebody who

believes in me, in *us*, in our future. I would never start a marriage preparing for divorce! I'd never marry a man unless I trusted him completely and couldn't imagine life without him *or* his children!"

Spence waved an irritated hand. "You're talking like a child, Betsy! That's the way Randy and Laurie think of romance. You've never been married, never fought tooth and toenail to hold on to your only son. That fairy-tale vision of true love you've got in your head is just for princesses who live happily ever after with white knights in medieval castles. In real life, businesses fail and children get torn apart in divorce! No man who's been through what I have would be foolhardy enough to risk going through it all again." Suddenly he took a step toward her and finished in a low, solemn tone, "Any woman who really loved me would understand that. She'd sign that contract just to give me peace of mind."

Stoutly Betsy countered, "Any woman who really loved you would *refuse* to sign that contract. To live with only half your heart would be worse than having to live without you altogether!"

The silence on the humid porch grew clumsy, oppressive, as Spence faced Betsy's dark eyes without a word. All the nights they'd spent together, all the almost-touches and not-quite-kisses, seemed to permeate this single, anguished moment, and for one full minute neither one uttered a sound. The nightly frog-and-cricket chorus grew louder and louder as the rhythm of their music kept time with the heavy thud of Betsy's pulse.

At last Spence straightened, jamming both tight fists into his pockets. "I don't see what you're getting so worked up about, Bets," he tossed out almost casually, as though he didn't realize that his next words were a brutal slap in her face. "This is only a hypothetical discussion, after all. Whether I ever marry again has *nothing* to do with you."

CHAPTER SEVEN

TUESDAY NIGHT was Randy's turn to do the dishes, but he'd been working in his room so intently since dinner that Spence had decided to go ahead and clean up the kitchen himself. Besides, he had some serious thinking to do, and he did that best in the silence of the big old farmhouse, where not one stick of furniture had been moved since his mother's death and a photograph of every Spencer born since 1873 still hung over the fireplace.

The scene on Betsy's porch the night before had greatly disturbed him, largely because he knew that the uncertain future of their relationship was something he could no longer ignore. For weeks now—maybe since the night they'd met—he'd been pretending that whatever twinges of loverly feeling he felt for her could be suppressed, if not destroyed. But now he had to consider the possibility of romantic feelings on *Betsy's* part, a possibility that made him squirm.

The fact that she'd never dropped any hints or exerted any pressure on him was no proof that she was tickled pink with the status quo. He'd been gratified to learn that Betsy had only had lunch with Mike Ralston once—he'd invited himself to join her when she'd been eating with a mutual female friend—and even more delighted when rumors had reached him that she'd turned down dates with two other local men on the grounds that her feel-

ings were "otherwise engaged." Yet Spence had also realized that if Betsy really was falling in love with him,
then he'd behaved abominably. He'd treated her like
somebody's old shoe, while she—woman of rare patience and insight that she was—had given him all the
room he'd needed, showering him with sympathy and irresistible desserts at the same time.

But what did she really think of this fellow who took
her company for granted, ate her out of house and home
and responded to a simple inquiry about his true feelings for her by launching into a diatribe on premarital
contracts? Did she think he was selfish, overly sensitive,
maybe a little bit neurotic? And when he'd started talking about marriage, had she imagined, for even a moment, that he'd been talking about the two of them? And
if she had, was it because he might have given her reason
to?

Who are you kidding, Spencer? he growled at himself. *You can lie to yourself till the cows come home, but
you know you don't end up on Scarlet Elm every Monday night just because Betsy's a terrific cook!*

He shook his head and tried to clear the fuzzy
thoughts. Angrily shoving Betsy from his mind, he hung
up the dish towel on the refrigerator door and marched
down the hall to check in on his inexplicably silent student. Normally Randy came out for a snack break about
every thirty minutes, but tonight Spence hadn't seen him
for over two hours.

"I've got to know what subject you're studying tonight," Spence observed from the doorway, leaning
nonchalantly against the frame. "Whatever it is, I want
you to major in it in college. It's obviously your forte."

Randy laughed as he waved a mimeographed handout
in his father's direction. "Sorry, Dad, but I'm not

studying for a class. Mrs. Mac gave us this stuff at one of
the faire meetings when you were chatting with Betsy. She
said we all needed to learn how to talk like this and we
should practice on one another."

Spence glanced down the front page and intoned melodramatically, "'Fie, O thou pernicious worm! May
vultures vile seize thy lungs!' When does she think a line
like that would come in handy? If you're planning to address your dear old dad in that fashion—"

"Oh, I wouldn't say that to *you*," Randy assured him,
his manly tone breaking into a squeak on the last word.
"It's the kind of stuff one guy says to another when he's
calling him out. It's sort of like a duel of words."

"I see." Spence pondered the rest of the page in
amazement. Modern profanity seemed so dull and un-
inspired in comparison! "'Lurking serpent, step aside!'"
he quoted. "'Your wit's as thick as Tewkesbury mus-
tard.'"

"Neat, huh?"

"Interesting, I'll give you that." He shared a grin with
his son. "The man who comes up with the most creative
cut wins?"

"Something like that." As Spence turned to the next
page, Randy added, "And it gets even better, Dad. Those
are things we're supposed to say to the girls."

Again Spence read out loud. "'My affection hath an
unknown bottom, like the Bay of Portugal.... No angel
ever sang a sweeter song in the merry month of May.'"
And then, with disbelief ringing through his deep voice,
he lay one hand over his heart as he muttered melodramatically, "'Run through fire would I for thy sweet sake,
or bare my chest to another man's sword!' You're supposed to keep a straight face and spill out a line like that
to Laurie?"

Randy hunched his bony shoulders in a less-than-successful imitation of a nonchalant shrug. "Well, gee, Dad, I'm going to try. I was hoping you'd help me memorize this stuff. Mrs. Mac says that during the Renaissance people talked that way to one another all the time."

"Good thing I was born in the twentieth century. I never would have had a thing to say."

Randy gave him an uncertain, pleading grin before he asked, "Do you think you could talk that way for just one night?"

Spence narrowed his eyes, knowing he was about to be suckered into something he didn't want to do. "Spell it out for me, kiddo. What do you have in mind?"

Randy fidgeted with the pile of papers on his desk. "Mrs. Mac was telling us about this restaurant in Columbus called Medieval Times and Tournament—the medieval period was the one just before the Renaissance—where they serve the kind of food people ate then while you watch a joust for a floor show."

"A joust? You mean on film?"

Randy shook his head. "No, I mean in real life. I guess they've got an arena. You know, like for a horse show?"

"An arena for horses to throw dust all over the food?"

"Well, I don't know about the dust. But I do know that all the waitresses are dressed like serving wenches and—"

"*Wenches?*" he echoed. Was this really his laid-back teenage son speaking?

"Oh, Dad, come on! Mrs. Mac says you've got to get into the spirit of the thing. And Laurie said she'd do *anything* to go to that restaurant and see two real live knights joust!"

"Ah," Spence murmured, reading the writing on the wall. "I doubt if she actually meant *anything*, Randy. Besides, there are other factors to—"

"Dad, come on! I'm not talking about sex. I'm talking about the four of us going out to dinner!"

"The four of us?" he repeated blankly.

"Yes. You and me and Laurie and Betsy."

"Betsy?" he repeated slowly, as though he'd never heard the name. Feigning complete disinterest, he picked up Randy's old yellow tomcat, who was stretched out on the bed, and leisurely scratched his ears. "You mean Betsy Hanover?"

"Of course I mean Betsy Hanover! What other Betsy do we know? Besides, what other woman are you dating?"

"Dating?" This time the word stuck on his tongue. "I'm not exactly dating Betsy Hanover. We've just ended up in the same place at the same time once or twice but—"

"Dad, come on!" Randy hooted. "Who do you think you're kidding?"

Spence actually felt his ears heat up. How had his little boy grown into a near man who could make his father blush? Deftly dropping Betsy from the conversation, he asked, "When did you want to take Laurie to this restaurant and how much is it going to cost?"

Taking the hint, Randy quickly replied, "It's going to cost a small fortune, but I've got enough lawn-mowing money saved up to pay for my date if you pay for yours. The real problem is the timing."

"Oh?"

"Well, the restaurant is closed for remodeling until the end of May. Laurie's aunt and uncle are coming to town, and since they live in Indiana they don't get here very often, so she can't very well go running off to Columbus the minute they show up. But the next weekend I'll be out of school and—"

"And with your mother for the summer," Spence finished for him, unable to mask his regret.

"Oh, Dad, don't look like that!" Randy pleaded. "I'll only be gone for six weeks. I always call you every few days, and even if she did try to run off with me, I'm old enough to get back here by myself, you know."

"I know," Spence admitted with a sigh. He tapped his temple, then continued, "I know that up here. But it just isn't that simple to let go of old fears sometimes. I miss you when you're gone, Son. It's always hard to let you go."

Before the conversation turned completely maudlin, Randy pointed out, "Well, if she'll let me go to Columbus with you, you'll get an extra Saturday night with me."

"*If* she lets you go," Spence replied, deciding to ignore the fact that it was Laurie, not him, who had prompted Randy to beard the lioness in her den for the joy of a single evening. "You'll have to work this out with her in advance. I don't want to end up haggling in court because of some petty misunderstanding."

Randy grinned. "I'll call her tomorrow and get it all set up. And if it's really too much of a hassle, we'll wait until I'm back in August. Okay? And if you really don't want to ask Betsy, you can always take Aunt Janet."

Spence studied his son carefully as he pondered his choices. Granted, Janet was his favorite companion for most outings with Randy, and he probably would have instinctively invited her to join him for this occasion if Randy hadn't mentioned Betsy. But now that he had, Spence had to give the idea some thought. He couldn't keep treading water with Betsy forever. Last night he'd hurt her badly, and he owed her an apology at the very least. But he didn't want to jump from the fire into the frying pan, either. Was he keeping her at a distance because he really didn't want to get any closer, or just because he was afraid to? And if he was afraid, was it time to triumph over his fear?

"Randy, I'll take care of my own date for the evening, thank you," he finally declared.

Randy shrugged and grabbed his "Elizabethan as a Second Language" handout back. "Sorry. I just thought maybe you needed a shove in the right direction."

"A shove?"

"Yeah, a shove. I mean, you always act like Betsy's some guy you meet to go bowling with or something, or maybe somebody's nice old grandma like Oma Potter. But it's all a con, Dad. Don't you think I can see through it?"

"A con?" Spence repeated, suddenly feeling a bit woozy. *Out of the mouths of babes.*

"Yes, a *con*. Any fool can tell that Betsy's number one on your *Billboard* chart. You go gaga every time somebody mentions her name! If I acted like that about a girl, you'd razz me something fierce and give me a lecture on the false promises of young love."

"Randy, if you—"

"Hey, Dad! I'm cool," Randy said, backing off with an incredibly smug grin, spreading both hands in an innocent gesture. "Your secret's safe with me."

"Kiddo, I don't know where you came up with this idea, but you're starting to sound like Oma Potter. She sees love on every street corner, passion whenever two pairs of eyes happen to meet."

"Well, I don't," Randy informed his father sagely. "But I'd have to be blind not to feel the ground shake every time you look at Betsy."

"The ground does not *shake*!" Spence protested.

This time Randy laughed out loud. "Maybe it doesn't exactly shake, Dad," he finally relented, feigning a sympathetic punch to his father's right arm as Spence turned to leave the room. Then, with a wicked gleam in his adolescent eye, he tossed out just before the door closed, "But you can't deny that it trembles!"

Spence shut the door behind him firmly, but Randy's laughter chased him all the way down the hall.

BETSY SPENT the next few weeks creating the perfect Renaissance dress for herself and one equally as lovely for Janet. Betsy's was a luscious shade of blue with a low, straight neckline and a huge gathered skirt. Janet's was similar in style, but it was forest green, a dramatic contrast to her dark coloring. Both of them were excited about the upcoming Renaissance faire in Pittsburgh and didn't talk about much else when they got together for fittings or lunch. Mrs. Mac and several other members of the Muskingum Renaissance Faire Committee were going to join them on the trip. Janet had pleaded with Spence to come along, too—just to help drive the enormous van his Uncle Clay was loaning her, if nothing else—but he'd stoutly maintained that he had no interest in seeing the Pittsburgh faire, especially if he had to "look like an idiot" to attend it.

Betsy hadn't prodded Spence at all. Ever since the night of their first fight—what else could she call it?—she'd treated him gingerly. They'd met by accident half a dozen times—three of them Monday nights at the theater—and he'd still come home with her and waxed poetic over her cakes and pies. But there was a tension in him now, a wariness that Betsy had not noticed since their early weeks together. She suspected that a single possessive word on her part might be enough to make him take flight. And that was the one thing she simply could not bear.

Betsy knew it was time to face the fact that she was falling in love with the rugged man who was a curious blend of tenderness and restraint, and despite his disclaimers, she had a strong suspicion that he was falling in love with her, too. His desire showed up at unexpected moments, which he always later managed to dismiss. Sometimes he'd casually sling his arm across her chair when they watched a movie, apparently oblivious when his fingers edged down to lightly caress her shoulders or toy with her neckline. Sometimes his gaze would linger on a particularly tight bodice or pair of jeans, and a rush of heat would color his face. But still he kept his distance, still he held on to his place in her world as best friend, casual buddy and all around platonic pal. At times she wanted to shake him, or throw herself in his arms. But she knew she couldn't rush him, and after his infuriating speech on premarital contracts, she was no longer sure that getting further involved with Spence was even particularly wise. If he really parceled out love with such parsimony, she knew she could never trust him with her heart, and she could never, ever become his wife.

And then one evening, when the sky was growing cloudy with the threat of a thunderstorm, he muttered casually as he prepared to leave her house, "By the way, Bets, Randy would like to know if you can join us for a trip to a medieval restaurant in Columbus a week from Saturday. Mrs. Mac's been there and has the kids all excited about it. Randy insists that they've got live knights on horseback who actually *joust* a few feet from the tables as a floor show."

"It sounds remarkable," Betsy answered, holding back her more intense response. *What's remarkable is that you're asking me for a real live date, no matter how backhanded!* "I'm flattered that *Randy* would like me to go."

Spence had the grace to blush. "Well, to set the record straight, Laurie's his date. I'm just the chauffeur, and I don't relish talking to myself for two hours each way while the two of them bill and coo in the back seat. I need some company." He smiled. "Randy suggested you."

Betsy's own enthusiasm dimmed. "So I'm Randy's first choice?"

He sobered. "Well, he's your first choice for me."

"I see. And who's *your* first choice for this outing, Spence?" she demanded with a touch of asperity. "Should I consider this an honor or just a victory by default?"

Spence opened the screen door and stepped back over the threshold to stand beside her on the tired beige rug. "Look, Bets, that didn't come out right. I meant to say that you and I always have a good time together. And you're so wound up in this Renaissance faire thing that I thought you'd enjoy this restaurant."

"I'm sure I would. The question in my mind is whether you'd enjoy taking me." Betsy knew it wasn't smart to be so blunt, but she was growing very tired of being sweet and patient. Besides, where had such altruism gotten her? "I'm not in the habit of going out with a man who won't ask me for a date unless somebody twists his arm."

Spence met her eyes and read the challenge there. She waited for him to shake his head, to turn away, to tell her to forget the whole thing. Instead he took a deep breath and said, "Gonna make me sweat, are you?" Then, to her amazement, he sheepishly reached for her hand. It was the first time he'd ever touched her in quite so personal a fashion, and the sheer force of his calloused fingertips brushing her palm supercharged Betsy's feelings. "Gonna make me toss out some of that Elizabethan mush Mrs. Mac's making the kids learn? Or beg on bended knee?"

"Nothing so dramatic," Betsy promised, relenting a little as she fought her body's instantaneous sensual response to his touch. "I just think that common courtesy would suggest you say something like 'Betsy, I'd really enjoy spending an evening with you.' You're basically a very polite man, Spence. It's hard for me to understand why something that simple sticks in your craw."

Spence pressed her hand between both of his and pursed his lips as he considered her question. She hadn't really meant to challenge him, but now that she had, she knew he was going to ponder her words and give her a serious answer. She just hoped it would be one she wanted to hear.

"It's like this, Bets," he finally confessed, his expression sobering as his glance caressed her face with surprising intimacy. "I'm kind of allergic to giving compliments to women."

"You've always admired my cooking," Betsy countered truthfully. "Is that because you're afraid I'll stop delivering the goods if you don't slather on the praise?"

He chuckled and shook his head. "No, that's different. That's the kind of praise I'd give to anybody who baked like you do—male or female, young or old. But the kind of flattery you're talking about—" he kneaded her fingers with his own strong hand "—makes me very nervous. It reminds me of what a fool I made of myself when I was young."

Confused but hopeful, Betsy wove her fingers through Spence's, rejoicing when he pulled her closer and made no effort to escape. *If I didn't know better, I'd think we were holding hands like lovers,* she thought, her heart thumping in hopeful triumph. *Is he finally ready to cross that magic line that shuts me out of his heart?*

"For years I mooned over Tiffany like a lovesick puppy, Bets," Spence admitted in a husky whisper. "Not just when I was in high school, but after we were married...even after the first time I caught her with another man! I brought her roses, satin nightgowns, music boxes, jewelry I couldn't possibly afford. I showered her with every kind of sappy compliment that any fool ever conjured up, and what's worse, I meant every single word. Sometimes to this day I'll hear somebody talk like that to a woman and I'll remember some crazy moment when I said the same words. My ears turn red just thinking about it!"

Betsy swallowed hard as she squeezed his hand and leaned a little closer. Her heart beat rapidly as she listened to the heavy thud of Spence's pulse. She was touched he was trying so hard to open up to her, and she realized belatedly that he'd treated their first real date so casually only to hide his own apprehension.

"I guess I...just don't want to take any chances, Bets," he conceded hoarsely. "I'm afraid of what might happen if I start talking sweet to you."

"I'd be glad to help you overcome your fear," she suggested with great gentleness, unable to stop herself from pressing his warm palm against her flushed cheek. "What's the worst that could happen if you admitted that you don't just come here because you have nowhere else to kill your time on Monday nights?''

Genuine regret shadowed Spence's rugged face as his calloused fingers trailed over her delicate skin ever so lightly. "Is that what you've been thinking all this time, Betsy? That I come here because I've got nothing else to do? Or because I can't resist your chocolate éclairs?''

She didn't answer right away, and the silence had grown distinctly uncomfortable by the time she confessed, "Frankly, Spence, it's crossed my mind. That's how it started out, and you've never, well, said or done anything to indicate that... if Laurie's poetry group dropped out of Randy's life, you wouldn't drop out of mine." She didn't add that with Randy out of town for the summer, he'd have no reason to come into Muskingum on Monday nights at all.

Spence met her eyes uncertainly as the thunder rumbled in the distance. "I've liked being able to come here without any... expectations," he told her quietly, tension crackling his tone as he released her. "I'm comfortable with you because you don't—at least you didn't—demand anything of me.''

Betsy knew they were crossing into dangerous territory now, but she didn't see how she could back up. Very gently she assured him, "I have no intention of *demanding* anything of you, Spence. Has it ever occurred to you that I might enjoy *giving* you something? Not just coffee and cupcakes, but conversation and a smile or two?''

Moths danced in the porch light behind Spence as he guardedly studied Betsy's face, pondering the depth of feeling that quivered beneath her softly-spoken words. Slowly, with the utmost of tenderness, his hand crawled up to cup her cheek, but she'd barely had time to rejoice in the wonder of his touch before his hand retreated to his

side. His wide sensuous mouth tightened, and a compelling sorrow eclipsed the hint of desire that had so briefly
lit his gray eyes.

When he finally spoke, his tone was cautious. "Betsy,
I'm very fond of you," he murmured uncomfortably. "I
look forward to spending Monday nights with you, and
maybe I should have said so sooner. I just didn't want to
give you the wrong impression."

The words hung painfully in the air, and Betsy didn't
quite know how to field them. She knew that Spence saw
the hurt on her face, and she didn't try to hide it. Instead she stood perfectly still, proud and strong as she
challenged him. "What are you really scared of, Spence?
That I'll fall in love with you? Or are you afraid you'll
fall in love with me?"

"Betsy, don't," he begged her, his words punctuated
by the spear of lightning barely visible in the darkness
behind him. "Don't make this any harder than it has to
be."

"Hard for whom? For you?" Suddenly Betsy's patience snapped. She loved this man! How much longer
could she go on pretending that she didn't? "For two
long months I've bent over backward to make it easy for
you! But I can't go on in limbo forever, Spence! You're
special to me. You surely know it! And there are times—
oh, God, Spence, I'm so tired of pretending—aren't there
times when you think I'm special, too?"

"Dammit, Betsy!" he swore in frustration, balling
both hands into fists. "I don't *want* you to be special! I
don't want anybody to be special! I don't want to get involved with a woman again!"

"That's not an answer. I want to hear the truth! Don't
you have the courage to tell me straight out? If you

weren't so terrified of getting involved, would you want me or not?''

Emotional lightning crackled in the air between them, and something inside Spence seemed to break. One minute he was standing there, glaring at her, half angry, half afraid, and the next he was gripping her shoulders, crushing his lips to hers.

It wasn't the kind of kiss Betsy had expected from this casual, gentle man, and it did nothing to assuage her desire for him. It was a mixture of fury and desperation, long-repressed hunger and aching emotional need. Where was the tenderness, the sweet caring, the genuine respect she'd always believed that Spence felt for her? Was it overwhelmed by his anger, or had she imagined it all along?

Betsy found her fingers grabbing his collar for support as his weight pushed her back against the open door, not quite certain whether she ought to be pulling him closer or pushing him away. But once again he stole the decision from her as his lips abruptly abandoned hers. He dropped his hands as though she were too hot to touch, and a flare of self-reproach consumed his features.

For a moment he just stood there, hands jammed in his pockets, his eyes full of fire. Betsy tried to meet his gaze proudly, but somehow her eyes focused on the hollow of his neck and couldn't seem to rise.

Oh, Betsy, you fool! she chided herself, knowing she'd pushed him way too far. *Is that really what you wanted?*

And then Spence whispered bleakly, "I'm so sorry, Betsy. I never meant to do that.''

"I know," she said, swallowing back a surge of tears. "I always thought you secretly wanted to kiss me, but I . . . guess that wasn't what you wanted at all.''

"Oh, God, yes, I wanted to kiss you!" He groaned hoarsely. "But not like that. If I ever kissed you right it wouldn't stop there, Betsy. I don't think I could stop at all!"

Her eyes opened wide at his blunt confession, and her heart started pounding double time a moment later when Spence framed her heart-shaped face with two gentle hands. The tender gesture threw Betsy off guard and filled her with a fresh rush of hope. She closed her eyes and bowed her head, awed and helpless against this demonstration of his true feelings for her. Unable to stop herself, she pressed her face against his chest.

This time his arms closed around Betsy with tender, aching need, cradling her against his body as though there were no other place for her to be. "Oh, Betsy," he whispered against her hair, his voice hoarse and low, "if you had any idea what it's cost me to keep my distance..."

As the murmured confession faded away, Betsy's chin raised with courage, and she heard herself admit, "I want you so much, Spence! Some nights I think I—"

And then his lips claimed hers again, with infinite tenderness this time. It was the kiss he should have given her the first time, a kiss of tender longing, a kiss of promise, a kiss of hope. Betsy lost herself in the magic of it, lost all sense of space and time. She wrapped her arms around him and reveled in the joy of his hard, strong body crushing hers, certain, for one single joyous moment, that the man in her arms craved her adoration every bit as much as she craved his.

But then, as though in replay of her erotic dreams, Betsy felt Spence slowly pulling away from her, slipping from her grasp. When she opened her eyes he was still standing there before her, but he was shaking his head and struggling to step back.

His voice was shaky as he whispered, "Betsy, if I were somebody else, if I hadn't been through what I've been through, I'd never stop with just one kiss. As it is, I don't know if I've got the strength to do what I should."

"Spence, I don't *want* you to stop!" Betsy burst out, desperate to finish what they'd started. "Don't you know how I feel about you? Don't you know that I—"

"Betsy, listen to me!" he begged, his voice ragged with torment. "There's so much more involved here than whether you want me or I want you! I am who I am, and I...I don't want you to expect anything from me that...well, that I'm not in a position to give you."

"I told you right from the start, Spence," she reminded him desperately. "I don't *expect* anything from you."

"That's what you told me. And that's what I tried to believe. But either you were shading the truth in the beginning or else your feelings for me have changed."

Bravely she countered, "We've known each other since early spring, Spence. Surely you didn't expect our relationship to stand completely still!"

To her surprise his fingertips drifted softly down her cheeks until they nestled against her neck, teasing her sensitive ears as they kneaded the white skin of her lobes. With every stroke Betsy's arousal grew harder for her to handle, and it took all her strength of will not to press herself against Spence and beg him to take her to bed...and to take her to his heart. "Maybe it was too much to expect, but I think it was what I was hoping for, Bets," he confessed in a ragged whisper. "I've needed this—this *companionship*, these quiet talks and evening walks with a woman of good wit and a keen mind."

Betsy swallowed hard before she asked him, "Is that all you need from a woman, Spence? Is that all you need from *me*?"

A shudder of barely suppressed desire racked his body. "My God, Bets, you know better!" He moaned, his resistance crumbling as he pulled her back into his arms. She clung to him, rejoicing in his fervor, still frightened that he'd pull away once more. In the porch lamp's light, which was filtering through the screen, they fit together like two matching parts of one perfect whole, and Betsy ached for the total union of their bodies and their hearts. For the first time since she'd met Spence, she was absolutely certain that he ached for it, too.

But still he fought the hunger. "Betsy, I made it clear to you right from the start that I couldn't afford to get tangled up in a complicated relationship." He breathed against her widow's peak, contradicting his own words with a kiss on her forehead as he pulled her even closer. "That hasn't changed, Bets. All that's changed is how very much I want to be with you."

Betsy wrapped her arms around him as tightly as she dared, afraid she'd never get the chance again. "I want to be with you, too, Spence, more than I've ever wanted to be with anybody in my life. Please don't keep telling me that it won't work out. Just give it a chance!" She kissed the hollow of his neck, her warm lips lingering against his erratic throat pulse. "It means so much to me."

It was far more than she had intended to say, far more than she had meant to confess. But the words were out and there was no way to recall them. And—for at least another moment—there was no way that Spence could bring himself to push her away.

His voice was choked as he clung to her. "If I were a man who indulged in casual sex, Bets, believe me, I wouldn't look any farther than your bedroom door. But with you and me—" his voice grew even huskier with the depth of his confession "—it could never be casual. It's hard enough for me to be casual about you even... even as it is."

Trembling, Betsy raised her head until her eyes met his. Gravely she stood on tiptoe to drop the softest of inviting kisses on his mouth before she asked hesitantly, "Why does it have to be casual, Spence? If we're both feeling the same... if we're both growing closer... can't we just... let our friendship grow?"

She wasn't sure what answer she'd expected, but she knew it wasn't the closed expression that masked his face as he slowly disengaged himself from her loving arms. It took a long time, partly because Betsy was so slow to release him and partly because Spence was so reluctant to let her go. When he finally shoved his hands back in his pockets and stepped away from her, his expression was distant. In that instant, she felt as though the past five minutes had been no more than a dream. Even the thunder and lightning had disappeared.

"I think that letting things between us take their natural course could be pretty risky, Bets," he said.

Urgently she reached out to touch his arm, unable to smother the throb in her voice as she admitted, "It's a risk I might be willing to take."

Spence took a deep breath. His eyes met hers with the greatest of longing, and when she read the anguish there she almost hurt more for him than she did for herself. Helplessly he whispered, "But I'm *not* willing, Betsy. I'm not willing to take any risks at all."

Before she could find the magic words that might have persuaded him, the screen door banged just inches from her face, and Spence disappeared into the emptiness of the night.

Outside, the storm was over, but the one in her heart still raged....

CHAPTER EIGHT

SPENCE PULLED UP at the Williams Number Nine drilling site ten miles east of Muskingum at seven o'clock the next morning with his emotions still in a whirl. He had eight deliveries to make before noon, and about the last thing he needed was a head full of guilt and a heart full of lead.

"'Morning, Spence," Sonny Barnes greeted him warmly from the rig floor high above the ground. "Beautiful day, ain't it?"

"Nice enough, I reckon," Spence answered, certain that it wasn't pretty enough for a grown man to wax poetic, especially with the earthshaking rig making every kind of ungodly noise known to man. Granted, the sun was barely visible above the fine mist on the poplars and elms, and the johnny jump-ups along the road were especially blue and bright. But the grin on young Sonny's face was even brighter.

"You look like the cat who swallowed the canary," Spence teased him as he climbed the crude steps up to the sheet metal "doghouse" and took the cup of bitter coffee the young driller offered him. "If you've got some good news, why don't you share it?" *But if you have another joke about Betsy, I suggest you keep it to yourself.*

The redhead grinned the way Randy did when he looked at Laurie—as though he had too many teeth for one mouth. "I'm getting married, Spence! Biting the dust next weekend."

"Sandra finally caved in?" Spence asked incredulously.

"You betcha!" Sonny literally bounced on the balls of his heavily booted feet. "That little gal's been giving me the runaround for months now. Kept saying she needed a little more time, no matter how I groveled. But last night I took her out to dinner—nothing fancy. Between the salad and the steak, she says out of the clear blue sky, 'Sonny, I think I'm finally ready to settle down.' Just like that!" He laughed out loud, a sound of joyful innocence that was rare among the tough roughnecks and roustabouts who peopled the oil patch. "Hell, Spence, I called the preacher the minute I got her home. Can't take no chances that she might change her mind."

Spence shook the other man's hand and found some words of celebration for him. "I'm happy for you, Sonny. I really am."

He was actually more apprehensive than delighted, if the truth be told. He'd never met Sandra, but from what he'd heard about her, she'd rather enjoyed keeping her smitten suitor on a short leash, and he suspected she'd manipulate him even more once she became his wife. A sudden memory of Spence's own wedding day—when his own grin had been even wider than poor Sonny's—filled his mind, snuffing out the vision of Betsy's anguished eyes for the first time since he'd left her last night.

I'm a damn fool, he told himself for about the sixteenth time. How had he let things get so out of hand? The only thing about that scene at Betsy's front door that really surprised him was that it hadn't happened weeks ago. Betsy wasn't cut out to be a wallflower, and Spence wasn't cut out to be a saint.

When he realized that Sonny was recounting his bride's capitulation once again, he thrust Betsy to the back of his mind and vowed to keep her there. With the sorrow that comes whenever one decides to say goodbye to a good memory or a good friend, Spence promised himself he'd forget the happy, carefree nights they'd spent together and give up the lie that they could always be "good friends." He'd laid out the rules for Betsy right from the start, but that hadn't kept her from falling in love with him. Now, nothing but time and distance—God help him—would protect him from falling in love with her.

I only hope it's not too late already, he warned himself. *You can't afford to take any more chances.* If Betsy didn't have the grace to cancel the trip to Columbus, he'd have to go through with it, Spence decided ten minutes later as Sonny dropped the catline down to the pickup. *But that's the end of it,* he vowed as he wrapped it around the scraper sub and waited for Sonny to hoist the thousand-pound pipe up to the rig. *I'll be friendly when we meet on the street, but from now on those marvelous Monday evenings are a luxury I just can't afford.* Reluctantly he realized that he owed it to Betsy to tell her that outright.

"So that's the whole story, Spence!" Sonny finished his tale ecstatically. "Now ain't that just like a woman?"

"You bet it is," Spence agreed as heartily as he was able to, shaking the other man's hand again before he climbed back down the steps and hopped into his truck. "Sounds like you've got a first-class bride-to-be, Sonny," he assured the young groom with less than genuine candor. "I'm sure you'll do just fine."

He'd already turned on the engine, when Sonny jammed the rig throttle and shouted down to him, "Hey,

Spence, what do you say to a double wedding? Unless you think that Betsy babe would turn you down?"

The laughing words dug an icy hole in the pit of Spence's stomach, and the fear that engulfed him eclipsed the sense of loss he knew he'd feel when he shut Betsy out of his life. "You'd better go ahead and get hitched without me, Sonny," he counseled his young friend, grateful that the groan of the drawworks made further conversation impossible. "I'm proof that you just can't teach an old dog new tricks."

Before Sonny could pursue the matter, Spence gunned the engine and took off down the gravel road.

"THE MERRY WIVES OF WINDSOR is not the best of Shakespeare's work from a literary point of view," Mrs. MacGillicuddy informed the group that was gathered at the gym the following Thursday evening, "but by no means is it the worst. The reason I have selected it for our intense scrutiny is that it is set among the country gentry in Elizabethan England, providing the rich linguistic texture necessary for us to master."

"I think she means it's got weird expressions we're supposed to learn," Laurie bubbled to her grandmother, who sat on Betsy's left. "Like that super list she gave us. Randy's memorized half of the 'sweet nothings' for me. His dad's helping him study them!"

Oma put one finger on her lips to shush the loquacious girl, continuing to focus on her old teacher as though she were still in class.

"We will, of course, play out the entire drama," Mrs. Mac continued in her booming voice, "going through one scene each meeting through the summer so I can help you practice your accents and other mannerisms of speech. But to get us started, would someone like to review the basic plot for us? Someone who graduated in—'' she lifted her eyes, thinking for a minute ''—1963?''

A communal sigh of relief swept the crowd as everybody younger and older than those in the designated year realized they were off the hook. After the obligatory ribbing, one woman who appeared to be in her forties stood up in the bleachers and did her best. ''Basically, there was this... well, sort of down-at-heels knight named Falstaff, who came to visit some families at Windsor Castle. Two of these families were quite well off, and Falstaff wanted some of the booty. But the men were sly and unapproachable, so he tried to get on the good side of their wives. But the wives realized that he was sending them identical love letters, and they set up a trap for him.''

''Excellent, Lucinda. Simply excellent!'' Mrs. MacGillicuddy said with rare praise. ''I'm sure it won't surprise any of you to recall that Lucinda was valedictorian in '63. I only hope that in twenty-five years, when we all get together, Howard Walsh will be able to perform as well.''

When Howard, the present year's top student, offered the crowd a smug, officious grin, his buddies cheered and Laurie swooned. ''Isn't he just the cutest guy you ever saw, Betsy? He's coming to my sister's graduation party.''

Oma shushed her again, just as Randy sauntered in the door. Spence followed slowly about ten paces behind him.

Betsy's eyes rushed to his; she couldn't help it. For three solid days she'd been replaying every instant of their last evening together, wondering why she'd pressed him so hard, wondering why she'd failed. *He wants me, dammit! I know he does!* she'd reminded herself over and over again. But that simple fact—a fact even Spence had admitted—did nothing to change their hopeless situa-

tion. He didn't dare love her a little because he was afraid
he might learn to love her a lot. And if he couldn't see his
way clear to loving her in the near future, Betsy knew she
could no longer carry on the pretense of their peaceful
platonic friendship. Not when she lay awake at night
aching for his touch.

As Randy bounded toward the three of them, Spence
trailed along in slow motion. Betsy didn't know if his lack
of alacrity was obvious to everyone, but it was excru-
ciatingly clear to her, especially when he clambered up the
bleachers to sit on the other side of Laurie and Randy,
even though he had to walk in front of Betsy to do so and
she'd left enough space for him beside her. For a frac-
tion of a second, he met her gaze with veiled eyes that
showed no memory, no promise, no grief. He shook his
head, just once, as if to tell her straight out that whatever dreams she'd had about him should be forever buried now. Granted, he did toss an offhand "'Evening,
Bets" in her direction, but it was only what small town
courtesy required of him, no more.

It's over, Betsy realized blindly, the pain so great that
breathing was a sudden burden. *I won't be spending
Monday at the movies anymore.* For a moment the hurt
filled up her chest and her throat and her eyes and then
threatened to spill over. Until that instant, that terrible
moment when he'd met her eyes with the blank look that
just said no! she had actually believed that there might
still be a shred of hope. But now there was nothing.
Nothing but the memory of a love affair that might have
been. A love that Spence had killed before it had had a
chance to live or die.

I love you, Spence, she longed to tell him. *It could be
so good between us if you'd only give us a chance!* But
the sturdy profile that met her longing gaze for the rest

of the evening confirmed everything she'd been dreading for the past three days. It was obvious that Spence had already erased her from his heart.

IT SEEMED TO SPENCE that the meeting went on forever. He'd never read *The Merry Wives of Windsor*, and despite Mrs. Mac's stern admonitions, he vowed then and there that he never would. He wasn't interested in the tale of a fop who had tried to con two married women with slick jargon solely to gain access to their husbands' purse strings. Any fool who went around saying things like "Thine own true knight, by day or night," deserved to get dumped in the Thames. Besides, he had no need to learn any more Shakespeare. If he ever wanted to memorize some choice insults or complimentary phrases, he'd just borrow Randy's Elizabethan English handout.

When Janet finally whisked Mrs. Mac off center stage, the meeting turned to more practical things—costumes, sets and tradesmen's booths at the faire itself, which would be set up at the high school between the rows of classrooms. An empty lot near the football field would serve as the jousting arena, with an old storage shed providing shelter for the horses' food and tack. One corner of the bus garage would be converted into a costume storage area for the duration.

At the moment, Janet was still struggling to fill up Threadneedle Row, which was supposed to consist of twenty-five different booths and so far had only seven. She was hopeful that she'd get more ideas when she attended the Pittsburgh Renaissance Faire on Saturday with the rest of the core planning committee.

"Now Clay Spencer's van holds eight people comfortably, and right now we've only got seven—Mrs. Mac, Paula Rickman, Jeff Melborne, Marvin Oates, Ila

Marsh, Betsy Hanover and me," Janet told the group. "If there's somebody else who wants to come along and get some ideas for new booths or activities, please call me sometime tomorrow and we'll pick you up around six. It's going to be a long day but a marvelous one." Excitement flushed her cheeks, and it pleased Spence immensely to see her so happy again. "Now when Betsy and I went to meet Paul Hardison before, we met a lot of interesting people and got some great ideas. Paul has invited us to his house for lunch—a Renaissance meal, of course—so anybody else who comes along will get to see his terrific collections of coins and costumes and other artifacts. Also, if you have any specific questions about the faire, you might want to mention them to one of us and we'll try to get an answer for you while we're there."

An hour later, Spence ushered Janet out to the parking lot and complimented her on her fine presentation.

"Thanks, Spence. I had my doubts about this whole thing when Mrs. Mac first drafted me, but I've got to admit I'm really getting into it." She started to fill him in on several minor details, but he had a rough time paying attention. His thoughts were still with Betsy.

"Our biggest problem," Janet told him bluntly, "is that we just don't have enough action activities for the faire. We have lots of Renaissance food and jewelry and plenty of period knickknacks for sale. Now we've got enough riders around here to put together a halfway decent horse tournament, and Paul Hardison has made arrangements for us to hire the lead jousters at a reasonable cost. But that's it as far as any kind of sporting event or chivalrous confrontation. I'm just desperate for a duel."

Guilt tugged at his conscience, but Spence held firm. "Honey, don't do this to me. I'm just not cut out to parade around in women's tights, gushing poetry! Besides,

I haven't fenced in over fifteen years and I was never too good at it to begin with."

"Spence, how good do you think the faire visitors are going to be? Most of them will never have fenced at all! They just want to get into the spirit of the day. John Percy—the head fencer at the Pittsburgh faire—explained the whole thing to me. He has one of his fencing students play the role of a young squire. The boy gives each 'combatant' a safety jacket, a mask and a ten-minute minilesson while John swaggers about and goads the next likely candidate from the audience into accepting a duel. He says it's a lot of fun."

"Then let *him* do it," Spence suggested. "And tell him to bring his own squire along. I'm fresh out of fencing students."

Janet gave him her sweetest smile. He remembered it as the one she'd used on Bill when she'd wanted him to do something... and the technique had usually worked. "Randy could be your squire."

"He wants to be a page at the horse tournament because you assigned Laurie to work there as an abigail."

Janet sighed in exasperation. "I can change her assignment, Spence."

Before he could conjure up yet another defense, Janet waved into the darkness and called out, "Hey, Betsy, got a second?"

Spence turned quickly to spot Betsy marching briskly toward her black Mazda, which was parked a few rows away. She was wearing a ruffled strawberry pink sundress with spaghetti straps. It showed just enough cleavage to be inviting but not indiscreet. *Why does she have to look so damn appealing tonight of all nights?* Spence raged inwardly. *I'll be up all night thinking about what's hidden beneath those ruffles.*

Reluctantly, it seemed to Spence, Betsy changed her course and threaded her way through the parked cars until she reached Janet's side. She didn't even glance at Spence.

"Betsy, I'm trying to convince Spence that he should run a fencing booth like John Percy's, and he's got a washtubful of excuses," Janet pleaded. "Please tell me he can play the role of a dashing bon vivant."

Betsy licked her lips while she pondered the question, as though it might take a lot of thought to answer. For just a moment she met his eyes, and the tender forgiveness he read there nearly undid him.

"I don't think you should pressure Spence into taking the booth," she said quietly to Janet. "He's a capable adult, and he should be allowed to make his own decisions about what's right for him. Besides—" her voice dropped perceptibly "—if you try to force somebody into doing something before the time is right, it's likely to blow up in your face, anyway."

Janet raised her eyebrows at this unexpected speech in her brother-in-law's defense, clearly not certain that all of it pertained to the issue of the fencing booth. Spence, of course, needed no footnotes or explanations, and he had to take his hat off to Betsy for so graciously letting him off the hook. Any other woman, he was sure, would have treated him to a scornful lecture on his cowardice.

"Betsy, we're not talking about running for the presidency or anything," Janet pointed out. "I just want him to wave a saber around in the air for a few hours on a lovely autumn weekend!"

"A foil," Spence corrected automatically. "A saber is a much heavier, curved instrument, originally used by a cavalryman to whack the opponent broadside from the back of a horse. A foil is light and very easy to maneuver. Much better for practice, but useless against a saber in a duel."

"See?" Janet retorted triumphantly. "You still remember!"

Spence waved her away indulgently, then kissed her on the cheek. "Good night, Janet. Have a good trip on Saturday. And go ahead and ask that Percy guy to help you out. It wouldn't hurt for you to spend some time with a man who hasn't known you for fifteen years."

"Thanks a lot, Spence," she countered playfully. "You might want to meet this fellow before you try to strike a match for me."

Spence grinned. "What is he, some ancient geezer with a beard down to his knees?"

"No," Janet corrected him saucily. "He's just my age and looks like a movie star."

"Which one?" he challenged her with a laugh.

Betsy, who'd been silent for a couple of moments, now piped up, "Tom Selleck. A certifiable hunk."

The wave of envy that swept through Spence caught him off guard, and he wondered whether Betsy was deliberately baiting him. But Janet immediately concurred, saying, "You're right, Bets. I knew John looked like some famous actor, but until you said it I couldn't put my finger on which one." She gave Spence an enchanting smile. "Maybe I will entice him to help us out here, after all." Before Spence could answer, she bounced off toward her car with a cheery good-night.

Despite the fact that a dozen other locals were drifting out to the parking lot, Spence suddenly felt as though he and Betsy were all alone on her front porch. A cloud of hurt and unabated desire enveloped the two of them, shutting out the rest of the world. Despite all of Spence's firm resolutions, nothing seemed to have changed in the past three days. He still ached to claim Betsy as his woman. He was still sure he never could.

Betsy's eyes were proud, with only a glimpse of hurt revealed in the depths. With studied nonchalance she said, "About the restaurant, Spence.... I hate to cancel out on Randy, but I'm sure you could find somebody else who'd like to go. If you're having second thoughts about taking me, I understand."

The amazing thing was, her tone conveyed the fact that she really did understand. She didn't like it—his withdrawal had hurt her badly—but she was doing her best to bow out like a lady. That was something Tiffany never, ever would have done.

Betsy had given him the perfect chance to cancel their date altogether, to cut the cord all at once. But his native sense of chivalry—or was it something stronger?—made the notion of taking the coward's way out stick in his throat. Instinctively he told her the truth. "Actually, Betsy, I think I'd feel worse if we didn't go than if we did. I know things are...awkward...between us right now, but I'd like to think that we'll still be friends. Just because we had our first fight—"

"It wasn't our first fight," she corrected him crisply. "It was our second. And if we try to pretend it didn't happen, we'll have our third the next time we're alone. We've cleared the air, Spence, and that's not all bad. You know how I feel and I know how you feel." Her calm words did nothing whatsoever to conceal the great pain that discovery had cost her; he could see it in her pinched, wan face. "I don't see any point in pretending that we'll ever see eye to eye, Spence, and I don't think I can bottle up my feelings for another whole evening just to make Randy happy."

Spence took a deep breath and jammed both hands in his pockets. He always wanted to kiss her when she looked like this—so angry, so hurt, so proud, so full of love for him. "Betsy, it's not that I don't think you're special," he protested, suddenly feeling as though all the Muskingumites flooding the parking lot were gathering behind him, ready to laugh or cheer. "Giving you up is going to be very hard for me." The words were slow, honest, painful. But he had to make the confession and Betsy had to hear it just this once, to put it all to rest. Then he was certain that neither of them would ever mention it again. "If I ever got involved with a woman again, Bets, you know it would be you," he admitted, his voice hoarse and low. "But as I told you right from the beginning, that part of my life is over."

"I know." She tried to keep her tone even, but Spence could see that her lower lip was trembling, and he longed to take her in his arms and kiss her pain away. As Randy trotted toward the truck, calling out one last love-drunken good-night to Laurie, Betsy's blue eyes seemed to darken in the moonlight, magnifying her poorly veiled anguish. "You told me the truth, Spence," she whispered brokenly, "but I never quite believed you. It's not your fault that somewhere along the line I deluded myself into thinking that maybe you wanted something more from me than—" she closed her eyes to ward off the threatening tears "—peach pie and chocolate éclairs."

BETSY DIDN'T SLEEP much that night or the next, and at three o'clock in the morning of the Pittsburgh Renaissance Faire, she found herself wide-awake and staring at the ceiling. After thrashing restlessly for an hour, she pulled on a robe and shuffled into her sewing room, determined to restitch the not-quite-perfect corners of the low, square neckline of her blue velvet dress. Nobody but a professional seamstress could ever have noticed a flaw in her glorious creation—once a source of great pride and excitement, now just another dress for a ho-hum day— but Betsy knew that keeping her hands busy might keep her mind off the great weight on her heart.

I don't know how I could have been so foolish, she upbraided herself in the predawn stillness of the empty little house. *He told me, he told me, he told me. But I never listened to him. I listened to my heart.*

Randy's abrupt arrival had kept Spence from backing out of the medieval dinner altogether, but she had no doubt that in time he would. He wouldn't be at the theater on Monday night, and he wouldn't sit with her at the next Thursday night meeting. He would keep a safe distance until he was "sure" she was no longer pining for him, which meant that it was essential for her to bottle up her anguish whenever he was present. The town was too small to accommodate broken hearts or feuding lovers. She'd have to get over him, at least on the surface, by the time they met again face-to-face.

That moment turned out to be much sooner than Betsy had anticipated. At daybreak, just as she finished adorning her multitude of tiny blond ringlets with blue satin ribbons and fake pearls and rubies, she heard a brisk knock at the front door. When she pulled back her living room drapes to glance out the window, she found Janet by the porch swing, dressed in yards of forest green velvet, looking utterly enchanting in the gown Betsy had sewn and designed. Behind Mistress Janet, on the driveway, was the van that Betsy presumed belonged to Spence's uncle, crammed with bodies clad in an equally exotic assortment of brocade, leather and lace.

At this distance, the only person she could see clearly was the driver, who wasn't in Renaissance dress at all. One glance at his green plaid shirt and thick black hair made Betsy's wounded heart do a flip-flop that she was powerless to restrain. But somehow she'd have to stuff her feelings deep into the "opal"-studded satin bag she planned to carry for a purse, because fate had played a cruel trick on her this morning.

No matter how much it hurt her, she was going to have to spend the day with Spence.

CHAPTER NINE

"YOU'D BETTER SIT in the front, Betsy," Spence heard Janet comment as the two women approached the van. "You need room for that flowing skirt and we're already pretty crowded back here."

Nice try, Janet, he observed in silence. *You've always prided yourself on your subtlety.*

His presence could have hardly been classified as subtle, not when he considered what a terrible fuss he'd made over denying his interest in the faire. It was more like a desperate attempt to find some middle ground between logic and desire. Common sense told him that he and Betsy had broken off completely and it was in the best interests of both of them. But for some reason, the knowledge that he would no longer be able to spend Monday nights in the homey comfort of her living room, swapping funny stories and sharing cakes made from scratch, had heightened his restlessness unbearably. Right now he desperately needed to spend some time with Betsy, whether it was a good idea or not. He hadn't the slightest idea how he was going to explain his attendance to her. He hadn't even tried to explain it to Janet. "Pick me up in the morning. I've decided to go," was all he'd told his sister-in-law when he'd called her the night before. Mercifully she'd said, "That's great, Spence," and had let it go at that.

When the passenger door swung open, Spence reached across the cavernous front seat of the van to give Betsy a hand up, knowing from long experience that it was a big jump for people who weren't used to it, even when they were dressed in jeans, as Spence was. He'd intended to greet her in a cheerful, nonchalant manner, but before he could speak, he made the fatal mistake of glancing at Betsy's Renaissance gown.

She looked like a queen. Folds of royal-blue velvet sailed around her, and her dress's low-cut neckline, more chaste than many he'd seen, could not begin to hide the elegant swell of her bosom, especially in the deep, revealing squared corners where her lovely breasts struggled to break free.

Spence might have weathered the enticing view if he hadn't allowed his gaze to drift up to her beautiful heart-shaped face. Those big blue eyes were staring at him, begging for a sign, no matter how tiny, that there was some hope of reviving their aborted friendship. The determined pride that had helped him keep his distance on Thursday night seemed to have disappeared. Clearly Betsy knew as well as he did that there were myriad unanswered questions between them...questions that he couldn't very well avoid for the hours and hours they'd be at the faire.

When she took the hand Spence offered, her touch was warm but hesitant; he had to tighten his grip to tug her in. "Good morning, Bets," he said casually as she climbed up. "I see the dress came out okay. Janet's looks real good, too."

A cautious smile warmed Betsy's lips for just an instant before she replied, "Good morning," as though even those two words were an effort. She closed the door with her right hand while Spence continued to hold on to her left. It occurred to him, distantly, that he had no good reason to keep on holding her hand, and certainly none to interlace his fingers with hers as though they were taking off on a Friday-night date. Yet he couldn't seem to retreat into safety, even when she nonchalantly pointed out, "I didn't expect to see you this morning, Spence. I thought you told Janet you didn't have time to spend on the faire."

He shrugged as casually as he was able. "Randy's with his mother this weekend, so I didn't have anything else to do." Deliberately he released Betsy's fingers and turned the ignition key.

As they pulled out of the driveway, she asked, "So you haven't changed your mind about the fencing booth?"

"Nope," he said without thinking. "I haven't changed my mind about a thing." The words came out a lot harder than he'd intended, and when he saw Betsy's lips tighten, he found himself reaching out once more to take her hand.

They were on the turnpike before he remembered to let go.

WHEN THE TRUMPETS SOUNDED to honor the queen as she was carried by, Betsy told herself it was only natural for a person to feel so giddy on her first trip to a Renaissance faire. The fact that Spence was hovering so close behind her—a cautious smile warming his rugged features—surely had nothing to do with her elation.

"I cry thee mercy, Mistress, but wouldst thou care to buy a garland for thy lovely hair?" asked a bearded young man clad in knee britches made of wool and heavy leather leggings. When Betsy's eyes lit up at the sight of the roses, bachelor's buttons and ribbons so artfully intertwined, the man turned to Spence, who was standing close enough to be taken for her escort, and tried another tactic. "Prithee, good sir, does not thy lady deserve the finest? 'Twould be a loss to leave one so lovely unadorned with the ripest blooms which spring canst give."

Spence looked embarrassed, but he asked good-naturedly, "How much do they cost?"

"A mere sixpence, my good sir," the flower seller answered cheerfully. "In foreign currency from the colonies, that would be ten of the green paper bills."

Without even glancing at Betsy, Spence took out his wallet and slipped the man a ten. "Give her a pretty one," he instructed.

Janet, standing by his elbow, whispered melodramatically, "You're supposed to say something like 'Let us find for Lady Elizabeth a living crown as befits a gracious queen.'"

Spence glowered at her, but the corners of his mouth hinted at a smile as he turned to Betsy and said without fanfare, "Pick out a living crown, Lady Elizabeth." His words weren't terribly Elizabethan, but his expression was warm as he tacked on, "I think blue flowers would look good with that dress."

Janet took his elbow and whispered sotto voce, "How about 'These flowers are the color of thine eyes, though they could never be quite so lovely.'"

"How about if you let me stumble through this faire in my own clumsy fashion before I take Uncle Clay's van back to Muskingum without you?" Spence teased her. "I bought the stupid flowers, didn't I?"

"Okay, I get the hint. I'm going to catch up with Mrs. Mac," Janet decided prudently, lifting her long green skirt as she sauntered past a sign that said Potwobblers Way.

Mrs. MacGillicuddy, already several booths away, was busily engaged in an animated Elizabethan conversation with another woman about her age. The two of them, both dressed as ladies of the court, genuinely looked as though they'd been transported to the twentieth century from another age.

Betsy herself felt as though she'd been transported to a fairy-tale world. A few hours ago she'd been deeply slunk in gloom; now—as though a miracle had landed in her life—she was glowing with the warmth of Spence's continuous smile. Despite Betsy's determination to take Spence's actions at face value, there was no denying that his decision to come to the faire today had something to do with her. Even now, as the other members of their party slowly disappeared in three different directions, he made no effort to catch up with them. Quietly, almost possessively, he stood by her side.

When Janet was almost out of sight, Spence muttered regretfully, "I guess I should have bought her some flowers, too."

"Maybe we can find something else she'd like and give it to her later," Betsy suggested, realizing that Janet was already too far away to catch without making a scene. "There should be a million things here to delight her."

"But nothing so delightful as fresh-cut flowers," the flower merchant reminded her, handing Spence a blue garland. "'Tis a pretty sight, m'lord. 'Twould be a great honor for thy lady to wear such a crown were thy strong hands to place it on her head."

"Are you guys all in on this together?" Spence asked, unable to restrain a chuckle.

"God's wounds, sir! Wouldst thou mocketh me?" Despite his jumbled mouthful of Elizabethan verb forms, he looked so terribly serious that Spence, apparently taking pity on the man, struggled to keep a straight face as he replied dramatically, "Nay, good sir, I mocketh thee not!" as he plopped the garland on Betsy's head.

Despite his nonchalant attitude, his fingertips lightly traced the trail of ribbons over her temple, then her ear, and it seemed to Betsy that they lingered on her neck a great deal longer than necessary. A moment later she felt Spence's warm, sweet breath graze her bare shoulder, and then he pressed his lips against her nape. She shivered from the impact—and from the implied intimacy of the unexpected caress.

What is he doing to me? she asked herself almost breathlessly. *Is he just playing the Renaissance game as Janet ordered, or is he trying to tell me something else?*

She got the answer to her question when Spence winked at the tradesman and said, "Is that better?"

Although Betsy knew she ought to be pleased that he was finally getting into the spirit of things, she couldn't stifle a twinge of disappointment when she realized that Spence's romantic overtures were only his way of playing the nobleman's role.

"'Tis a fine tribute to pay to such a lady," the flower seller answered. "Good morrow to ye both. May all joys be yours as ye go a-mayin'!"

As Spence led Betsy up Gaming Hill, she thanked him for the garland in the calmest voice she could find. Casually he answered, "If I'd known I was going to have to work so hard, I probably wouldn't have bought it." Then his eyes met hers for just a moment, and he added warmly, "But it really sets off that gown, Betsy. I've never seen you look any better, and you look...well, you look just terrific most of the time."

Another jolt of wild hope and hunger zigzagged through Betsy, and she had to take a quick extra breath.

Awkwardly she answered, "If I'd known you were coming, I could have designed a costume for you, too, Spence. Something dashing and heroic."

"I'm neither one, but thanks all the same," he replied. Then, without warning, he wrapped his warm, callused fingers around her hand. It was the third time today that he'd done it, and this time there was no way he could pretend he'd reached for her by accident. The joy inside Betsy erupted in a radiant smile on her face, and though Spence looked a little red-faced, he smiled right back at her.

By mutual consent they slowly began to wend their way through the crowd of faire visitors clad in old muslin shirts and baggy wool britches, full-hooped farthingales and jewel-laden hats. Many of the women had garlands like Betsy's, and a number also sported a single flower tucked between their breasts, held in place by a tightly laced bodice. They passed a unicyclist, a strolling minstrel and a falconer with a grim-visaged bird on his arm. Spence stopped to pick up a teddy bear that a darling baby girl had dropped, and fussed over Betsy while a tarot card reader promised her a long and joyful life with a tall, dark, handsome stranger. And at one point they stumbled over a genuine bride and groom dressed in Renaissance clothes, who were apparently exchanging real-life vows in the middle of the faire. The wedding guests were all clad in velvet and satin, also, and each wore a paper ring imprinted with the same words that were engraved on the bride's ruby-studded ring: "My heart and my fortune I do render unto thee." A young girl tried to give one to Spence, too, but he stiffened when he saw the words and brusquely told her that he and Betsy weren't part of the wedding party.

Overall, it was a wonderful, rollicking morning, and except for the unavoidable misery of wearing heavy velvet on a humid midwestern day, Betsy thoroughly enjoyed the hours she spent with Spence, and he showed every sign of enjoying her company, too. It was almost noon—the hour they were scheduled to rendezvous with the others at Gaffer Paul's—when Betsy's eye fell on John Percy's fencing booth.

John was really a sight to see. He wore bright turquoise tights with silver-and-red slops, and a jewel-encrusted sword sheath hung from his belt. Row after row of gold chains adorned his doublet-covered chest, and his plumed felt hat was so heavily peppered with fake jewels that it was hard to see what color lurked beneath. He brandished a brilliant silver saber and tossed his ermine-trimmed red cape over his shoulder with a dramatic flourish as often as he could get away with it.

"Oh, Spence, you've got to see this!" Betsy crowed, eagerly rushing toward the sound of the booming voice announcing that "Sir Percival" was about to engage in another duel. "This is the Tom Selleck look-alike Janet was telling you about. Let's see how he handles a sword."

Spence followed reluctantly, and he was still a pace or two behind her, when the teenager at the gate who helped would-be duelists strap on face masks and protective jackets called out to him, "Art thou a fencer, good sir? Wouldst thou like to try thy hand against the invincible Sir Percival?"

Betsy could feel the resistance in Spence's fingertips as they lightly grazed her arm, but his tone remained light as he answered, "I'm afraid it wouldn't be a fair fight."

"Alackaday!" the young squire answered. "Afraid thou art of being brought to thy knees in battle?"

Betsy grinned. "I hope you realize he's calling you a coward," she pointed out to Spence.

"I realize that," he replied with a sardonic lift of one eyebrow. "I don't like it, but I think I'd rather look like a coward than be proved a fool."

"Sir Percival would destroy thee in a moment!" the boy taunted, obviously goading his prospective customer as he'd been trained to do. "There is no power greater than my lordship's sword!"

Before Spence could answer, John Percy spotted Betsy and swaggered grandly to her side. "Lady Elizabeth!" he swooned. "What joy to see thy fair visage once more! What bliss! No happiness could be greater than to greet thee with a kiss!"

To his credit, John did a great job of keeping a straight face while he recited this brief rhyme, but Betsy found herself laughing out loud when he reached for her hand and dramatically pressed his lips against the back of it.

Her laughter stopped when the master fencer laid eyes on Spence, who was mutely watching this flowery exchange with a tense, dark scowl on his face. "And what have we here, young squire?" John asked the boy by the front gate. "A knave who lacks the courage to face me man-to-man?" His feigned supercilious tone gave Betsy chills, and she knew that even in sport, it would be hard for a man like Spence to ignore the deliberate challenge.

Still, Spence held his ground. Incredibly he responded with an Elizabethan insult that sounded quite authentic from a man clad in blue jeans and a plaid shirt. "A silly question, and fitting well a sheep."

John tried to look outraged, but it was obvious to Betsy he was delighted to have found somebody to join him in a verbal duel. To the crowd he called out, "That great baby you see there is not yet out of his swaddling clouts!''

"Blasts and fogs upon thee, thou paper-faced villain!'' Spence shouted back, almost sounding truly angry now. "You lie, up to the hearing of the gods!''

John gave a marvelously evil laugh before he hollered to the giggling crowd, "God made him, and therefore let him pass for a man, but the tartness of his face sours ripe grapes!''

"A blister on his sweet tongue!'' Spence roared back, then whispered to Betsy with a wink, "Let's get out of here. I've just about used up all my lines.'' But apparently a couple more zingers occurred to him, because he tossed back over his shoulders, "Zounds, but I was ne'er so bethumped with words! Would thou wert clean enough to spit on!''

With that last insult, he took Betsy's hand to lead her away, but John was having far too much fun to let him go. "Go, thou mongrel, thou beetle-headed, flap-ear'd knave! Take with thee my most grievous curse!''

All in all, Betsy considered it a fair exchange, and she was delighted that Spence was playing his role so vigorously. They were going to be a few minutes late to meet the others, but she knew that nobody would mind when they found out that Mrs. Mac's Elizabethan English handout had been put to such good use. She was just about to congratulate Spence on his superb performance, when John called out again, "Lady Elizabeth! Wouldst thou leave me without a tender word?''

Instinctively she stopped and turned around just as he reached down to pick up a white rosebud that had fallen from her garland and gotten stuck on Spence's boot. Before Betsy could stop him, John leaned forward to sandwich the flower securely between her tightly laced breasts, his fingers lingering fractionally longer than was absolutely necessary as he finished, "If this hand were to die this morrow, 'twould be to die most happy now."

In an instant Spence was transformed. He'd played his role so well for the past few minutes that Betsy would have thought he was still having a good time if his instinctive grip hadn't all but crushed her arm. The intensity of his reaction took her by surprise. At once he grabbed a foil from the fence behind the squire, his fierce scowl indicating that he was a man about to engage in mortal battle. John tried to look equally angry, but his smiling eyes revealed his delight that he'd goaded a faire visitor into battle. After all, that was his job.

Spence, it seemed, had decided that he also had a job to do, and Betsy wasn't at all sure the faire had anything to do with it. She wasn't sure whether she was thrilled or alarmed when he swore, "Fie, O thou pernicious worm! Soil not the white skin of this fair lady!" He tugged on a protective face mask as he hurled epithets at the other man with all the rancor Mrs. Mac had taught him. "May vultures vile seize upon thy lungs!"

By now the crowd was howling and pressing closer, clearly delighted by the drama unfolding before their eyes. While the squire handed Spence a white fencing jacket, John, artfully playing Sir Percival, continued to taunt him with ribald suggestions and increasingly raunchy insults to his manhood. He used the word "cuckold" again and again, which seemed to especially incense his rival. Though a regal saber was part of John's attire, Betsy noticed that he seized a specially tipped practice foil from the rack behind his squire before he stepped back onto the greensward to challenge Spence.

The duel began in earnest when Spence followed, and John shouted, *"En garde!"* thrusting his foil in the air.

Instantly Spence's foil collided with the other man's and they darted back and forth in the roped-off ring.

"Kill him, Sir Percival!" the young squire shouted. "Show this knave that thou art the finest swordsman in the kingdom!"

"Nay, not he!" Betsy cried, eager now to play her part in this impromptu street theater. "Sir Geoffrey will draw first blood as sure as bark on a tree!"

And so it went; the foils clashed, the two men leaped forward and scrambled back and the crowd shouted boos and huzzahs. Betsy didn't have to feign her excitement. She knew that the scene would never have been so compelling if it had been rehearsed. She also knew, in some secret part of her heart, that the knowledge that these two men were fighting over *her*—even in jest—greatly accentuated her pleasure.

The duel went on for about five minutes, the scores of each man implying that they were almost evenly matched. But it was obvious to Betsy that Spence wasn't as light on his feet—he had more strength than agility—and she wondered if John was engineering a faire guest's victory. Nonetheless, when John sprawled into the dust as Spence scored the final point, Betsy burst into cheers along with the crowd. With a dramatic swagger, Spence thrust his foil toward his rival's throat, just close enough to make clear his warning without doing his defeated foe any harm. "Take thyself off into some dark hole!" he commanded. "From this day forward, whoever sees this lurking serpent must shield his eyes!" He tossed his foil back to the squire, then hurled the mask and jacket in the same direction. Then he glared at John—who was doing his best to scowl even though his sides were shaking with laughter as he lay on the ground—and ordered, "Knowest thou this. Should thy hand ever again dare to soil my lady, I will cut out thy black heart and toss it into the fire to fry!'' On that dramatic note, Spence swaggered over the rope boundary and took Betsy in his arms, sweeping her backward into a melodramatic kiss.

She knew that he was only claiming "Sir Geoffrey's" prize. She knew that the crowd expected the kiss. She knew that it was the only logical ending to the feigned 1588 duel between two lords over the favor of a lady. But her knowledge did nothing whatsoever to prepare her for what happened when Spence's mouth claimed hers.

The moment she felt the fierce warmth of his hunger, Betsy left the sixteenth century. She left the faire. She left the whole state of Pennsylvania.

She closed her eyes as her heart lurched, and her hands gripped Spence's old plaid collar for support. She felt the warmth and power of his sensual lips—the lips that had denied her what she'd ached for just a few short days ago. But now Spence delivered what he'd kept from her then. Betsy's desire for him flared into an inferno, and she clung to him with the certainty that she would never, ever let him go.

As his kiss deepened, Betsy pressed Spence's broad muscular chest, reveling in the urgency of the hands that cradled her bare back. She could feel the power and hunger of his own need in every line of his body; she could feel the tension in the corded muscles of his arms. The warmth of his soft, yearning mouth seemed to invite her tongue to slip out to tease him. But the instant her tongue touched his lips, Spence began to pull back.

The crowd was still huzzahing and Sir Geoffrey's slain opponent still lay "defeated" on the ground when Betsy opened her eyes and stared urgently into Spence's. She could barely think; she had no recollection of where they were or what they were doing here. All she was sure of was that she was in Spence's arms once more, and this time she was going to do everything in her power to stay there.

But Spence didn't look the least bit dazed. If anything, he looked surprised and a little embarrassed. In a whisper that only she could hear, he reminded her gently, "We're still at the faire, Bets. We're just playing a game for all these people." Ever so briefly he touched her face, as if to remove any sting from his prosaic words. "I'll cover for you while you get yourself together," he promised.

Red-faced and mortified, Betsy was still reeling when Spence placed her on her feet, one arm cradling her firmly, and called out victoriously to the crowd, "'Tis as 'twas meant to be. My lady's heart belongs to me!"

And then, as though to squelch any lingering doubt about the question, he tugged out the rose that his rival had tucked between Betsy's breasts, crumpled it into a sodden ball and threw in on the ground just inches from John Percy's dirt-smudged face. In that instant, Betsy got a glimpse of the possessive gleam in Spence's eyes, and she knew that in the secrecy of his soul there was no way he could pass off this duel—or the kiss that had followed it—as only a meaningless game.

He'd fought a duel for Betsy's honor, and he'd won her fair and square.

SPENCE WAS FEELING a little shaky by the time they reached Paul Hardison's mansion. He'd really thrown himself into the fencing bout—physically as well as mentally—and his bad knee was acting up again. Worse yet, he'd been as badly shaken by that kiss as Betsy, only he'd managed to hide his reaction better, thanks to all the practice he'd had steeling himself against the potent need she aroused in him.

It wasn't easy to maintain his composure during the six course Renaissance meal of hand-held turkey legs, baked yams, Banbury cheese and ippocras, put together by Paul's new housekeeper, Velma, an elderly widow who was gaunt and taciturn and looked as though she desperately needed a day off. Fortunately Mrs. Mac and the old man did most of the talking, so Spence wasn't called upon to recycle his half a dozen Elizabethan phrases. Equally fortunate was the fact that he was sitting next to Janet and across from Marvin Oates, so he didn't have to face Betsy. The instant he'd released her, after their kiss, Spence had realized that coming along to this shindig had been a big mistake. It just wasn't possible for him to spend time with Betsy without fireworks exploding between them, and he couldn't handle those fireworks at all.

Spence tried to focus on Gaffer Paul, who was a fascinating character. He was frail and somewhat crippled by arthritis, and took so long to answer questions that Spence sometimes feared he'd forgotten the subject altogether before he came up with an appropriate response. But he was a gracious host and ex-globe-trotter who was more than eager to share with his visitors all his recollections and his prized collections gathered from around the world. When they'd first arrived, he'd taken one look at Spence in his blue jeans—the only one of the Muskingum group who was out of costume—and insisted on finding something suitable in his private Renaissance wardrobe. He'd promptly forgotten this suggestion but recalled it again after the meal, at which time he insisted on leading all eight of his visitors to the back room where he kept his costumes. Janet gave him a fierce look that meant "You be nice to this old man, Spence!" so he didn't demur.

He supposed he should have been grateful for Betsy's interest in the matter. She had favored him with neither a glance nor more than a dozen words since he'd kissed her. He suspected that she felt just as ridiculous as he did.

How could I have made such a fool of myself? he berated himself again and again. *It's none of my business who touches those lovely breasts. None of my business who crawls between Betsy's sheets at night. I've been invited and said no, and that's the end of it.*

But it wasn't the end, not by a long shot, and he was certain that Betsy knew it as well as he did. But he did his best to push the dilemma away from his mind when he spied Paul's extraordinary collection of coins. There were over a dozen separate collections, half of which Spence recognized. He was impressed with all of them, but especially entranced by the English monarch series that Betsy had mentioned. How exhilarating to view a thousand years of history in one set of coins!

"Mr. Hardison! What a sight!" he gasped in genuine pleasure.

Behind him, Janet whispered, "'Gaffer Paul.' Call him 'Gaffer Paul.'"

"Uh, Gaffer Paul, my son has a coin collection, too," he began again, wishing there were some way he could show these beauties to Randy. "Nothing so dramatic, of course, but he's very proud of the ones he's got."

Gaffer Paul hobbled over to his coin case and tugged out one of the displays. "This is my English monarch collection," he announced with pride, plucking out one heavy coin by its ridged edges. "This is the sovereign they were using during the reign of Queen Elizabeth I."

"It's beautiful," Spence said truthfully. "My boy would give his eyeteeth for even one of these."

"Oh, they're not all expensive," Gaffer Paul informed him. "Some of these—" his trembling fingers gestured toward two or three of his prized possessions "—are worth a small fortune, of course. But this little coppernose—" he picked up a Henry VIII shilling "—wouldn't bring more than a hundred dollars. It's the sort of coin you could find in any—"

He broke off abruptly as grim-faced Velma ushered in a man in familiar turquoise tights and red-and-silver slops. Spence would have known that smirk anywhere. His whole body tensed for another verbal battle.

"Ah, John, good of you to drop by!" Gaffer Paul greeted the other man, ambling toward him without locking up the coins that still sat on the display case. "These are my friends from Muskingum, who are putting on their own Renaissance faire." Quickly he introduced all the Muskingum visitors by name—with a little help from Janet, then tacked on, "And this is my good friend John Percy, who runs the fencing booth."

"Some of us have met," Percy answered, grinning warmly at Spence and Betsy as though they were all the best of friends. "You're pretty handy with a sword, Spence. Had some training, have you?"

"A long time ago," Spence admitted, knowing perfectly well that he'd won the duel only because Percy, in the spirit of the faire, had allowed him to. "Fencing's never been my best sport."

Percy laughed a bit harder than Spence thought was absolutely necessary. "Well, you put on a good show, and that's what matters. So did you, Lady Elizabeth," he added, his eyes dropping to her deep neckline as though in memory of the flower he'd placed there. "I think you convinced the crowd you'd never been kissed before."

When Betsy started to color, Spence said quickly, "She's a good actress. From the first moment Mrs. MacGillicuddy put a script in her hand, she knew what to do." Quickly he turned to his old teacher, who was poring over a bookcase full of original copies of the classics. "Didn't she, Mrs. Mac?"

Mrs. MacGillicuddy, oblivious to his plea for help, took her eyes off a seventeenth century volume of *The Taming of the Shrew* in her hand only long enough to correct him. "'Gammer Mac' to you, Sir Geoffrey," she muttered, then continued to lovingly caress the book's engraved leather cover.

John didn't seem troubled by Mrs. Mac's reaction. In fact, he didn't seem troubled by anything as he sauntered over to Janet, grinning, and took her hand. "What joy to see thy fair visage once more! What bliss! No happiness could be greater than to greet thee with a kiss!" he oozed as he kissed her fingers.

That line was bad enough the first time, Spence groaned inwardly. *Don't you know any other way to greet a lady?*

But Gaffer Paul, still hunched over next to Spence, beamed approvingly. "John studied Shakespeare at Oxford, you know. His mother was born in England, and his father was one of our most generous sponsors when we were first getting started. The whole family participated in our faire for years." He sighed nostalgically. "What a blessing that we still have John."

"Yes, isn't it?" Spence replied out of courtesy to the old man. Inside, he was still steaming over the familiar way Percy had touched Betsy's breasts, and he couldn't help but sneak a glance at her now, anxious about her

response to the other man as Percy dropped Janet's hand
and sauntered over to Betsy's side. But to Spence's surprise, Betsy's eyes weren't trained on John but on Spence
himself, and the moment she realized that he'd caught her
staring, she flushed and looked away.

Dammit, Betsy, what do you expect from me? he
wanted to holler, already knowing the answer. *It was just
a show-biz kiss, nothing special. Is it my fault you got
carried away?*

But he knew it hadn't been that simple, and he knew
that Betsy hadn't been the only one who'd forgotten John
Percy and the crowd. And she certainly hadn't been the
only one who'd desperately wished that that kiss could
have been the beginning of a long, intimate night together, instead of another bittersweet memory they were
both better off forgetting.

"Has thou supped, my good man?" Gaffer Paul asked
his younger friend. "I could provision thee with a turkey leg and a tankard of ale."

"Twoudst be a sweet moment, Gaffer Paul, but return to the greensward now I must. I came but to leave
my saber as it grows heavy in the battle."

As he whipped off the jewel-laden sword sheath, it occurred to Spence that even though Paul's house ad-
joined the grounds of the faire, it was a bit of a hassle to
hike over a hundred acres of oak-studded hills just to
drop off a sword. But before he could dwell on that,
John, sword in hand, slipped easily into the walk-in
closet, leading Paul to remember that they'd gone to it to
look for a costume for Spence.

"What findest thou for our good man to wear, Sir
Percival? He is of noble blood, indeed, if he woudst face
thee with a sword!"

John's words to Spence were a bit more blunt. "I think this would suit you just fine," he declared, tossing a fringed leather vest and chaps out the door. "A natural image."

"He'll look like a cowboy," Janet said.

"Exactly." John laughed again. "What goes better with blue jeans?"

"Let me pick something out for him, John," Betsy announced crisply, so crisply, in fact, that everyone in the room turned to stare at her. She ignored them all, her head held high as she pointed out, "I know you're in a hurry to get back to the fencing booth."

John met her eyes briefly, as though he were surprised at her snappy tone. "Actually, Betsy, neither one of us can do much for him. All the Renaissance costumes are already out on loan."

"Oh, that's right!" Gaffer Paul groaned, as though it were a startling thought, one of many he seemed to be having trouble holding on to. "Remind me, John, to send them all to Muskingum after the faire is over next week."

"Send them to Muskingum?" John repeated, his sharp blue eyes briefly meeting Gaffer Paul's.

The old man nodded. "I'm not well enough to travel that far to help these folks, but I'm going to send what I can to help them get a good start."

Slowly John straightened, smoothing the lines of the fringed leather vest in his hands. "Why, that's a great idea, Paul. Maybe some of the rest of us can help." His eyes darted to Betsy, dropping quickly to glance at her partially exposed breasts. Then, more slowly, he turned to Janet, infuriating Spence with the sudden, knowing warmth of his smile. "When's your faire scheduled, Jan?" he asked, exacerbating Spence's resentment by his casual use of the nickname nobody but Bill had ever used to address his wife. "Maybe I could run the fencing booth for you."

"Oh, could you, John?" Janet cried, edging toward him with palpable excitement. "We've just been desperate for help with our action booths. I can't tell you how grateful we'd be."

John's grin was so smug that Spence wanted to grab a foil again, but he restrained the impulse. He'd already made a fool of himself once today, and he was hoping to avoid a repeat of the morning's folly. Still, he suspected that even when he cooled off, he still wouldn't want John Percy working on the faire with his sister-in-law, and he *knew* he didn't want the bastard within a hundred miles of Betsy.

To his dismay, Spence heard himself declare, "That's a generous offer, John, but we know it's too far for you to come. Now that I've seen your fencing booth in operation, I'm sure I can run it by myself."

Janet whipped around to face him as though his hair had just turned green, and though Spence didn't dare look at Betsy, he heard her suddenly gasp in disbelief. He didn't know if it was pride or stubbornness or just plain jealousy that had caused him make such a sharp reversal. He did know that even if word got out in the patch that he'd worn purple tights in public, it would be worth it to keep John Percy out of Muskingum.

"Hey, that's great," John answered, no trace of distress on his smiling, too-pretty face. "But you let me know if you need help with anything, Spence." He turned back to Janet, and giving her a visual caress that implied she was the only woman in the world, he offered, "And if there's anything else I can do to help you, Jan, you just let me know."

Stop calling her "Jan"! Spence wanted to shout. *That would help us all a great deal.*

But Percy had one more farewell to offer, and he slithered right up to Betsy's face to give it. "The sun will not shine until I gaze upon thy fair face once more, Lady Elizabeth," he intoned dramatically. "I shall see thee anon." Again he took her hand, this time turning it over to kiss the inside of her delicate wrist.

While Spence seethed, Betsy dropped a deep curtsy, which, in her low-cut dress, offered a tantalizing view of what lay hidden beneath the tight bodice. His hunger for her flared again, intensified by his unreasoning fury with John Percy.

As the other fencer strode away, Spence faced the fact that he'd been lying to himself all day. He'd come on this trip because he couldn't stay away from Betsy, and he'd gone berserk because another man had encroached on his imagined rights. Now he'd volunteered to do something he detested—and couldn't do very well—just to protect his status with the woman he claimed did not belong to him and never would.

That wasn't Sir Geoffrey who had kissed Lady Elizabeth this morning! he was forced to admit. *That was Spence kissing Betsy, and Betsy who had kissed him back.* And that kiss had been even hotter than the ones they'd shared the other night at her house! If it had happened in Betsy's living room and the shades had been drawn, Spence was certain they'd be in her bed right now.

He swallowed hard to fight the hunger, but he was betrayed by both his body and his heart. Deliberately he pushed past Betsy, desperate to escape from the power of her spell. *I've got to get over her,* he vowed. *I've got to keep her from getting a grip on my heart!*

It was a fine resolution, and one he fully intended to honor...until Betsy's eyes met his, and her vibrant longing for his touch gripped him from clear across the room.

It took every ounce of self-control Spence possessed to march through the doorway without reaching out to touch her.

CHAPTER TEN

BY SATURDAY NIGHT when Betsy fell into bed, she was weary to the bone. It wasn't just the long drive and the busy day, or even the accumulated fatigue of too many dream-filled, sleepless nights. Her exhaustion stemmed from the heaviness of her heart.

Spence was driving her crazy. On Monday night, he'd kissed her, then pulled away; on Thursday he'd confessed that he cared for her deeply, but he'd vowed that he'd leave her alone. And then, when she'd almost accepted the inevitability of their parting, he'd shown up Saturday morning and had commandeered her day. In the space of a single hour he'd taken her in his arms and kissed her as she had never in her life been kissed before, and then he'd brought her back to earth with a hearty thump and all but tossed her away.

Spence had kept a rigid distance from her ever since the duel, even finagling the group's seating on the way home so she ended up sitting next to Mrs. MacGillicuddy, who recounted every minute of her joyful day on the way home. His toneless "Good night, Betsy" had been the only discordant note in the otherwise communal chorus.

Betsy knew he was teetering on the brink; there was no way he could deny that he wanted her. But he'd also made it clear that the next move had to be his, and there was nothing she could do but wait. But *where* she waited was up to her, and Monday evening found Betsy waiting at the Muskingum Movie House at 7:25. If there was any chance at all that Spence wanted to give their stillborn affair another chance to live, she knew he'd meet her there.

He didn't.

Betsy sat perfectly still through two hours of mindless cartoons featuring an obnoxious duck while great, dry sobs slowly racked her body. By the time the show mercifully ended, she was able to stand up, dry-eyed and straight spined, determined to get on with her life. She masked her grief with a plastic smile as she said goodnight to Hal and Hattie, then walked on home. Alone.

"DAD?" Randy prodded his father when Spence failed to respond to his first call from the kitchen. "Mom wants to talk to you."

"Tiffany's *here*?" Spence barked in surprise, finally aroused from the self-directed fury that had gripped him all evening as he'd battled visions of Betsy at the theater by herself. "What the hell is your mo—"

"She's not *here*, Dad. She's on the phone. The phone in the kitchen," he explained patiently, patting his father on the arm. "You remember the phone? It rings every now and then when—"

"Randy, I'm not in the mood," Spence snapped, referring to both his son's adolescent patronization and the grueling prospect of talking to his ex-wife. "Tell her I'll call her back later in the week."

"Dad, I can't tell her that! I'm the one who called her! Remember you told me to straighten out the details with her ahead of time so she wouldn't make a fuss on Saturday night?"

Spence eyed Randy dimly, struggling to thrust the haunting image of Betsy from his mind. "I thought the court order required you to go over there Friday night. Your mother always whisks you off for summer vacation the instant you're done with school."

Randy tossed up both hands in a gesture of exasperation, then leaned over to lightly rap his knuckles on the side of his father's skull. "Hello in there. Earth to Dad. Earth to Dad. This is your son, Randy, reminding you that we have reservations for the Medieval Times and Tournament in Columbus on Saturday night. I groveled to Mom for hours to get special permission to give you one of 'her' nights less than twenty-four hours after I'll arrive there, and—"

"*We?*" Spence repeated blankly, suddenly zeroing in the true subject of conversation.

"Very good, Dad. We, as in you and me and Laurie and Betsy. Remember Laurie? Remember Betsy? Remember *me?*"

Spence groaned as he realized that common courtesy wouldn't allow him to dodge Betsy forever. *Oh, hell, do I really want to?* he asked himself sharply. *How many nights can I live through like this, staring at the walls, seeing nothing but her exquisite face?*

"Remember Mom, who's still waiting on the phone?" Randy prompted, his voice less sarcastic now as he studied his father intently. "Dad?" His tone now reluctantly revealed some genuine concern. "Are you okay? Maybe I ought to tell Mom that—"

"I'll talk to your mother," Spence declared firmly, taking command of his feelings with a great, angry rush as he stood up. "And then I want you to disappear for a while. I've got another call to make and I *don't* want an audience. Is that clear?"

Randy started to make a joke, took one look at his father's eyes and swallowed back the ribald suggestion.

"Perfectly clear. I'll be in my room working on my science report."

Spence watched him go, wishing there were some way he could explain to Randy what was going on without betraying Betsy's private longing and grief. But there were some things he just couldn't talk about to Randy, such as why it was that by the time he was done talking to his ex-wife, he knew he'd need two or three days to find the courage to place that second call.

OMA ALWAYS TOOK her lunch from twelve to one, a fact almost everybody in town was privy to. Betsy, holding down the fort alone, was busily altering a hoop skirt for the faire, when the phone rang at precisely 12:31 on Thursday afternoon.

"Ye Olde Fabric Shoppe, Betsy Hanover speaking. How may I help you?" she greeted her unknown caller with determined cheerfulness.

It had been a grim couple of days, but Betsy was never one to stay down too long. She loved Spence, and she had an uneasy feeling that she always would. But loving him and pining over him day and night were two separate things, she'd decided, and she'd vowed on Monday night that no matter what she was feeling inside, she'd get back into the swing of things before life passed her by. She'd even decided to start dating.

"Black Gold Supply, Geoffrey Spencer speaking," came the quick response, which tried but failed to convey a note of humor. "Do you have a second, Bets?"

Betsy closed her eyes, reeling a moment as she gripped the counter top. Spence had never, for any reason, called her. He'd met her at the theater and had periodically dropped by the shop when he was "in the neighborhood," but he had never called; not to ask how she was, nor to arrange to meet her somewhere, nor to firm up plans. The fact that he would call now—when she had just accepted the fact that there wasn't a hope in the world of melding her life with his—was more than a little ironic.

"I don't have any customers at the moment, Spence," she told him truthfully, "but that could change anytime."

"Understood. I'll be brief. Randy just reminded me the other night that we've still got reservations for that medieval hoop-de-doo in Columbus on Saturday evening. I don't think we ever decided whether we were going when we talked about it before. In the interest of protocol, I thought I ought to get back to you." Not one ounce of either warmth or sorrow colored his bright, brusque tone.

"I don't know what more there is to say," Betsy said bluntly, suddenly furious that he'd stirred up her hopes again for such a prosaic reason. "I see no point in going through such a farce even for Randy's sake."

Spence took a deep breath, then said in a softer voice, "Ah, Bets, have mercy. Please don't make this any harder than it has to be. I'm *trying* to be diplomatic. Can't you just say yes or no?"

Betsy could have pointed out that *he* was the one who had trouble giving simple answers where their relationship was concerned, but she held her tongue. Instead she replied honestly, "If you have a genuine interest in spending some time with me, Spence, I'd still be delighted to go to Columbus with you and your son. But if you're contemplating going through with this out of some misguided notion of chivalry, then believe me, I'd really rather skip the whole thing." And then, unable to help herself, she added, "I've already got a date for Friday night and I don't think it would be too hard to drum up another one for Saturday.''

A stunned silence greeted her from the other end of the line. *Oh, Betsy! How childish of you to try to make him jealous!* she chastised herself. But surely he realized, if he'd ever given it any thought, that she'd been turning down dates ever since they'd been meeting on Mondays, and her reputation as ''Spence's woman'' had nearly precluded any further invitations. When Wade Carlson had called her the night before, she'd accepted his dinner offer at once. She barely knew the man and didn't have the slightest idea whether she liked him, but he was a friend of a friend and she knew he was safe and decent, which made him a godsend, as she was facing a long, lonely weekend nursing a shattered heart.

But Spence didn't seem enthralled by her news. ''Betsy,'' he commented crisply, ''I can't say I like the idea of your... dating somebody else.''

She knew it was a hard confession for him to make, so she swallowed her hurt and admitted gently, ''I'm not crazy about it, either, Spence, but I don't see that you've left me any choice.''

At that moment the front door opened and Trudy Olson bustled in, greeting Betsy with the news that she had just a few minutes to get another yard of that ''gold, glittery rickrack'' before she had to get back to the bank.

''You've got a customer,'' Spence said, obviously hearing the other voice in the background, ''so I'll let you go.''

Betsy struggled to think of a way to tell him how desperately she longed to be near him, how she'd happily give up a date with any other man in the galaxy for the privilege of a single night by his side. But she wasn't sure she could have risked another rejection even if she could have made her confession without an audience. With Trudy waving the roll of gold trim in her face, it was impossible.

"Spence, about this weekend. I—"

"Wear your Renaissance dress, Betsy." There was a sudden change in his tone. Authority replaced the uncertain pleading she'd heard a moment before. "Randy wants us all in costume. We'll pick you up at six, okay?"

Before she cold think of a sensible answer, Spence hung up the phone.

TWENTY-FOUR HOURS LATER, Spence sauntered into Janet's office just as she was finishing off a ham-and-rye. She looked flushed and excited, as she often did these days, and he couldn't help but observe, "If I didn't know better, honey, I'd think you were falling in love again."

Janet laughed. "Well, it's a good thing you do know better. Even if I were ready—which I'm not—there's certainly nobody around here who sets my heart aflame."

"Is there anybody in Pittsburgh?" he asked, cringing as he considered the possible implications of her answer.

"Hardly. Though I think there's somebody there who'd like to."

"Meaning?"

Janet smiled. "I got the most extraordinary letter from John Percy the other day, reiterating his willingness to come down here to help us with the faire. It's written entirely in Elizabethan English and I must admit it's enough to thrill a woman's heart." She plucked an envelope out of her In basket and handed it to Spence. Silently he read the mushy letter—in calligraphy, no less—then laughed out loud when he got to the concluding poem.

Thine own true knight
by day or night
or any kind of light
with all his might
with thee to fight—

He stopped, pondering the ludicrous words. "For some reason this cornball stuff sounds familiar, Janet."

"It's from *The Merry Wives of Windsor*," Janet informed him with a laugh. "It's in one of Falstaff's letters."

"I'm sure you're very flattered," Spence teased her. "If any of the Spencers were rich, I'd be worried."

"I guess we're safe there," she said with a chuckle. "I have to admit that his style is a bit much. Nonetheless, it's been a long time since I've had a man tell me that the birds can't sing at sunrise until they see my face."

"While that may be true," Spence answered diplomatically, "I certainly think there are men head and shoulders above John Percy who also hold you in such high esteem. We don't need the likes of him helping us put on this faire. Personally, I know that I'll run that damn fencing booth a lot better without worrying about him. If you need advice from anybody else in Pittsburgh, why don't you stick to Paul Hardison? He's a nice old guy."

"He's adorable. He's also a tiny bit senile and losing his grip. Betsy's afraid he'll forget to send those costumes on Sunday night." Her tone gentled somewhat as she tossed Spence an apple before taking another bite of her sandwich. "Speaking of Betsy, have you seen her lately?"

"No," he answered quickly. "Why?"

Janet's eyes darkened with concern. "There's something wrong with her, but I don't know what it is."

"Wrong?" A quick jab of concern pierced his heart. "What do you mean, wrong?"

"Well, I've talked to her on the phone two or three times this week for various reasons, and each time she's sounded the way I did right after Bill died." Genuine compassion warmed her tone. "She says she's just tired, but any fool can see that it's a great deal more than that."

Spence sighed heavily, then lowered himself into the nearest plush chair. "Are you talking about fools in general, or any one fool in particular?"

"If the shoe fits, wear it," Janet replied without missing a beat.

"It fits." The minute the words were out he felt better. Relieved, at least. He'd come to ask Janet for advice, but he hadn't had the slightest idea where to begin. "Janet, I'm going crazy," he admitted miserably. "I just don't know what to do."

"Well, you came to the right place. It's pretty obvious to me."

"Is it? With everything you know—I mean, everything you know about me—can you really tell me it's safe to... well, to fall in love with Betsy?"

"Spence!" Janet groaned. "You don't fall in love because it's *safe*. Sometimes it isn't even smart! And in your case, I think it's too late to be asking yourself whether it's a good idea! You've been in love with Betsy for months!"

He opened his mouth to protest, but no words came out. He leaned forward, hands on his knees, and whispered hopelessly, "Oh, God, honey, I don't *want* to be in love with her!"

"What do you want then?" Janet asked him boldly. "What do you really want?"

He pondered the question with a sigh. "I guess I want an ironclad guarantee that I won't get hurt again. That Randy or some other poor Spencer kid won't get tangled up in litigation... that my libido won't bring Grandpa's business to its knees." He shook his head. "Fat chance of that. Once I mentioned the idea of a premarital agreement to Betsy and she went berserk. She's so logical about her business but so romantic when it comes to—" he nearly choked on the word but finally got it out "—well, dammit, when it comes to *me*."

Janet's smile was wide. "She adores you, Spence. She does her best to keep her feelings under wrap, but as my mother always used to say, 'I'm a woman and I know a woman's heart.' Her love for you is pretty plain to see."

"At the moment," Spence clarified grimly. He exhaled heavily, then threw up his hands in defeat. "Okay, I admit it. I'm... attracted to Betsy. And she's drawn to me. Right now it looks like everything is coming up roses. But what about tomorrow or next month or next year? The last time I felt like this I made a total idiot of myself, Janet, and I'm not sure I'm doing much better this time around. On Saturday I actually fought a duel for this woman, for Pete's sake! That's when I realized I was in over my head. I never even did that for Tiffany."

"I was wondering when we'd get around to Tiffany."

"Pardon?" Spence asked, as if he didn't understand.

"You know what I mean. None of this—the fear, the business, the premarital agreement—really has anything to do with Betsy Hanover, Spence. At least not the Betsy Hanover I know. It's true that your life would have turned out a lot differently if you'd signed a premarital agreement with Tiffany or had had enough sense not to marry her in the first place, but you're trying to lock the barn after the horse has been stolen." Her tone grew firm as she added, "You're also punishing Betsy for all of Tiffany's sins."

"I know." Spence was nothing if not an honest man. "And I know I've put her through hell this past week, Janet. Ever since it all came to a head and I told Betsy it was over, I haven't been able to stay away from her. I managed to stay home on Monday night, but I nearly went crazy thinking about Betsy, and tonight I'm afraid I'm going to lose my mind altogether."

"What's happening tonight?"

"She's got a date!" he ground out bitterly. "She's actually going out with some other fellow."

"Does that surprise you? Have you any idea how many dates Betsy's turned down since she came to Muskingum? Ever since word got out that she was taken?"

"Taken?"

"Spence, everybody thinks of her as your woman. Everybody but you."

He leaned forward again and dropped his face in his hands. "I've got to make a decision I can live with, Janet. And I've got to do it before I take her to Columbus tomorrow night."

Janet reached out to pat his shoulders, then gave him a moment of peace to contemplate his choices. At last she questioned, "Do you really want my advice, Spence?"

Slowly he nodded. "Yes, I really think I do."

"In that case, I think it's really time for you to let her go," Janet recommended stoutly.

"Let her go?" He glanced up, startled. "I thought you were on Betsy's side. I thought you wanted us to be together!"

"I do!" Janet insisted. "*She's* not the one you need to get rid of! I'm talking about your ex-wife."

"Oh, come on, Janet! I gave her up years ago. I don't even *like* her anymore!"

"Spence—" Janet stood up to lend height to her diminutive stature "—there was nothing you could do when Tiffany left you. There was nothing you could do when she took your son. There was nothing you could do when the court costs she made you pay for practically tore the business apart. But this time, Tiffany isn't even *trying* to do battle with you, and you're still letting her win. My God!" she burst out with sudden vehemence, "she's already taken so much of your life away from you! Are you going to let her deprive you of Betsy, too?"

CHAPTER ELEVEN

ON SATURDAY NIGHT, Betsy felt like a young girl going out on her first date. Even though she didn't have to fuss over which dress to wear, she spent hours debating over the attendant Renaissance accessories—especially the garland Spence had bought her. It was beautiful, and doubly so because it was a gift from Spence. But in the end she decided not to wear it because she still didn't know what his intentions were tonight, and she didn't want to look like a romantic fool.

I should have insisted that we talk this out first, she told herself for the hundredth time since Thursday. She was accustomed to running her own life, making plans in a timely and orderly fashion; it seemed bizarre to leave something as vital as her future with Spence to pure chance. But after the speeches she'd given him on trust as the basis of love, how could she refuse to give him a little latitude? Wasn't it possible, remotely possible, that his brief spate of jealousy over Wade had cast a new light on the situation, helped him to see that he really did love her too much to imagine her with anybody else?

I'll know the minute I see him at the door, she told herself, taking a deep breath when the bell finally rang at six o'clock. *If he's really sure this time I'll read it in his eyes. If he's still waffling, I'll keep my distance this evening and never, ever be foolish enough to go out with him again.*

Betsy summoned her courage and corralled her hopes as she swept grandly toward the front door. But when she flung it open, it wasn't Spence who stood before her but a radiant Laurie Potter.

"Well, what do you think?" Laurie gushed, gesturing at the skintight red bodice of her floor-length velveteen gown, then sailing on before Betsy could answer. "I'm sorry we're late, but I had trouble lacing up the bodice 'cause it's so tight and my mother almost said it was indecent and I couldn't go and by then Spence was outside and waiting and so when we got here I jumped out before he even turned the motor off and isn't this just so exciting you could die?"

Betsy was breathless by the time Laurie flounced off the porch, but her consternation turned to mirth when she saw Spence opening the passenger door of his '57 Chevy.

He was wearing the purple tights he'd repeatedly lamented about from his high school days as Romeo, with slops of silver and a lighter shade of purple. His legs were so muscular that he looked anything but effeminate in the ridiculous getup, and his broad chest looked even more solid in the padded doublet crisscrossed with gold chains.

"I hope to God this is how everybody else in this restaurant is dressed, Bets," he greeted her sheepishly. "I hope I won't embarrass you."

Her tension ebbed as she laughed at his red face. "You look just fine, Spence. Most authentic." Then, unable to resist teasing him, she tacked on, "I never imagined you had such attractive legs."

"Betsy, please," he begged her, rolling his eyes as she slipped into the car.

"How do I look, Betsy?" Laurie piped up from the back seat as Spence closed her door behind her. "Grandma said you were the expert."

"You look great, Laurie," Betsy was kind enough to answer, though secretly she thought the bodice was tight enough to split at any second. "Randy will be delighted. Speaking of Randy—" she did a double take as she realized that Laurie sat alone in the back "—where is he?"

"He's still at his mother's," Laurie answered cheerfully. "She lives in Bremer, about fifty miles from here. He's only been gone since last night, and all of a sudden I feel like he's been gone a year. It's going to be such a long summer without him!"

From the other side of the car, Betsy could hear Spence's long, quiet sigh. Then he said, "Believe me, Laurie, I know just how you feel."

Betsy wanted to reach out to squeeze his arm in consolation, but she didn't dare. She also wanted to ask him outright what role he expected her to play over the course of the evening, but she didn't dare do that, either. And if she was actually going to meet the much maligned Tiffany...

Spence made courteous responses to Laurie's constant stream of conversation until Randy joined her in the back, saying—to Betsy's relief—that his mother had already gone out for the evening. After that the elder Spencer fell silent as the two kids billed and cooed in the back. Betsy made a few feeble attempts at conversation herself, but Spence gave her brief, airy answers that didn't give her any clues as to what he was feeling. By the time they reached Columbus, she was sure he was just as tense as she was. And just as confused as ever.

IT WAS NOT UNTIL the intermission between jousts that Spence had a chance to talk to Betsy alone, which was just as well, since he didn't really know what to say. He wanted to tell her that she looked incredibly delectable. He wanted to tell her that he ached so much he felt as though his loins were on fire. He wanted to tell her that if anything had happened on her date last night—anything at all—he'd never forgive her for betraying their love. He'd never forgive himself, either.

"Well, it's been quite an evening, Spence," Betsy commented coolly when Laurie and Randy left the table for a walk around the "castle." "I can't say I've ever had one quite like it."

Spence tried to smile as he followed her lead. "I thought Randy went a bit overboard when he started hollering 'Gig the froggie,' when it looked like the Frenchman was going to beat the English chap."

"It's not much worse than 'Crush the limey,' Spence. Honestly, such passion over two men on horseback!"

This time his smile was genuine. "I bet you're a real wet blanket at a football game."

Betsy managed to laugh. "And here I've always thought of myself as a good sport."

He could have answered with equal humor, but he let his tone grow solemn again. "You are, Bets. You're a very kind and patient woman."

"Thank you," she replied without warmth.

"Betsy, I meant that as a compliment." He felt the need to assure her, certain that she'd misread him again.

"I know." Her beautiful blue eyes, tense and unhappy, met his across the round wooden table graced with tin cups full of sack and ippocras and platters of Cheshire cheese. "I'm sorry. It wouldn't take much for you to hurt my feelings right now, but I'm determined not to fight with you tonight.''

"I didn't bring you here to fight, Bets," he assured her, wondering why it was so very hard to tell her that he'd finally made up his mind. Ever since he'd picked her up he'd been exceedingly friendly, but she'd remained stiff and unyielding throughout the evening—warm enough to the kids, but no more than civil to Spence himself. She was clearly laboring under the illusion that tonight would end up like all the other aborted evenings of indecision she'd suffered through because of him. He couldn't blame her. But tonight—dammit, tonight *would* be different. He'd faced his demons, had battled with them all night and had slain them just before dawn. He loved this beautiful, compassionate woman, and he wanted to enfold her in the heart of his life. But after so many months of denying his feelings, even to himself, he couldn't seem to find a way to let her know. "Betsy—" again the right words failed him "—I've been trying to tell you all evening that . . . oh, hell, Bets! I want to clear everything up between us, but I can't very well fuss all over you in front of Randy.''

"Ha!" she burst out bitterly. "You're not about to fuss over me under any circumstances. If you really wanted to clear things up between us, Spence, you would have come to see me alone.''

He swallowed hard and met her firm gaze. "That's not entirely true, Betsy. I do want to straighten things out between us. Very much." His voice grew low and hoarse. "I guess I just don't know how.''

Her eyebrows raised in disbelief. "You don't know how? I offer you my love and you scramble for the door, and you don't have a clue as to where you went wrong?''

"At least I didn't run straight to somebody else!"

"And you think I did?"

"Well, I'm not the one who was out on the town last night, Betsy," he pointed out, suddenly realizing it was her unexpected declaration that she was seeing somebody else that had left him feeling so tongue-tied and set adrift. What if her feelings for him had changed? What if he declared his feelings this evening, only to be told it was too late? "Randy went to his mother's house, but I stayed home alone."

"Don't expect to get any sympathy from me, Spence," she retorted. "I've known you for three months now, and in all this time, have you ever once sought me out? Ever asked to go anywhere on purpose? No. And don't try to count this evening—you only did it for Randy, and even then you tried to back out. You just saunter into that damn theater when you're in the mood, expecting me to pant and wag my tail with the joy of seeing you." Her tone grew sharp, but she kept her voice low. "What do you think I've been doing between Mondays? Putting my life on hold while I wait for the next show?"

She stared at Spence defiantly while he struggled for a reply. He'd always looked upon their Monday nights as a regular date, and he was certain that she did, too. That was why it had been so damn hard—and so important—to skip the film last week. So hard to imagine her there alone. So hard to imagine her there with someone else.

"Who is he, Bets?" he asked abruptly, as though her unanswered questions didn't linger in the air. "Who were you with last night?"

Betsy's eyes narrowed. "I don't think that's any of your concern."

"Dammit, I want to know! In a town the size of Muskingum I could find out with half a dozen phone calls and you know it."

"Then make them! Find out everything you want to know. Where we went, when we got home, what time he left in the morn—"

"Don't, Betsy," he begged her, the image of her naked form intertwined with some other man's simply too terrible to bear. "I know I deserve it, but please don't...don't twist my guts like that when you know that it's not true." And then he looked at her, really looked at her—proud, determined, terribly hurt by his betrayal—and remembered the intensity of her passion when he'd kissed her at the faire. "My God, Betsy! Tell me it's not true!"

Slowly she shook her head, and it seemed to Spence that it took her a thousand years to answer his desperate question.

"You're a fool, Geoffrey Spencer," she said sadly. "At times like these I can't imagine how I could have fallen in love with you."

"Betsy!" he begged her.

Again she shook her head, but too gently now to scare him. "Oh, Spence! Don't you know by now that the only man I have the slightest desire to make love to is you?"

He closed his eyes and released a great breath, feeling like an idiot. He couldn't even look at her as she continued tonelessly, "Wade Carlson. Glen Tavern for dinner ten miles to the east, home at nine, fed him some leftover apricot pie I made last Sunday, sent him off at eleven o'clock without so much as a good-night kiss, went to bed alone and had a good cry." After a long, terrible moment she added, "I plan to have a lot longer cry tonight. This time I didn't even bother with a pie."

He saw her then, saw the woman Betsy Hanover truly was and not the Tiffany Atkinson clone he'd once imagined her to be. Tiffany would never have told him the truth about the night before; she would have relished seeing him tied up in knots. And she would have slept with the other man just to spite him, whether she had any interest in him or not. She would never have taken the risk of confessing how much she loved Spence, not once but several times, and never, after the wishy-washy way he'd called on Thursday, would she have given him another chance. But not even Betsy, he realized, would cut him any more slack after tonight. He was going to lose her if he held on to his fears too tightly to take her in his arms. He had only two choices now, he suddenly realized: he could cling to the shadows with which Tiffany had darkened his life, or he could step boldly out into the bright rays of Betsy's sun.

When Randy and Laurie returned to the table, the joust was starting up again. Laurie had a rose stuck between her small breasts, flattened by the tight bodice. While she bubbled about meeting the queen of the court in all her royal finery, Randy presented Betsy with the most exquisite lavender rose Spence had ever seen.

"A gift from the queen," he intoned dramatically.

"A gift *for* a queen," Spence corrected, suddenly finding the strength to speak the truth. Betsy flashed her dark, suspicious eyes in his direction as he took the flower from Randy and quickly dethorned it. He ran his fingers over the short green stem to make sure it was smooth enough to suit his plan, then boldly leaned across the table and slipped the rose down Betsy's laced bodice, ensconcing it firmly between her invitingly full white curves.

Her bosom heaved—in surprise, desire or indignation—as he retreated from the implied caress of her breasts. He let his hunger sweep across his face without the slightest effort to conceal it from her. Betsy's eyes met his with wonder, smoldering not with anger this time but with newfound hope and cautious passion.

Trembling, Spence reached out to grip her hand, which was lying idly on the table. With that one simple gesture, he promised her that she would not sleep alone tonight.

As THE OLD CHEVY chugged its way through the darkness toward Muskingum, the lavender rose insinuated itself between Betsy's breasts as though it were Spence's own hand. His fingertips lay on top of Betsy's left knee in the most casual fashion, but there was nothing casual about the effect of his touch on her rising hunger.

Laurie and Randy cuddled in the back seat, exchanging flowery words of Elizabethan love they'd learned from Mrs. MacGillicuddy. "'Thy beauty is too rich for me, for earth too dear!'" he'd tell her thickly, and she'd sigh, then answer, "'Thy lips, those kissing cherries, tempting grow.'"

"Don't forget 'Thou art the goddess of my idolatry,'" Spence suggested wryly to his son. "I understand that works especially well with the ladies."

"Have you tried it on Betsy?" Randy asked.

"Can't say as I have."

"Well, Betsy?" the boy prodded. "What do you think is the best line Mrs. Mac's taught us so far? I mean, that a man would say to a woman he really wanted to impress."

Betsy gave the question a moment's thought before she recalled the phrase Spence had whispered in her erotic dream. "'Run through fire would I for thy sweet sake, or bare my chest to another man's sword.' It's the perfect expression of chivalry, a man's power, his vulnerability and his tender humility while under the spell of his lady."

It took an effort to say the words with a straight face, but Randy assumed she was deadly serious.

"Okay, I'll try it. Laurie," he began in tones of high dram, " 'run through fire would—' "

"It's Lady Laura May, if you please," she corrected him, giggling before she gave Randy a noisy kiss. "Now try it again, Squire Randall."

Betsy couldn't see Spence's eyes in the dim light of the car, but she heard him suppress an indulgent chuckle. "I suppose we'd never catch you making a sentimental confession like that, would we, Sir Geoffrey?" she observed dryly.

Spence laughed. "Not with an audience, Betsy. But you might entice me to try it later when we're alone."

Confidently he took her hand in the darkness, weaving his warm fingers through hers. Another wave of arousal swept through Betsy as his thumb moved lightly over her palm, back and forth in slow, promising strokes, and she reveled in a sensation that was utterly new to her: subtle foreplay with Spence. After months of restraint, he was suddenly willing to give her a thousand hints of his long suppressed desire. There was erotic power in his touch, the tone of his hungry voice and the warmth of his breath. Even the rose that was wedged so tightly in her bosom seemed alive with the memory of his fingertips brushing her aching breasts.

He didn't even let her go when they reached Bremer, but held her hand firmly while Randy and Laurie said their mushy good-nights in front of Tiffany's house. An hour later Spence left Betsy in the car for maybe two minutes while he walked Laurie to her door, then took her hand again as he drove to Scarlet Elm and parked possessively in the driveway. In the same ripe silence, he followed her up the walk, waiting until she'd unlocked the door, then slipping inside and flicking on the living room light as he'd done so many Monday evenings after the show.

But this time he didn't ask for a piece of pie, and Betsy didn't offer him one. She stood perfectly still behind the door that now closed out the world, quivering inside, unable to invite Spence to make love to her, terrified that he might yet decide against it.

And then, in slow motion, he turned around to face her, eyes solemn, mouth tight. When he spoke his voice quaked with uncertainty and passion, and his words took her totally by surprise.

"Lady Elizabeth," he murmured with all the drama he could muster, "'run through fire would I for thy sweet sake—'" slowly he took hold of both of her hands "'—or bare my chest to another man's sword.'"

Betsy stared at him, helpless and confused. Nothing would have surprised her this evening, not even hearing Spence drop that line in jest. But he didn't look the least bit playful. He looked as though he were about to embark on a journey that would change his life.

"'When I see thee smile 'tis as though the very dawn has commenced to shine upon thy face,'" he tried again, struggling bravely for a smile but falling a little short of it. "'Oh, that thou couldst teach the torches to burn so bright.'"

By now Betsy recognized the subtle Shakespearean game Spence was trying to play with her, and she struggled through love-soaked thoughts to come up with equally appropriate Elizabethan phrases. "Brightly I burn in the heat of your fire, Sir Geoffrey," she replied softly, trying to follow his lead. "Wouldst I to search for the paragon of earthly man, I would no farther go than one step to take thy hand."

For the next few shining moments, they struggled for the finest of Elizabethan sentimental phrases, showering each other with adoration in a way that neither would ever have risked in normal dress in the light of day. By the time they'd exchanged another half a dozen phrases, Betsy knew she'd just about exhausted her repertoire. So had Spence, but she couldn't quarrel with the way he ad-libbed in words she *knew* he hadn't learned from Mrs. Mac. "Never hath a man laid eyes on a more perfect snow-white bosom," he vowed in a husky tone that didn't sound feigned at all. "O what joy 'twould be to lay but a single hand on the ruby-red rosebuds of brightest spring, which lie hidden from my view. How I should like to gently coax them to stand upright and greet the dawn."

Betsy's "ruby-red rosebuds" rose the instant he named them, with a matching urge somewhere deep below the skirt of her billowing blue gown. Surely, *surely* he wouldn't play this game with her—tonight of all nights—if he hadn't decided to stay? Randy was gone for the weekend...for the summer, if she remembered correctly...but her memory was fleeting. Nothing else seemed real but what was happening in her living room.

Her body was buttery soft with need, her voice a mere croak as she suggested bravely, "'Tis time I called the abigail to unhook my gown, Sir Geoffrey. Should you deign to help, instead, perhaps your need and mine could be as one."

Spence barely stifled a shudder as he absorbed the meaning of her words. Unbridled desire for Betsy flared in his dark gray eyes.

At moment later he circled behind her. His fingers were slow and clumsy as he did battle with the archaic fabric hooks and eyes Betsy had so painstakingly created to convey authenticity, never imagining they'd pose an ob-

stacle at a time like this. She couldn't suppress a moan as
Spence's hands slipped beneath the back of her gown
when the first closure was released. A moment later she
felt his lips against the same patch of skin, warm and
tempting as they aroused her with half a dozen tiny kisses
that trailed up and down her spine, ending on her nape.

Bowed against the force of her rising passion, Betsy
didn't say a word as Spence continued to unhook the
gown—seven closures, one by one—sensuously stroking
every inch of skin he uncovered until the bodice began to
slip off her shoulders on its own. Ever so slowly his hot
palms covered the naked skin above her breasts, brand-
ing her with his fire as he pulled her back against him till
her body touched his own.

His fingertips, so magical, so firm, gently swept to her
chin, her collarbone, then edged inexorably back toward
the upper curves of her breasts, now fully revealed to his
view. When her rigid nipples were pinpoints of desire,
Betsy swallowed a groan of desire that broke the spell.

"Betsy, this is Spence," he whispered huskily, his lips
actually grazing her passion-inflamed ear. "We're not
playing a game anymore. This is *real*."

Quickly, hungrily, she whipped around to face him,
heedless of the bodice that now fell open clear to her
waist. "So is my love for you, Spence," she promised him
fervently. "And I swear to you, *it's not going to go
away*."

He shook his head, but his hands reached out to pull
her closer. His palms pressed great circles of passion on
her bare back as his lips claimed the hollow of her throat.
"Oh, Betsy! I want you so much I'm shaking," he confessed in a raw, hoarse whisper. "I can't stay away from
you another minute, but I can't *promise* you anything
past tonight." His kisses grew more hungry, more ur-

gent, as he nibbled her chin and her ear. "I've been trying so damn hard to be fair, Bets. To both of us."

"If you want to be fair, don't try to plan the rest of our lives before we even give our love a chance to get off the ground," she begged him. "Let's just take it one day at a time."

"And that's enough for you?" he asked uncertainly.

What would he say if I told him it will never be enough? Betsy asked herself through a haze of escalating desire. *He can't believe how much I already love him. He'll never believe that I'm his for life.*

Instead she managed to whisper, "It's enough for right now."

She waited interminably for Spence to kiss her, to commit himself to the rest of the night. His gray eyes smoldered with desire and indecision, but desire won the battle in his heart. When his lips claimed Betsy's a moment later, she had no further doubts about his feelings. He wasted no more time on Elizabethan flattery, and Betsy was certain that he neither knew nor cared what century he was in.

Spence's outfit was easier to manage than hers had been, and he discarded it in bits and pieces between the living room and the foot of her bed as she led him silently through the darkened hallway. He eased himself down beside her on her hand-pieced quilt as though his body had known hers all his life, and slid one leg over her thighs as he gathered her into his arms. For a moment he just held her close, sheltering her naked body with his, as though to make up for all the hard, lonely nights he'd left her crying in this very bed.

Then, slowly, as though he had a lifetime to share with her now, Spence kissed her warm lips, her throat, one sensitive ear and then the other. And then, with infinite gentleness, his searching tongue lifted Betsy's aching nipples to the peak of sensual pleasure.

She slipped her fingers deep into his thick black hair as the ripples of arousal threatened to overwhelm her. But beyond her own passion, beyond her own need, she was aware of the deep satisfaction of inciting Spence's overpowering hunger. He'd tried so hard to stifle his love for her, so hard to quell his desire! But she had won him in the end, and she vowed to make this night so extraordinary that he would never forget it...and never, ever forget *her*.

After waiting so long for this precious moment to occur, it now seemed to Betsy that their lovemaking was suddenly rocket fast. In a matter of moments she was begging him to merge with her, only dimly aware of his whispered, "Are you sure, Bets? I don't want to rush you." In answer, she pulled him closer and wrapped both legs around his back. Quickly he accepted her tacit invitation and plunged deeply within her like a man who'd gone on a long journey and could hardly hold himself back, knowing he was almost home.

The power of his hunger stirred something uncontrollable inside Betsy. Surrendering all her apprehension and pride to her overwhelming love for Spence, she rode the bold tide of his desire for her. A moment later, the ever-tightening knot of erotic joy burst apart deep within her.

Then Spence cried out, "Betsy!" as he reached the height of passion, too.

CHAPTER TWELVE

THE NEXT THREE WEEKS were so perfect that Betsy felt like Cinderella at the ball; she kept expecting to find a pumpkin in the parking lot instead of her car when she left the shop at night. The hours she spent immersed in the fantasy world of the Renaissance only heightened the romantic illusion. Paul Hardison did remember to send her the costumes after the Pittsburgh Faire was over—he even sent along that fringed cowboy vest and chaps by mistake. Betsy and Oma divided up the clothes—women's at Betsy's house, men's at Oma's—because there were just too many to fit in the back of the store and they wouldn't have the use of the bus garage until about a month before the faire. A few days after the outfits arrived, Betsy got a very flowery letter from John Percy, promising to be her own "true knight, by day or night," in a corny poem that Oma, reading over her shoulder, identified as William Shakespeare's. The upshot of the letter was that John was once again offering to help at the Muskingum Faire—*insisting* on helping was more like it—but Betsy and Janet agreed that Spence could probably carry off the fencing booth on his own and would most certainly prefer it. Mrs. Mac had scheduled a practice faire for the end of August—a one-day event with just the principal players, no guests—and if the whole thing started to look insurmountable, they could still call in the big guns after that. Janet volunteered to write John an equally ornate letter graciously declining his kind offer.

Betsy hated to admit it, but in a way she rejoiced that Randy was staying with his mom for the summer. Although she missed his sunny smile and dutifully saved him every old coin that crossed her counter, she loved the fact that Spence was now free to join her whenever the spirit moved him—which was often—and to spend the night without making any special arrangements for his son. From time to time they were interrupted by an emergency call from one of his customers' oil rigs, but he often took Betsy with him to the drilling sites and proudly introduced her to every man who came within a dozen yards of his truck. They never talked about the future, and Spence never came right out and told Betsy how he felt about her with words. But his love wrapped itself around her in a hundred wordless ways, and she basked in the joy of their togetherness.

She pushed to the back of her mind their unspoken agreement to avoid three topics of conversation—Tiffany, marriage and prenuptial agreements—as well as the curious omission on Spence's part of ever inviting her to his own home for dinner or the night. She told herself it had something to do with Randy, but since Randy wasn't there, that line of logic had some gaping holes. And it wasn't that Spence was determined to take advantage of her hospitality, either, because the first three weekends that his son was gone he took Betsy away—once to Columbus, once to Kent and once to a lovely country inn just over the West Virginia state line—and always insisted on picking up the tab. On the first weekend Betsy had suggested that her income was more than sufficient to cover her half of the expenses, but he pointed out that he never paid for groceries at her house even though he

ate there half the time, and this was his way of paying her
back. When he sent her a dozen red roses the next day—
which she knew he couldn't possibly afford—she realized that in his own way he was trying to make up for all
the time they'd spent together when he'd denied her the
pleasure of feeling courted. After that she just thanked
him warmly for whatever he gave her and tried to order
economical meals.

By mutual consent, they abandoned Monday nights at
the show during July. In fact, the last time they'd gone—
a few days after Oma had knocked on Betsy's kitchen
window one morning while Spence, dressed only in his
underwear, was having breakfast—they hadn't stayed
more than half an hour before Spence had pointed out
that he'd seen the old western several times before. When
Betsy had commented that Hal and Hattie Marshall
would think they were rushing off to consummate a passionate love affair if they left early, he'd reluctantly
agreed. But when Betsy had wrapped her ankle around
his a moment later, he'd stood up abruptly and said,
"Let's go." He'd actually put his arm around her right in
front of Hattie as they'd marched out the door.

All in all, it was a gloriously romantic summer, and
Betsy pushed from her mind the questions that still
plagued her at dark, quiet moments. Spence had never
said he loved her, had never promised her a future beyond the coming weekend. He showed no sign of relenting on his vow to marry only if his wife-to-be signed a
premarital contract, and he rarely mentioned the possibility of marriage anyhow. While Randy was gone, they
didn't need to resolve any of these questions right away;
things could take their course. But Betsy knew that when
Randy came home from his mother's, Spence couldn't
act like a bachelor anymore. Once again he would be liv-

ing the life of Randy's father, and the only way Betsy was
likely to fit into their small, cozy family was if she became Spence's wife.

"DADDY?" whined the shaky voice on the phone. It was
Randy's voice, but it sounded like the little-boy Randy
Spence had known in years past—scared, almost tear-
ful, terribly alone.

"Where are you?" Spence asked at once, his voice
tight with fear as a dozen worst-scenario scenes suddenly galloped through his mind. He gripped the receiver with cold, sweating hands. "What's wrong?"

Randy began to cry. "She left me, Dad," he mumbled. "I just can't believe it. I've never felt so alone."

Something in Spence's heart seemed to give way. Was
there no end to the misery that hateful woman could
cause? He'd actually believed that things were on an even
keel after all these years! "Are you still in Bremer,
Randy?" he asked. "I can be there in an hour."

"Oh, I don't think you should come over here, Dad!"
Randy protested. "I don't want Mom to get mad. She
just suggested that I call you because I was so upset."

"*She* suggested you call me? I thought she'd run off
again!"

Suddenly Randy broke into great sobs. "Not *her*, Dad!
Mom's been great about the whole thing! It's *Laurie*
who's left me! For Howard Walsh!"

Spence closed his eyes and took several deep breaths
while he tried to stuff his heart back in his chest. While
he had no doubt that in Randy's eyes, being abandoned
by his girlfriend was a far greater calamity than being
dumped by his mother, to Spence the relief that little
Laurie was Randy's only problem was simply overwhelming. Randy had wept through another three or four

paragraphs of explanation—Laurie had been bored and lonely since he'd been out of town, Howard Walsh had taken note of her at her sister's graduation party, he had his license and had been squiring Laurie around, she had lied to Randy about it, but a friend had checked out the rumors and told him the truth—before Spence was sufficiently coherent to start giving his son the loving support he so desperately needed. Spence had always known that this moment was inevitable—in fact, he was surprised that Randy's first romance had lasted as long as it had—but he knew that mentioning this fact wouldn't do a thing to ease Randy's immediate pain.

"I'm sorry, Son," he said gently. "I know it hurts. All I can tell you is that my love for you just keeps on growing, and someday the pain won't be quite so bad."

"How can you say that?" Randy moaned. "You never got over the girl you loved when you were my age!"

Spence swallowed hard and tried to field that one. "That was different, Randy, because we had a child. It was never the loss of Tiffany that I had a problem with. I was just afraid of losing you."

He wept a little more, but quietly now, before he said, "How could she do that, Dad? She said she loved me! I was so sure that she did!"

"Some girls are just like that," Spence replied helplessly. "Someday you'll find one who'll love you till the end of time."

"You never did," Randy pointed out, too miserable to realize his words might be painful to his father. "Why should I?"

For a moment Spence considered telling Randy that he had found such a woman. There were moments when he was so sure of it that he forgot everything that stood between them, every complication that might keep them from becoming man and wife. But there were days like this—when the memory of Tiffany's betrayal still loomed large—when he found it hard to believe he'd ever let Betsy past the last of his defenses. To marry her would mean more than risking the business, even more than sharing children. It would mean he'd have to trust her with all his heart. *And even then, I'd have to wrap myself in that legal document like a medieval knight in armor.* A legal document that Betsy claimed she'd never sign.

ONE SWELTERING TUESDAY MORNING in July, Betsy was helping a particularly persnickety patron choose a dress pattern, when Oma called her to the phone.

"It's a girl who works in your Pittsburgh store," the older woman informed her. "She says it's an emergency and she's got to talk to you right away."

Since Wilma Cox, her Pittsburgh manager, was a grandmother of six, Betsy was sure that somebody else was calling for her, and she knew instinctively that something was wrong. The first thing her managers told the other employees was how to reach Betsy in an emergency, but none of them had ever needed to do so before.

"Betsy Hanover here," she greeted her unknown caller. "How can I help you?"

"Miss Hanover, you don't know me, but I work at Ye Olde Fabric Shoppe in Pittsburgh," a young frightened voice blurted out. "I've only been here about a week, and Mrs. Cox was teaching me what to do. But Mrs. Cox—" the next words were muddled by tears "—just had a heart attack or something right here in the store! I called an ambulance and they took her away. The paramedic said they got to her in time, so I think she's going to be okay, but I'm here all alone and I've got a class in three hours and I don't know how to lock up or anything!" She babbled on, almost hysterical as the shock set in, while Betsy nursed her through her fears, arranged for a more experienced employee to hurry to the shop and promised to leave for Pittsburgh within the hour.

"WHAT DO YOU MEAN she spent the night in Pittsburgh?" Spence demanded, wondering if he'd heard Oma right when he called the shop twenty-four hours later. He'd spent Monday night at Betsy's and she hadn't mentioned a word about her trip. Mainly they'd talked about Randy, who was no longer in shock but still nursing a slow-mending heart. "Betsy wouldn't go away overnight without telling me!" *Unless she didn't want me to know,* a ghostly voice within him added.

"It was an emergency, Spence," Oma clarified, then proceeded to tell him everything she knew about the problem, tacking on the news that Betsy had called her around eight o'clock to say that Gaffer Paul had offered to put her up for the night. And then, as though it weren't earthshaking news, she added, "She also asked me to tell Janet that John Percy's going to come help us with the practice Renaissance Faire on the twenty-second, after all. If you see her before I do, would you relay the message?"

Spence couldn't stifle the flare of anger that seared him at the mention of the other man's name. "What do you mean he's coming? I thought Janet wrote and told him we didn't need him!"

"I know, Spence, but that was before he wrote that marvelously mushy letter to Betsy."

"You mean to Janet," he corrected her. "I read it."

"You mean he wrote to Janet, too?" Oma questioned. "Was it written in Elizabethan English, full of flowery words about her beauty and all?"

"Are you telling me that's what Percy wrote to Betsy?" Spence demanded. "Did it end with that stupid poem about the day-and-night knight, too?"

"Well, yes," Oma replied a bit uneasily, as though she just realized she'd let the cat out of the bag. "I'm surprised Betsy didn't tell you, Spence. But I don't think it was a secret or anything."

By now Spence was livid. "Did she tell you when she'd be back, or is that a secret, too?"

Oma giggled. "Why, Geoffrey Spencer, surely you're not jealous! Don't you know by now how much Betsy adores you?"

"When is she due back, Oma?" he repeated tersely. "Did she say?"

"She said she'd be back tonight if everything went okay at the shop and Gaffer Paul found his missing coins."

"His missing what?"

"Coins. I think that's why Betsy called John Percy. I guess the poor old man misplaced part of his collection, and she hated to leave him alone when he was so upset."

With one part of his mind, Spence understood why Betsy might have turned to Percy for help with Gaffer Paul. After all, she didn't know many of the old man's friends. But another voice said, *Why him? Surely there was somebody else!* And another voice, even louder than the first, demanded to know, *Why didn't she tell me he wrote to her? And why did she tell him he could spoil our mock faire?*

Spence's jaw tightened as he fought against his senseless jealousy. Hadn't he made a fool of himself with

Percy once already? And hadn't he acted like an idiot when Betsy had gone out with Wade Carlson? *Of course, I wasn't sleeping with her then,* he remembered sharply. *I was still trying to deny the fact that I was in love.*

It occurred to Spence, with a dull, anxious clamor near his ribs, that he still hadn't admitted it to Betsy, not in so many words. *But she knows! I haven't tried to keep it from her!* another voice protested. *Then why haven't you told her outright, told her how rich she makes your life?*

It was a question he couldn't answer. But it paled beside the question that haunted him all that evening, even more so after midnight, when he dialed Betsy's number for the fifteenth time and reconciled himself to the fact that she'd be gone another day.

Is she still at Gaffer Paul's tonight? Spence asked himself as he tossed restlessly for hours after he went to bed. *Or has she received a better offer?*

He told himself that Betsy loved him and he had absolutely nothing to worry about. But his sleep was troubled and he woke up at 3:00 a.m., thanks to a dream about a rematch of the duel at the Pittsburgh faire. But this time Spence was the loser, and Betsy ended up kissing John.

IT WAS ALMOST SIX O'CLOCK by the time Betsy returned to Muskingum on Thursday. She found a note on her door from Spence that said he'd pick her up for dinner at seven. The thought of spending an evening with him filled her with warmth, but after all the confusing activities of the past two days—both at Gaffer Paul's and at the Pittsburgh store—she knew she was simply too exhausted to do anything tonight but go to bed. Reluctantly she called Spence to say she'd see him Friday, but she had to leave a message with his answering service. Then she headed for her bedroom.

"Boy, I really must have left here in a hurry," she observed, surprised at the general chaos of her clothes. "I haven't kept house like this since I was twelve." Actually, she wasn't sure she'd been this messy even then. Most of the dresses that were still on hangers hung by one strap or sleeve, and nothing in her drawers was well folded. She *had* been in quite a hurry when she'd rushed home to pack her bag, but she didn't recall rifling through so many of her possessions. Neither did she recall going into her sewing room at all, but it was a mess. The chemise she'd just finished for Rhonda Watson was lying in a heap by the closet door.

Too tired to clean up, Betsy decided she'd rest for a while before she did anything else. She'd just slipped into a nightgown and robe, when the doorbell rang.

It was Spence. "Decided to skip dinner and go straight to dessert, I see," he greeted her with an appreciative glance at her lingerie as he slipped inside the door. He gazed fondly at her tired face and tousled hair, but he made no move to touch her as he said, "Aren't you going to kiss me hello?"

Betsy summoned up a smile, solely because the joy of seeing him was even greater than her fatigue. She melted against him like a purring kitten and gave him a single, resounding kiss. He put his arms around her, hesitantly at first, then more tightly, and he rested his chin on her head.

"I missed you," he confessed. "I guess I've gotten kind of used to your always being here when I'm in the mood."

"In the mood for what?" she joked, then kissed him again. Before he could answer, she tacked on, "I take it you didn't get my message."

"That you went to Pittsburgh?" He said each word with care. "Sure. Oma told me."

"No, I meant the message I left with your answering service that I was too tired to go out tonight."

Spence pulled back, clearly surprised. "No, Bets, I haven't checked in for about an hour. It never even occurred to me that you wouldn't want to see me this evening. You've been gone for nearly three days."

There was just the barest hint of hurt in his tone, and it took Betsy by surprise. As close as they were, it had never occurred to her that Spence wouldn't understand why she was too tired to see him tonight. If anything, she'd been afraid that he might be getting restless, be feeling hemmed in by all the time they spent together. Something in his attitude, though carefully veiled, struck her as not quite right.

"Spence, I *always* want to see you. I've just had a rough couple of days and I thought it would be smarter to get some rest. I'm not complaining, mind you, but I don't do much sleeping when you spend the night. But now that you're here—" she gave him her most engaging smile "—why don't I rustle up something for dinner?"

"No." His tone was clipped. "If you're too tired to go out, you're certainly too tired to cook. I should have made a proper date with you before I showed up here. I'm sorry."

"Don't be sorry," Betsy told him, feeling a little uneasy with the tension in his tone. "Why don't we just bake a frozen pizza? Or we can just make some soup and sandwiches."

He studied her quietly for a moment, his eyes troubled but warm.

"Spence, what is it?" Betsy asked with some alarm. "Is something wrong with Randy?"

He shook his head and lifted one hand in quick denial. "No, nothing's wrong. At least not with Randy. Or with you. I think I'm the one with the problem."

Betsy reached out quickly to take his hand, apprehension flooding through her. "What is it, Spence? You know I'm always here for you."

Slowly, uncertainly, he nodded.

"You don't look too sure of that."

Again he nodded, raising his eyebrows apologetically. For a moment he was silent, then he burst out, "I had a dream last night that you were getting awfully chummy with John Percy."

"Chummy?" Betsy repeated, not quite certain what he meant. She *had* been with John quite a bit the past two days—not by design, certainly, and she'd taken no pleasure from his company. In fact, it was safe to say that the more time she spent with the man, the less she liked him. But knowing how much Spence resented John, she realized that he might have another vision of her trip to Pittsburgh in his mind. "Chummy the way I'm chummy with you?"

Without meeting her eyes he said, "I guess you could put it that way."

Betsy quickly slipped her hand in his and squeezed it lightly. "We all have strange dreams now and again, Spence. Why, before you and I were close, I used to have dreams about you that—"

"Betsy, this is serious. Not the dream, but—" He broke off, angry with himself. He exhaled heavily, then inhaled again before he confessed sheepishly, "Betsy, I had a rough time with your little trip to Pittsburgh. I didn't like the fact that you left town without telling me, and I especially didn't like the fact that you went to the town where Percy lives. On top of that, Oma said you'd called him for some reason—a good reason, I know... something to do with Gaffer Paul—but when she added that the bastard had actually written you the same kind of sixteenth century hogwash he'd written to Janet and I realized that you hadn't even told me... well, for a little while there I kind of went berserk.''

"A little while?'' Betsy repeated cautiously. "Does that mean you've returned to your senses now?''

He exhaled slowly. "Yeah. More or less.''

Quickly Betsy kissed him, then shook her head. "You're crazy, Spence. You know that?''

He nodded. "No argument there.''

Betsy rubbed his neck with her free hand, then led him over to the couch and curled up snugly beside him. "Are we talking about a blind moment of jealousy or did you start cleaning your dad's double-barreled shotgun?'' she asked.

Spence managed to smile. He even squeezed her hand as he admitted, "I tried to call you here last night. The first few times I just wanted to make sure you got home all right. After ten, I suspect that I was really calling because I so badly needed proof that you weren't with him.'' Bravely he met her eyes before he finished, "I'm ashamed of it, Bets, but I know it's true.''

Betsy knew she should have been angry, but the fact that he'd already worked through his unreasonable suspicions by himself and was willing to confess them to her went a long way to ease her distress. "I wish you had more faith in me, Spence, but at least you didn't come in here making a lot of wild accusations. It takes a big man to admit he's a fool."

A sheepish grin split Spence's broad face as he slipped both arms around her. "I'm sorry, Bets. Really, I am. But it's really got me thinking about . . . well, about a lot of things. About us."

"Us?" She kissed him on the neck and cuddled closer. "Would you care to elaborate?"

He laid one hand on her face, his eyes warming hers, before he quietly returned the kiss. "I'm still working on it, Betsy. Why don't you tell me about your trip and then we'll try to sort out my feelings, okay?"

"Okay," she agreed. "But there's not all that much to tell. I spent the afternoon getting my store in order. I had to calm a young girl's shattered nerves, rearrange the week's work schedule and give the assistant manager a crash course on running the shop. Then I went to the hospital to see Wilma, who's going to be okay provided she slows down a bit. The doctor and I ordered her to take a month or two off. I called Gaffer Paul to see if he could meet me for lunch the next day because I thought it would be nice to return the favor—I mean, he fed eight of us, Spence—virtual strangers. I know he's incredibly rich and Velma did most of the work, but he's been very kind to me and I wanted to do something for him."

She went on to explain how confused Paul had sounded on the phone. At first he couldn't seem to place her name, but once he did, he'd gushed out a confusing collection of alarming facts. His beloved English monarch coin collection was missing—all of it, this time—and Velma was out of town, so he couldn't ask her if she'd put it away somewhere. He'd searched and searched and had even considered calling the police, but he hated to report the coins as stolen when he was sure he'd find them any minute. Unable to calm him down, Betsy had volunteered to come over and help him look, certain she'd find them on top of the coin cleaning table or perched on top of some antique hutch.

"But I couldn't find them, either, and Gaffer Paul was so upset by then that I just couldn't bear to leave him alone," she explained to Spence. "He's got a zillion guest rooms and offered me one. But I felt the need to report his situation to somebody in Pittsburgh who knew him well—a family member or close friend—especially since Velma was gone. It was possible that nobody would check in on him for several days. The only name I recognized in his private phone book was John Percy's. I called him in desperation, and he came right over. To my great relief, he really calmed Gaffer Paul down. John wasn't all that gentle, but I guess that man-to-man 'get yourself together' stuff was just what Paul needed. I was so grateful that I couldn't bear to refuse John again when he still seemed so determined to come help us with our faire. It just seemed rude. I mean, I owed him one."

Ignoring the subject of John Percy for the time being, Spence asked, "So where were the coins?"

Betsy shook her head. "We never found them, though John and I searched the house both nights. He suggested to me—out of Gaffer Paul's hearing, of course—that it was possible Velma had taken them. She's only been working there a few months, you know, and it's curious that she should leave town to see a sick sister right about the time the coins turned up missing."

"That's possible, Bets," Spence conceded. "That monarch collection is worth a fortune, you know. Some of those coins are worth five thousand bucks apiece."

"I realize that. But the first time Janet and I went to see Gaffer Paul, he thought he'd lost some of those coins and they were right in front of his eyes. The day of the faire when we all ate lunch there, he left them out again while he wandered off. I can just see him tucking them under one arm and drifting from one room to another. They could be inside a suit of armor or stuffed behind a potted plant.''

"They could also be doubling the worth of some other numismatist's collection by now,'' Spence added. "If he leaves them outside of that locked cabinet very often, it wouldn't be too hard for somebody to walk off with them.''

"Only somebody who has a good reason to be in the house. What burglar would brave those vicious dogs and the burglar alarm? John suggested we try to find out if anybody else had been there lately—you know, delivery men, cleaning crews and the like—but Gaffer Paul doesn't keep records of that kind of thing and his memory isn't worth a hill of beans. He doesn't even have nosy neighbors.''

It occurred to Betsy that they were milking the subject of the coins to avoid tackling the more crucial issue that still lay unresolved between them: Spence's distrust. Apparently his thoughts were running along similar lines, because a moment later he asked, "Why didn't you tell me about John's letter?''

Betsy shrugged with genuine innocence. "I'm not sure, Spence. Partly because I thought you might respond like this, I suppose, but mainly because I had so many more important things on my mind than John Percy! I did mention it to Janet, and we had a good laugh when we realized that he'd written the same letter to both of us almost word for word. After that, I forgot about the whole thing.''

Spence sighed and looked away. "I believe you, Betsy. Honestly I do. There's just this part of me, this part that feels so sick when I imagine another man with you . . ."

"Spence, we've been over all this before," she reminded him gently. "I've told you about every man I've ever dated more than half a dozen times, and I haven't looked twice at anybody since the first night you spent with me. Even when I didn't think you wanted me, there was never any question—"

"I know. You're Betsy Hanover, and you love me. You only look like Tiffany."

Betsy had to glance away on the last word, one she never liked to hear. And this time it heralded more bad news; she was sure of it.

"Look, Bets, I came to grips with this about three o'clock this morning. I think what bugged me the most was that I didn't feel I had a right to be jealous, to tell you how to spend your time, because I haven't . . . well, exactly *claimed* you. I haven't really told the world you're mine."

"But I am yours, Spence. Surely you know that—"

Tiredly he stood up, abandoning her on the couch. "You're missing the point, Betsy."

Betsy stiffened. He wasn't angry with her, she was certain, but by no stretch of the imagination was he his usual tender self. Something was eating at him, and Betsy didn't know quite how to ease his pain.

"What *is* the point, Spence?" she asked gently. "Let's just get it out in the open and maybe we can work things out."

He jammed both hands in his pockets and slowly licked his lips. "Okay. Let me try to let you inside my head. I'm not sure just what's going on, but I think it's something like this." He crossed the room till he stood by the window, addressing the glass pane rather than the woman on the couch. "I love you something fierce, Bets, but I've never admitted it right out loud. Since Randy's been gone I've shown up here every other night, but for some reason I've never invited you to my house. Not even once. I'm not that ungracious a host—not really. It can't be just an...oversight." He paused for a moment, then swallowed hard. "I think...in a lot of ways...I'd like for you to be my—" he nearly choked on the word "—wife. But I can't imagine being brave enough to ask you to marry me. And even if I did, I'd nail down every single corner of a prenuptial agreement so tight that I know you'd squirm even if you'd sign it. And if you meant what you said before—"

"I did."

This time he whipped around to meet her eyes, and their gazes locked for an interminable moment of angry, hurtful silence. When he released a heavy sigh, Betsy couldn't tell whether it was a sound of relief or despair. At last Spence confessed, "I guess that's what scares me, Betsy—that you'll never agree to marry me on terms I can accept. How are we ever going to get any closer if we keep pushing each other away?"

Quietly Betsy rose and crossed the room until she stood by his side. She didn't touch Spence, but her voice throbbed with warmth as she assured him, "I'm not pushing you away, Spence. I want to be as close to you as I can get."

He met her eyes with a relieved smile, then slipped one arm around her and pulled her tightly against him. Betsy snuggled closer, thrilled that he was even willing to *consider* asking her to marry him. Maybe in time...

And then he said coolly, "Are you sure you couldn't find a way to live with some kind of a contract, Bets? You've got so much more money to lose than I do."

Betsy's blue eyes flashed as she stepped back and threw her hands in the air in exasperation. "It's got nothing to do with *my* financial situation," she replied with poorly veiled bitterness. "In fact, it's got nothing to do with me at all. It's Tiffany you want a premarital contract with. She's the one you needed protection from. You won't get it by humiliating me."

His eyes, frustrated and enraged, met hers as he reached out to take her hand and pull her back beside him. "Dammit, Betsy! I wish you could understand."

"I do understand!" she snapped, her fingers stiff and cold in his. "That doesn't mean I have to like it. Besides, I'm not pushing you to marry me, Spence! I have to admit the idea appeals to me as a possibility somewhere down the road, but what's the hurry?" She swallowed hard, fear now superseding anger. Earnestly she squeezed his fingers. "We're doing fine just the way we are," she reminded him in a low, pleading tone. "Why rock the boat?"

He dropped her hand and balled his own into a tight fist. "We've got exactly ten more days of this carefree romantic bliss, Betsy," he pointed out tersely. "Ten more days until Randy comes home, and then we won't be doing fine at all." His eyes grew dark with frustration. "Now I won't leave him alone while I cavort with you every evening—especially when he's feeling so down—and I won't take you to bed with my son in the same house. Before you came to Muskingum, I was happy living with Randy, spending what free time I had with my family and friends. That's not the case anymore. I want you, dammit! I want you deep in the heart of my life. But not enough to push Randy out of front and center stage, where he belongs.''

And not enough to take the risk of asking you to be my wife. He didn't need to say the words for Betsy to hear them, and he didn't need to spell out what they implied.

"I'm very fond of your son, Spence," Betsy heard herself say in her own defense. "And I think in time he might grow fond of me. As for any other children the two of us might decide to have someday...I think that's something we could work out when the time was right.''

"I know.'' Spence turned away from her and started to pace back and forth across the room. "I know there wouldn't be any insurmountable problems with Randy or...any other kids...if we actually got married." *And stayed married,* his wary tone implied. "But unless we do, I see all kinds of choices to be made, all kinds of problems.''

As Spence continued pacing, Betsy returned to her place on the couch. She knew this was a very delicate moment and she needed to choose her words with care. But she was tired and terribly disheartened. They could spend hours going round and round on this issue, and nothing would ever change.

"We only have one real problem, Spence,'' she admitted sadly. "And it seems to me there's only one solution.''

Slowly Spence turned around, his biceps rigid as he waited for her next words.

When he finally met her eyes, Betsy bluntly told him, "You're afraid to marry me unless you're armed with a prenuptial agreement that's as cold and hard as steel. But if you don't have enough faith in me to get married without one—'' she swallowed hard before she whispered the awesome truth ''—then I don't think I really want to be your wife.''

CHAPTER THIRTEEN

WHEN RANDY CAME HOME a week and a half later, he clung to Spence all the time. In the daytime he moped around in the truck and halfheartedly helped with deliveries, and in the evening he dogged his father's heels like a love-starved puppy. He called none of his friends and never did anything alone in his room—he even built models and cleaned his coins on one end of the kitchen table while Spence did paperwork on the other. While Randy was perfectly willing to let Betsy tag along with the two of them, he wasn't about to let his daddy out of his sight, and by the time Muskingum held its Saturday practice faire, Randy had been home for over three weeks and Spence hadn't seen Betsy alone for more than an hour or two at a time.

Spence arrived at the high school at eight o'clock in the morning with mixed emotions. He was eager to help Janet and Betsy and glad to do his part for the hometown, but he still didn't relish prancing about in a pair of tights, waving an old foil in the air, with or without John Percy by his side. Randy, of course, had begged to drop out of the faire altogether once Laurie had dumped him, but Spence needed Randy to assist him as a squire.

"Look, Randy," he'd told his son truthfully, "I got into this because of you, and Aunt Janet needs both of us now. Besides, do you really want Laurie to think you're pining away for her?"

Randy had slouched, both hands in his pockets, and moaned, "Oh, Dad! She knows that. I told her I loved her all the time."

"You're not the first man to have fallen flat on his face for an unfaithful woman, son, and I don't think you'll be the last," his dad had counseled. "The smartest thing you can do now is start looking for some other girl to keep you company. I think Owen Markson's eldest daughter has a lot of class."

Spence had realized as soon as the words were out that he'd put the kiss of death on Ellen Markson by his complimentary remark, but it had gotten Randy thinking.

"Barbara Peterson's going to be selling clay flutes at Mongers Crossing," he'd mused. "I always thought she was kind of cute."

"Cute?" Spence had repeated, desperately trying to recall the Peterson girl's face. "She's adorable. Do you think she might be interested in you?"

Randy had shrugged. "I don't know, really. Last year we used to do our geometry homework together in study hall and we had a good time. She's a lot better than I am in math."

"There you go. Ask her to help you. Then you'll owe her a favor. The least you can do is take her out for a soda or—"

"Dad!" Randy had laughed, his first genuine chuckle in a month. "You crack me up. Do you really think I need *your* help to get a date?"

Now, in the gym with Randy at his side, Spence swallowed his smile and turned away. With Randy following, he eased his way through the crush of farthingales and feathered hats that blocked his path to the bus garage, where Betsy's costumes were now stored. Even though this practice day lacked the crowds Mrs. Mac had

promised them for the genuine faire, there was plenty of
hustle and bustle just among the local staff. It had taken
some doing to get the whole community involved, but
once the core group had gotten the ball rolling, little
Muskingum had put its whole heart into the fund-raising
event.

The high school grounds had been transformed into an
exciting layout for the faire. Glaziers Row, between the
history wing and the math rooms, was a line of booths
that sold pottery, gourd drums and stained glass; the
Road of the Celts, near the gym, led the faire goer to the
marvels of basketry, woodwork and pewter cups. Naturally dyed silk was available at the Potters Market, and
the Pedlars of the Shire proudly gave a weaving demonstration while live musicians performed on harps and
ocharinas.

Spence was almost getting into the Renaissance spirit
by the time he and Randy crossed the threshold of the bus
garage. But before he could even call Betsy's name, a familiar male voice cried out behind him, *"En garde!"*

So much for my Renaissance spirit! Spence moaned
inwardly as he turned around to spy John Percy. "Hello,
John," he said as calmly as he could.

John, however, was still in the mood for melodrama.
"I was seeking for a fool and I found thee!" he crowed,
grinning triumphantly.

Spence struggled for courtesy as he introduced his son
to the other man, who was wearing his turquoise tights
and red slops and had actually drawn his heavy silver saber from the jewel-encrusted sheath. He made a mental
note to make sure that John had remembered to take one
of the foils they'd borrowed from the fencing school in
Columbus before he called him a "plague sore," an
"embossed carbuncle" or any of the other new insults

Randy had helped him memorize. At the moment, however, civility was in order, so he forced himself to say, "Nice of you to come help us out, John," even though the lie stuck in his throat.

"No trouble at all," Percy responded, slipping his cherished weapon back into its glittery sheath. "Are you prepared to be humiliated again on the greensward?"

"Again?" Spence asked, finding it difficult to keep his smile in place. "Seems to me I took home the huzzahs the last time we dueled." *And the lady, too,* he might have added.

"Ah, yes. I guess you did," agreed John with a smirk that left no doubt whatsoever it had amused him to let Spence win. "But this is a new day, so don't expect me to do you any favors."

Having no interest in John, Randy quickly excused himself and set off in search of Barbara Peterson. At about the same time, Percy asked Spence, "So where's that lovely lady you had on your arm the last time we met?"

It was on the tip of his tongue to say, *You lay one hand on that lovely lady and I'll run you through with your own silver sword,* but he swallowed the impulse. Besides, all the protests in the world didn't equal the worth of a single wedding band, prominently displayed by a woman who carried herself like a man's devoted wife. Though how was he ever going to get a ring on Betsy's finger if he couldn't get her to sign on the dotted line?

"Betsy's not here yet," he answered with all the nonchalance he could muster. "But last night my son and I brought most of the costumes she made over here, if you'd like to take a look at them."

"I already have. Wonderful hands, that woman has."
His grin was so broad Spence wanted to smack him in the
mouth. "Simply wonderful."

Spence was too irritated by that wry comment to figure out how Percy had had time to give the costumes
more than a cursory glance so early in the morning. Today Mrs. Mac had been the only one authorized to use
the key to the bus garage, and she'd arrived only half an
hour ago. *Maybe he isn't really all that interested in the
faire,* Spence decided, fighting the green-eyed monster
within him. *Hell, I would have joined the crew for Betsy
myself if I hadn't already done so for my son.*

"And that other charmer, the one who carries your last
name—the lovely Mistress Janet. Where might I find her
this morning?"

Spence's brother had been dead for almost three years,
but he still felt the need to defend Bill's wife. "She's very
busy with the faire arrangements," he declared stoutly.
"I doubt she'll have much time to socialize."

Percy gave him a knowing grin that stripped Spence
naked, and he wondered, *How can he be so friendly? He
must know how much I hate him.* Struggling for a safe
topic of conversation, Spence asked, "Did Paul Hardison ever find those missing coins?"

"You mean the monarch collection that disappeared
while Betsy was in town?"

It seemed an odd way to describe the theft, but Spence
let it pass. "Betsy was pretty sure he'd just mislaid them.
We were hoping they'd turn up by now."

John shook his head. "Not a sign. And not a sign of
Velma, either. She called the employment service to say
she'd decided to stay in Idaho, but she conveniently forgot to leave her number." John made it clear he thought
Velma had stolen the coins, but mentioned that Paul still

believed he'd misplaced them...when he remembered they were missing at all.

Fortunately the sound of Betsy's hearty greeting saved Spence from extending the odious conversation. He watched her through Percy's eyes as she slipped eagerly into the bus garage, her golden hair bouncing freely around her shoulders, her blue eyes sparkling with the joy of life. She was carrying a sewing basket and three enormous dresses that nearly obliterated the fine shape of her hips, but nothing could hide the exquisite curve of her breasts in that lacy T-shirt top.

She smiled when she saw Percy, a smile of greeting to a stranger, or possibly an acquaintance. A moment later she spotted Spence beside him, and the change in her expression cleared Percy's face of his smug grin.

It was no "Hi, there, buddy" smile that curved her lips in greeting. It wasn't even an "I'm counting the minutes till we can share a bed again" smile. It was definitely a "You're here, darling. My life can begin" smile.

Abruptly Spence forgot John Percy as he hurried across the dusty concrete floor. He reached for the dresses to unburden Betsy, but when he took them in his arms, she didn't quite let them go. They kissed with the clothes between them, as though the dresses were the rumpled covers of a bed. It took all the strength Spence had to stop with that one kiss of greeting, the only one he'd been free to claim from Betsy in more than ten long days.

"I miss you," he whispered, too low for John to hear. "And I don't just mean the way you kiss."

Betsy grinned, eyes shining with love for him. "Is Randy still going to see his cousin next weekend?"

He nodded solemnly. "Praise God for relatives." Then he forced himself to acknowledge the inevitable. "We're not likely to get much time alone today with Percy here."

She kissed him again, in a redundant note of reassurance, before she turned to greet the other man. John instantly asked her to show him all of her costumes, and when she agreed to lead him to the wardrobe in the back, he fell into step beside her and casually slipped one arm around her waist.

Without the slightest hesitation, Betsy dislodged it by bending to fetch a needle that had fallen on the floor. When she stood up again her smile was as bright as ever, but Spence noticed with great pleasure that she kept a pointed distance from Percy as she led him through the door.

IT WAS A LONG DAY but a rewarding one. Betsy spent most of it fitting costumes and adding frills. She didn't see much of Spence, who was playing jack-of-all-trades, solving problems with the booths when he wasn't fencing, but John Percy was her constant companion. Granted, there was a reason for his constant presence—he was making sure that the appropriate knickknacks were properly displayed with every costume—but he seemed to take remarkable delight in her company. He even tried to impress her by demonstrating that he'd learned how to sew—albeit crudely—when he'd been in the army.

"Such a knowledgeable young man!" Mrs. MacGillicuddy crowed in delight after he'd greeted her in silver-tongued Elizabethan English. "His high school literature teacher must have been awfully proud of him!"

Betsy relayed this compliment to John when he said goodbye an hour later, and she added her own thanks for all the help he'd given them.

"Truly, John, you were just what we needed," she told him honestly. "An old hand who knows what to look for, what to expect. I feel a lot more secure about the authenticity of my costumes after today.''

'' 'No gift could cast more sunshine than thy words of humble praise,' '' he quoted grandly. He gave her a measured, lascivious stare that was as subtle as a steamroller, then asked rather pointedly, ''Could you tell me where I might be able to get a good meal in Muskingum, Betsy? It's a long trip back to Pittsburgh and I wouldn't want to make it on an empty stomach.''

Ignoring the obvious fact that he was angling for an invitation, Betsy answered smoothly, ''I suggest Charley's Café. It has a nice, homey atmosphere and the food's not half-bad.''

He raised his eyebrows. ''I don't suppose you're in the mood for a nice dinner out yourself? I don't know too many folks in town, and I really hate to eat alone.''

Betsy did feel she owed the man her gratitude, but she didn't like him enough to risk upsetting Spence. ''I'm sorry, John, but I'll be here pretty late cleaning up. If you want to reach Pittsburgh at a reasonable hour, you better get a move on. Charley's is a friendly place. You won't be lonely there.''

He studied Betsy's firm breasts rather brazenly, then pushed a little harder. ''You know, it is an awfully long way to Pittsburgh and I've put in a hard day. It might be smarter to spend the night in Muskingum and go back in the morning.''

Betsy shrugged as indifferently as possible. ''Your choice, John. We have only one motel—right next to Charley's—but it's never full. You shouldn't have any trouble finding a room for the night.''

He grinned in what he surely thought was a beguiling fashion. ''Motels are so . . . impersonal. I don't suppose you have a guest room, Betsy?''

This time she gave up clinging to courtesy. "No, I don't, John. And before you ask—the other side of my double bed is already taken."

John laughed. "I must be losing my touch."

Assuming you ever had it, Betsy wanted to snap back. Instead she lied diplomatically, "Nothing personal, I assure you. I'm just wearing another knight's colors today."

"Sir Geoffrey?" he asked, as though this involved some extraordinarily brilliant deduction on his part. "Just because he wounded me in battle?"

"That was the clincher," Betsy confessed dryly.

This time his laugh was slightly hollow. "In that case, my sweet lady, next time I shall be triumphant. I shall pierce him through the heart."

"Nothing so dramatic, hopefully," Betsy retorted lightly, enormously grateful to spot Spence and Janet coming through the door.

"Oh, there you are!" Janet called out cheerfully to John. "I wanted to thank you again before you left for the night."

"An honor 'tis been to pass time in thy service, Mistress Janet," he greeted the other woman with a courtly bow, "and a privilege 'twould be to so serve again."

Janet smiled, trying not to look at Betsy, since every time they discussed John Percy one or both of them dissolved into laughter. "You really were a big help today, John," she assured him, dispensing with the archaic English. "If there's any way we can repay the favor—"

"And here I thought you'd never ask!" His triumphant grin consumed his too-pretty face. "I was hoping—"

"He was hoping to get a room at the motel tonight, Janet," Betsy cut in quickly, knowing that Janet was uncomfortable dodging John's manipulations. "I assured him that he'd have no trouble, but I think it would be very kind if you'd call ahead and ask Lyle Macy to give him that extra large room with the view in the back."

Nobody could really call the pair of elms behind the motel a distinguished view, but Betsy's words did serve to warn Janet of the trail John was sniffing out. "What a thoughtful idea, Betsy! I'll go do that right now. Thanks again, John. We'll see you next month at the real faire!" In a flurry of good-nights and messages for Oma and Randy, Janet fled.

For just an instant John Percy met Betsy's eyes with ill-concealed reproach, but he masked the emotion so quickly she wondered if she'd imagined it altogether.

"Well, now that you've planned my evening so nicely, I guess I'll get on over to Charley's. Unless you'd like some help cleaning up?"

It was obvious that he'd posed the question only to make conversation, but Spence instantly replied, "That's my job, Percy. You've done enough for one day."

Those two sentences, subject to two very different interpretations, stopped John in midstride. He met Spence's eyes boldly, and each man took the other's measure. The hostility between the two bristled, and Betsy was reminded of circling bulldogs. She was glad that neither man was armed with a foil tonight.

"It was my pleasure, Spence," John said evenly. "I'm looking forward to working the fencing booth with you on faire day."

Betsy couldn't prove there was a threat in those words, but she didn't like the look on John's face. Spence held his ground and kept up the pretense of courtesy—for her sake, she was certain. "It'll be an interesting experience, John. One I'm sure we'll both remember."

John said his farewells and sauntered out the front door of the dimly lit gym, leaving Betsy and Spence completely alone for the first time in days. The instant he was out of sight, Spence pulled Betsy into his arms. "I thought I'd go crazy if I had to wait one more minute to be alone with you!" he confessed, pressing his warm, strong hands against her back as he echoed her own tumultuous feelings. "My God, Betsy, I can't take this too much longer."

He kissed her then, a hard, hungry kiss that instantly fanned her smoldering ardor into flames. Oblivious to their surroundings, she buried her fingers in his thick black hair and pulled him closer, savoring the melding of his mouth with hers.

"Hold me, Spence. It's been so long!" she begged him, rejoicing when his palms slid possessively over her taut breasts. "Please, just for a minute."

They both knew they couldn't risk such reckless kisses for much longer than that. At the moment they were alone—everybody else had supposedly left for the evening. But neither Spence nor Betsy were about to make love in the high school bus garage on a Saturday night.

"When do you have to go home, Spence?" she asked breathlessly, burying her face in his chest.

"I've only got about two hours," he moaned while his fingers circled her turgid nipples. "Randy's gone to a friend's house to watch a movie on TV. It'll be over at ten."

Hungrily Betsy pressed herself against him, and the hard lines of his body proclaimed that his urgency was no less than hers. Intensely aroused, she begged him, "Let's go to my house, Spence. It's been so long!"

Deeply torn, Spence shook his head. "Believe me,
Bets, I wish we could, but it'll take too long to clean up
here."

"Forget about that!" she pleaded. "I'll come back
later. I was planning to do it by myself, anyway."

Spence looked downright shocked. Despite his own
palpable arousal, he managed to say, "Sweetheart, did
you really think I'd leave you out here alone this late at
night? Randy and I were planning to help you all along.
I just let him go with his buddies because he's been so
morose over Laurie it was good to see him perk up. Not
to mention the fact that—"

He stopped abruptly as the door behind them opened,
and they leaped apart like two miscreant teenagers.

"Well, well, if isn't Back-seat Betsy and Jealous
Geoffrey groping in the dark," John Percy greeted them
sarcastically. "Don't you kids have some better place to
go?"

Spence glared at the other man and seized Betsy's hand
almost defiantly. "One might ask you the same question. I thought you were going to stop for dinner on your
way out of town."

John's lips tightened. "I was just about to order, when
I remembered I left my saber here. It's pure silver, you
know. Besides, it was a gift from my grandad."

"I'm sorry, John. I hope it didn't get mixed up with
the rented foils back there," Betsy told him as graciously
as her frustration would allow. "Do you want me to help
you find it?"

John gave her an oily smile and shook his head. "No
problem. I remember where it is. I'll pick it up and get
back to my cold soup in no time."

"I thought he said he hadn't ordered yet," Spence
whispered under his breath when John had disappeared

into the storage room. "How can his soup be getting cold?"

Betsy shushed him before John reappeared, then blessedly said goodbye and left for the night.

Seething, Spence said, "He didn't forget that damn sword, Betsy! He hardly ever takes it off, even when he's fencing! He just left it here so he could come back and irritate me."

"Let's not go overboard, Spence. That's really not logical," Betsy pointed out. "I know he's not your favorite person, but—"

"You can say that again! I swear to you, Bets, if I weren't so civilized, I would have taken off his head for calling you 'Back-seat Betsy.' If I get through this faire without taking a swing at that guy, it'll only be—"

"Because you're so much more mature than he is, Spence," she finished for him sweetly. "And because you've got what he wants, and you know it."

A triumphant grin washed the irritation from his face. He kissed her again, and this time he took his time. It was a slow, thorough, lover's kiss that almost made up for all the nights they'd been apart. His hands slid lovingly down her back and over her hips as he pressed his hard, hungry body against her feminine curves, and it took all the willpower Betsy possessed not to start taking off his clothes.

"Do you remember," he murmured in her ear, "what I had to say to you the first night we played Romeo and Juliet?"

Too stimulated to think about Shakespeare, Betsy shook her head and pressed her mouth against the hollow of his throat.

"'O, wilt thou leave me so unsatisfied?'" he quoted, tugging on her sensitive lobe with his warm, moist lips.

"I know how the guy felt, Bets. If I have to go one more night without making love to you, I think I'm going to go nuts."

Knowing she'd gone as far as she could possibly go and still bring herself to stop, Betsy laid one hand on Spence's chest, gently pushing him away, while she struggled to get her breath. "I think I've already passed that point," she confessed raggedly.

Spence took a deep breath and released her. "I'm going to encourage Randy to spend the day with a friend tomorrow," he promised. "I think he's moped around long enough."

Betsy couldn't hide her hope that Spence was serious. "Should I stay by my phone all day?" she asked provocatively.

He laughed and kissed her once again, being careful to stop with a single light caress. "I won't waste my time on the phone, Betsy. The instant he leaves the house I'll be over at your place like the speed of light."

"In that case," she promised, "I won't bother getting dressed. I'll just wear my quilt and wait for you in bed."

BETSY WASN'T WAITING for Spence in bed when he arrived the next day. He found her watering her pansies and johnny jump-ups in the backyard, wearing a pair of pink shorts and a floral halter top, which were far more beguiling than a patchwork quilt. She'd pinned her hair up to escape the heat, but wispy curls kissed her nape and several loose strands brushed her temples.

"Spence!" she cried out when he poked his head over the back gate. "Don't tell me you really have a few free hours?"

"I'm free as a bird," he sang out with a grin. "From now until six o'clock, do with me what you will."

A sunbeam of joy warmed her heart-shaped face. "What I'd like to do with you—" she stopped abruptly, glancing at the house next door, then lowered her tone to a discreet whisper "—isn't something we should be discussing out loud in the backyard."

Spence grinned. He was always delighted when Betsy admitted how much she enjoyed making love to him, and today, when he was so eager and had been denied the joy of sleeping with her for so long, it was good to hear that she was also in an amorous mood.

When he held out his hand and raised his eyebrows, Betsy turned off the hose and scampered quickly to his side. She opened the gate and pulled him behind it, then slowly and seductively pressed her body against his as she placed her hands on both sides of his face. Somewhere behind him a blue jay was squawking and a neighbor's screen door banged, and he heard nothing but Betsy's eager breathing. She pulled him closer as he leaned down to claim her lips, and the kiss they shared took on a life of its own.

A steamy two minutes later, Betsy whispered, "Spence, we've got to go inside."

He knew she was right, but he could hardly bear to let her go for even a moment, and he knew that no one could see them in this corner of the yard. The aroma of gardenias enveloped the garden, and Betsy's clean, soapy scent made him ache somewhere deep inside.

"God, how I've missed you," he whispered eagerly, trying to figure out how to unhook her halter top. "If Randy hadn't gone off on his own today I think I would have gone stark raving mad."

Betsy pulled his hands away from her hooks but kissed his fingers as though to soothe the rebuke. "Follow me,

Spence," she whispered, her eyes wide with barely suppressed desire. "I want you now."

He grinned delightedly at her playful demand but offered no opposition as she led him through the cool hallway and pushed him gently down on the bed. Usually they undressed each other slowly, as need and pleasure moved them, but today she tugged off his boots, belt and jeans before she unbuttoned his shirt and pulled the T-shirt underneath over his head. A moment later she had thrown her own clothes over the chair by the bed and joined him on top of the quilt, straddling his chest.

"Would you mind terribly if I seduced you in a hurry, Spence?" she asked, her tone low and urgent as she lowered her breasts into his waiting hands. "Would you mind terribly—" she slid down the length of his hard body "—if I told you that you were a totally irresistible man?"

He kissed her, hard, then flicked her nipples with short, masterful strokes while she moaned and moved against him. Her lips wreaked havoc with his sensitive throat, then trailed hot kisses across his chin to his ear. Her probing tongue slid over the lobe, then darted above it.

"Betsy!" He moaned as she moved up and over him, taking him inside her. "Betsy, it's been so long!" She rolled back and forth, up and down, side to side, until he lost all sense of control. "Sweetheart!" he gasped in a hard cry of pleasure. "I can't wait if you're going to do that!"

Almost before he got the urgent words out, Betsy breathed in his ear, "Neither can I."

The bed rocked under them—harder and harder and harder—then kept rocking for a moment even after they lay still. Within minutes Spence was aroused again and so was Betsy, and they celebrated their rediscovered pleasure all over. They'd been in bed for nearly two hours before Spence realized he hadn't had lunch, and Betsy quickly volunteered to feed him.

While he watched her work in her short seersucker robe—elbows neatly tucked by her sides as she sliced ham and cheese for his sandwich—a strange, poignant feeling came over him. He'd just spent the most incredible afternoon in her bedroom, but he felt sad, bereft... as though he were going away on a long journey. After a while the silence alerted Betsy, and she asked, "What is it, Spence? I always worry when you're quiet like that."

She handed him the sandwich, but he set it aside and pulled her onto his lap. "I've missed you," he whispered as he held her close.

"I've missed you, too, Spence. It seems like—"

"No, I don't mean I've missed you like, gee, I wish we could spend some time together, or even wow, I wish we could go to bed. I mean—" he stopped as he struggled for words to explain the depth of his feelings "—ever since Randy came home, I thought that everything would be okay if I just had an hour or two to hold you. And now, here we are at last, and... it's not."

As Betsy stiffened, he knew she'd misread him, and he dropped a quick kiss on her jaw while he searched for better words. "I'm not saying that our bedroom romp hasn't been just super, Bets. Making love with you is always great, and it's never been better than today. But sitting here in your kitchen, watching you work, I just feel like..." Helpless, he let the words trail off.

But Betsy seemed to understand him. As one gentle hand brushed his love-mussed black hair out of his face, she said softly, "It's just not enough."

Slowly he nodded. That was it exactly. "I love sleeping with you, Bets, but I need so much more from you than that. I want to take country walks with you after supper and watch old reruns on TV. I want to know I'll see you every night without making a date. I want to wake up every morning and find you sleeping next to me."

He knew, even as he said it, that he was describing the married state. He wanted her now and for always, but he wanted to have her without taking any risks. He also knew, from her point of view, that he wasn't being very fair, and he hated to bring up his prenuptial demands again while they were nestling so quietly together. But he also knew that they'd never be able to seriously consider marriage until they hammered out a contract.

"Betsy, I really wish you'd give some more thought to some sort of legal agreement," he finally suggested, dropping a kiss on her neck to soften the words he knew she dreaded. "All it would say is that if anything ever went wrong, we'd both leave with what we had going in. Anything we earned along the way, we'd split down the middle."

Her whole body stiffened against him. "And what about the children we might have?" she asked tersely. "Are we going to split them down the middle, too?"

Spence scratched his neck and tried to come to grips with her question. "Let me ask you this, Bets," he continued soberly. "If we were married and had, say, two small kids, and we broke up, what would you do? I mean, if you could do anything you wanted."

"If I could do anything I wanted, I'd live with my children's father." Her tone was even, crisp, but she couldn't hide the tiny tremor in her lower lip as she said the words.

"Okay. Let's say that the guy walks out on you—" bravely he extended his analogy "—for another woman.

But otherwise he's been a decent chap in the years you've been together and you really believe he's a good father." He waited until Betsy met his eyes and he knew she was going to take him seriously. "What would you ask for in court?"

Betsy's eyes darkened, and she tried to slide off his lap. When Spence put his arms around her more tightly and dropped a kiss on her shoulder, she froze and sat perfectly still for a moment. Then, as she studied his earnest expression, her muscles began to relax.

"I'd ask for joint custody," she finally declared, her expression tense but not hostile. "I'd try to live close enough to my ex that the kids could see both parents comfortably with a minimum of fuss. I'd do everything in my power to make the whole divorce as civilized as possible, and I'd always put the children's needs first— before mine *or* my adulterous ex-husband's."

Her tone was even, calm, and as Spence listened to her, he felt his own fears recede. He knew she'd do exactly what she promised, and it seemed phenomenal to him that he'd ever suspected she might do anything else.

"That's all I'd ask of you, Betsy. Just put it on paper and sign it. Would that really be so hard to live with?"

Betsy's jaw tightened. "I can live with almost any kind of agreement between the two of us, Spence, as long as it's based on mutual trust. I've told you what I'd do about the kids in case of a divorce. I just want you to believe me." Suddenly her eyes clouded over. "Better yet, I'd like you to give some thought to how wonderful it would be to live together and *raise* those great kids we're already fighting about, instead of *assuming* that it would all fall apart for us!"

A wave of chagrin swept over Spence as he lowered his cheek to hers. "Oh, Bets!" he murmured. "Don't you realize the only thing that could hurt me more than losing you would be giving up your baby?''

Betsy's mouth opened in shock, then closed as she realized the enormity of his confession. Quickly her arms swept around his neck as her eyes grew wide with tender passion. "I'd *never* steal your children, Spence. Never!" she vowed. "When I think of a baby that's part of the two of us, a product of our love—" suddenly her voice was thick with emotion and each word broke with a sigh "—it just feels so *right* to imagine myself as a mother. So right to be your wife!"

After that words seemed to fail her, and she hugged Spence tightly, burying her nose in his chest. Quietly he rocked her back and forth, determined to find a way to make her see his point of view. In this fragile moment, he felt as though they were halfway home, and he wasn't at all sure what he could say that wouldn't spoil the mood. He didn't dare press the contract issue any further.

Then, to his surprise, Betsy sat up straight and said, "The way I see it, Spence, we've got two choices." As she met his eyes, her expression changed, and she started tugging mischievously on the curly hair of his bare chest. "One—we can spend our last hour together this afternoon fighting over something we don't have nearly enough time to resolve."

He sighed, wondering if he'd imagined the progress he thought they'd already made. "I don't think I like that option."

"Well, cheer up, because I think you'll like the other one." Deliberately she twisted in the chair until she was straddling him and looking him straight in the eye. "Two—as soon as you've finished your sandwich, we can go back to bed and negotiate in good faith."

Spence found a smile as he stood up, clutching Betsy's thighs against him with broad hands. "I vote for number two."

Betsy giggled as he stumbled through the doorway, setting her down after half a dozen steps. As he put his arm around her and steered her toward the bed, she asked, "Don't you want your sandwich first? I thought you were hungry."

"I am," Spence admitted as his fingers fanned out over her shapely hips, fondling the curves he found there. "But I've finally figured out that I don't come here just for food."

CHAPTER FOURTEEN

ABOUT THREE DAYS LATER, Spence called to ask Betsy if she'd like to join him for a trip to Columbus on Saturday because Randy had saved up all the money he hadn't spent on dates over the summer to buy some more coins for his collection. He'd found a dealer who specialized in Renaissance and medieval artifacts—costumes and jewelry in addition to rare coins—and had suggested to his father that Betsy might like to come along.

"It was really his idea?" Betsy asked, pressing the receiver a little closer to her ear. "He really wants me to go?"

"Yes, he does," Spence replied with obvious satisfaction in his tone. "He remembered your mentioning that you've had trouble getting all the hats you need for the faire, and he thought maybe we'd stumble onto some."

"What a considerate boy. You may tell him he's got a date."

"How about me? Do I get to come?"

"Sure," Betsy answered with a smile in her voice. "I guess we'll need a chaperon."

Spence gave her a low growl to signify his unmet need.

"My sentiments exactly, Sir Geoffrey," was her honest reply.

Oma agreed to take over the shop for Betsy on Saturday in exchange for an extra Monday at home, so Betsy set off for Columbus with a clear conscience when the two Spencers wheeled up to her house at ten o'clock.

"Dad said I could drive if we took the Chevy," Randy told her proudly. "That way we can all sit in the front seat."

Betsy stifled her apprehension. "I'm sure you'll do a fine job, Randy," she assured the boy with more hope than genuine confidence. "How much longer till you get your license?"

"Three weeks and two days!" he sang out joyfully.

"But who's counting?" said Spence.

"Laurie isn't, that's for sure," came the glum reply from the driver. "Howard Walsh owns his own Fiesta."

"Howard Walsh is a pompous jerk," Spence reminded him. "And he'll be going off to college in a couple of weeks, anyway."

Betsy, who was sitting between the two, reached out to squeeze Randy's shoulder. "If I were fifteen, I wouldn't look twice at Howard Walsh with Randy Spencer in the same state."

Randy turned grateful eyes on her and managed a limp grin. "Thanks, Betsy, but you're prejudiced. You just think I'm handsome 'cause I look so much like Dad."

"You could do a lot worse!" Spence countered, causing all three of them to laugh.

When the hoopla died down, Betsy said more gently, "Seriously, Randy, I think you're a great kid. I'm sorry Laurie hurt you and—" She stopped herself before she could fill his ear with soothing adult platitudes that were true but would very likely be untenable to a teenager who had just lost his first love. Instead she said with equal parts of truth and compassion, "I really am sorry, Randy, and I wish I could do something to make the hurt go away."

This time his smile was genuine. "Thanks, Betsy. Let's just have a good time today, okay? That'll help as much as anything."

Betsy warmed him with a grin. "Consider it done."

That set the tone for the day, and Betsy was certain that Randy enjoyed himself as much as she and Spence did. They were all buoyed by the sense of family that bound them, as they chatted and sang traveling songs and shared old stories they'd all heard before. They reached Columbus in time for lunch and stopped at a hamburger joint across from the Ohio State campus that had a sign out front promising The Best Hamburgers in the History of the World. Randy amused himself by creating hypothetical tests for comparing the merits of one hamburger with another, and Spence contributed some good ideas for requirements for the position of Professional Hamburger Taster. Betsy pointed out that the cute blond coed who served them had returned to their table at least two extra times—once to borrow a bottle of catsup and once to return it—solely in hopes of getting an extra glance at Randy, who *surely* could pass for a college freshman himself. He knew she was pulling his leg, but he seemed to enjoy her praise nonetheless.

They reached the artifact shop about two o'clock, and it was truly a paradise of marvelous things. The wall near the door was filled with glass cases full of ancient coins, and Randy crouched before them in wonder. The middle of the building was full of old costumes on racks, and Betsy headed there at once, while Spence ambled toward the medieval weapons in the back.

Six months ago she would have seen nothing but brightly colored fabric, but now she knew just which people needed a farthingale, a doublet or a chemise with removable sleeves. She found three of the wildly plumed hats she'd been looking for and bought one on the spot so she'd have a model to copy. And then, while Randy and Spence analyzed the merits of each and every coin in the shop, she sauntered over toward the jewelry counter and came to a full stop.

She hadn't been looking for anything in particular, but the instant she laid eyes on the jewel-laden ring in the corner, she knew it belonged on her own left hand. It wasn't gaudy, like so many of the period, but had five tiny perfect rubies, set like a flower. The ring was not unlike the one she'd seen on the bride's hand at the Pittsburgh Renaissance Faire. In addition to the exquisite setting, the engraved back was enough to make a sentimental woman weep: "A faythfulle wyffe, my wealthe in lyffe."

"It's pretty, isn't it?" Spence asked, suddenly materializing beside her. "Looks like the one we saw at the faire."

"Even nicer," Betsy replied, deliberately avoiding mentioning the engraved sentiment that seemed to express Spence's needs so perfectly. "See the delicate curve around the rubies?"

Spence nodded. "I bet the ring costs as much as a new house," he pointed out pragmatically.

"Oh, no, sir!" the bright-eyed shop owner denied. He was a middle-aged man, round like Humpty Dumpty, who drummed the glass top with his fat fingers while he spoke. "For such a beauty, it's reasonably priced. And if you're looking for a sound investment—"

"I'm not," Spence cut him off. "It's just a nice ring, that's all."

"That's *all*?" The man was scandalized. "Why, this ring represents the finest craftsmanship of the Renaissance! It's more than a wedding ring, sir," he oozed, quickly pulling the ring out of its case to slip it on Betsy's left hand. "It's a lifelong tribute to a gracious wife."

"Dad doesn't have a wife," Randy pointed out helpfully, joining in. "But he does have a son who'd like a cash advance to get this George III cartwheel. Would you come take a look, Dad? I've never seen anything quite like it."

Although Spence had glanced at the cartwheel before, he cavalierly abandoned the ring that still graced Betsy's finger and followed his son over to the coin counter. After a heartfelt sigh—both for the beauty of the ring and what it signified—Betsy slipped it off and followed him. Randy waxed poetic over the heavy coin—which looked just like the one Gaffer Paul had lost—and even Spence sounded quite impressed with the chubby salesman's rendition of the cartwheel's history. He gave every sign of seriously considering Randy's request for a loan, but in the end he shook his head. "Son, I'd really like to help you out, but I just don't have that kind of cash to spend on a coin. It's about double what I can afford."

Betsy knew he was telling the truth. The price was prohibitive.

But Randy didn't see it that way. "Please, Dad! You could make it my birthday present," he suggested, sounding desperate. "I'll be sixteen in three weeks and—"

"I know when you were born, Randy. I was there."

When Randy slouched into silence, Spence added gently, "I do have something special in mind for your birthday, son. I thought I'd buy you a new key ring...with your own set of keys to the Chevy."

Randy's eyes lit up at this prospect, and he resigned himself to picking out a less costly Henry VIII coppernose groat. But as soon as he followed the salesman to the cash register to buy it, Betsy whispered to Spence, "I was going to buy him something for his birthday. You want to go halvsies on the cartwheel?"

She expected him to say no—she was sure he would have if she'd offered to pay for the whole thing. But splitting things fifty-fifty seemed to be a concept that gave Spence comfort. He studied Betsy for a moment, then glanced fondly at his only son. For just an instant he touched her face with the back of his hand in the most tender gesture of unity. "It feels right somehow, sharing him with you," he whispered, his warm glance heating up her face. He gave her a wink and then disappeared. A few minutes later, as though they'd planned it for weeks, Spence distracted Randy while Betsy went back to the shop to retrieve her "forgotten" purse. She returned with the purchased coin, carefully wrapped in a padded envelope hidden in her wallet, and Randy never suspected a thing until he found it on his breakfast plate next to his own set of car keys the magical morning he woke up to find himself sixteen years old at last.

"I THINK," Randy declared a couple of weeks later, finally the proud possessor of an Ohio State Driver's License, "that I should thank Betsy personally for giving me half of that terrific coin."

"Good idea," Spence agreed. "You can call her at the shop now or wait till she gets home. Or, if you want to be really formal, you could write her a nice note."

A sheepish grin seized Randy's face. "Uh, actually, Dad, I was thinking that I ought to do it in person."

"In person?" Spence repeated. "That's a good idea, but I'm not going to see Betsy until Friday, and you, as I recall, have plans to go to the homecoming game that night."

Thank God, he added silently. He adored his boy and loved spending time with him, but he was missing Betsy more and more each day. Nothing that they did together seemed to satisfy Spence anymore. While their time together was always happy, always warm, it wasn't nearly enough.

"Well, yeah, Dad, that's why I thought...well, now that I'm sixteen and all and I've got my license... maybe I could just, you know, drive over there by myself."

"By yourself?" Spence repeated, feeling the first gray hair sprout in his paternal head. "You want to drive into Muskingum by yourself?"

Randy gave him a disarming grin. "It's daylight, Dad. The weather's great. I don't have any teenagers in the car." He ticked off the requirements his dad had laid out for his first solo drive. "I'm not tired and I'm not in a hurry, and there's never any traffic on that old country road, especially at four o'clock on a Monday afternoon."

The lighthearted plea couldn't fully mask the desperation in Randy's young eyes. It hadn't been all that long since Spence himself had turned sixteen, and he hadn't forgotten what that first solo trip meant to a boy. Even the ownership of a valuable coin paled beside that breathless moment of euphoria.

"Okay, Son," he relented uneasily. "I guess you've earned it. But for Pete's sake—"

"I know!" Randy cried, rushing out the door. "Be careful!"

Spence counted the minutes. It would take thirty to get there; he'd be ten or twenty at the shop, and a half hour later he'd be home, in time for supper at six o'clock.

By 6:30 he was standing in the gravel driveway, wringing his hands.

IT WAS ALMOST CLOSING TIME on Monday afternoon when Oma dropped by the shop to pick up a teddy bear she'd bought for her new grandson and had accidentally left behind the counter. She'd covered for Betsy over the weekend when she'd returned to Pittsburgh to check on Wilma Cox, who'd just gone back to work the week before. Everything seemed to be okay in Pennsylvania, except for the fact that Gaffer Paul still hadn't unearthed his misplaced coins and seemed even more befuddled than usual. In fact, if Betsy hadn't remembered that he'd forgotten her name once before she would have described his greeting on the phone downright cool.

Unbeknownst to Oma, her boss was feeling decidedly cool toward her. When Betsy had returned to the shop on Monday morning, she'd found it too messy to open for business. Considering how clean and orderly Oma normally was, the condition of the store had been shocking, and Betsy hoped that Oma had some extraordinarily good explanation for leaving the store in disarray. She'd planned to confront her assistant the next morning, but now that they stood face-to-face with no customers in the store, she decided to get the unpleasant task over with.

"How did it go on Saturday, Oma?" she asked carefully as Oma scurried about, looking for the paper bag. "Real busy toward the end?"

"Mmm?" Oma replied absentmindedly, digging through a stack of patterns stored beneath the counter. "No, real slow, as a matter of fact. It was so hot that nobody in his right mind went out of the house all day. By the time I left I would have given my eyeteeth for a dip in that old swimming hole we used to play in when we were kids."

Betsy was not in the mood for nostalgia. Her mind was on the store. "I take it you were too troubled by the weather to tidy up here with your usual efficiency?"

Oma stopped her searching and glanced at Betsy's tense expression. "In the summer I'm troubled by the humidity and in the winter I'm troubled by the snow. But that has nothing to do with the way I do my job. When I left here Saturday night everything was spick-and-span, as usual."

Betsy's eyes narrowed. She liked the chatty lady, admired her efficient if loquacious style. For nearly six months they'd spent the better part of every day together, sharing hopes and dreams and even financial plans for the business. It wasn't easy to berate her now. "Oma, I hate to say it, but this store was *not* spick-and-span when I walked in here this morning. To be perfectly honest with you, it was a mess. If I hadn't shown up half an hour early to work on Rhonda Watson's costume, I'm not sure I could have opened the doors on time. I spent twenty minutes cleaning up."

High color flared on Oma's cheeks and she struggled for breath. "I do my job, Miss Hanover!" she snapped, hurling the formal name at Betsy like a spear. "I've worked overtime more days than I can count to clean up extra, to wait on a late-minute customer, even to listen to *your* heartaches or plans for the faire! Not once have I ever shirked my duty! And that includes last Saturday night!"

It was precisely the reaction Betsy had expected, but that didn't make her job any easier. Facts were facts, and the facts were pretty clear. The store had been unacceptably messy when she'd walked in this morning. "Oma," she said sternly, "I don't mean to hurt your feelings. You were probably just tired when you locked up. But the store was not ready for business this morning. There's just no getting around it."

"Tell me what was wrong! You tell me what wasn't up to snuff!"

"Okay, I will," Betsy answered, struggling to remain calm in the midst of Oma's fury. "The bolts were all a mess, for one thing. The pins had fallen out of that blue calico on the end and about a yard of it had spilled onto the floor. A pile of patterns had been stuffed back in the drawer upside down, one of those giant button boards was jammed under the spools of thread and several stacks of zippers were in the wrong place. And worst of all—" by this time she could hardly look at Oma's crimson face "—the costumes we've been working on in the back were just tossed any which way on the couch. That jeweled bodice I'm making for the queen was lying on the floor."

Flabbergasted, Oma shook her head so vigorously that her short white hair bobbed up and down. "No," she protested hoarsely. "No!"

"No? Oma, I saw it with my own two eyes. I spent twenty minutes picking it all up!"

"Maybe you did, but I didn't do it!" Oma cried out. "Betsy, I'd never leave the store with fabric lying on the floor! I always straighten the bolts out one more time just before I leave. And on Saturday—" she grabbed Betsy's wrist to emphasize her point "—I never even *touched* the costumes. None of them! I was in the office a couple of times, and I thought about redoing Caroline Scott's hem, but I was just too hot and tired to bother."

"I know you were tired, Oma," Betsy tried again, losing the heart to wage this battle. "But the fact remains that—"

"The fact remains that I never touched the costumes!" Oma insisted, her voice taking on an eerie tone. "Don't you understand? Somebody else must have messed them up!"

A sharp bark of laughter bubbled out of Betsy's throat. "Come on, Oma! You're an adult. The least you can do is own up to your own mistakes. I'm not going to fire you or anything. Just tell me you're sorry and promise that it won't happen again!"

"I'm sorry that you don't trust me, but I can't promise you a thing!" Oma burst out, tears choking her exclamation. "I don't know how it happened this time, so how can I keep it from happening again?"

Suddenly Betsy thought of dear old Gaffer Paul, whose memory came and went so freely. Oma was too young to be going senile! But there were other diseases that caused such forgetfulness. Was it possible that...

"Betsy," Oma implored her, weeping freely now, "you've got to believe me. Somebody must have broken in here after I locked up that night."

"Broken in?" *Her fantasies are growing wilder by the moment,* Betsy thought with a mixture of sadness and disgust. "Don't be absurd. There's no sign of a forced entry and nothing is missing. The cash register wasn't disturbed."

Oma lowered herself into the chair by the counter and pulled out a tissue from her purse. "I don't know what happened, Betsy. All I know is that *I* didn't do anything wrong! If you were really my friend, you'd believe me," she insisted, dabbing ineffectually at her tears. "I'm not so sure I want to work here anymore."

"I DID IT, Dad!" Randy crowed as he pulled the old Chevy into the yard with a swaggering pride that his discreetly slow speed could not conceal. "I proved that I'm a man!" He stopped the car and leaped out of it joyfully.

Spence was too relieved to laugh, but he did conjure up a feeble reprimand. "Dinner's getting cold, Son. What took you so long?"

To his surprise, Randy stopped dead in his tracks while his ears flamed a brilliant crimson. "I . . . I had to parallel park. There wasn't quite enough room, and I—" his wobbling Adam's apple said far more than words "—I had to start over a couple of times."

Spence had to work at withholding a chuckle then, but somehow he made it. "I've always said we need more parking space downtown," was his only comment before Randy continued his explanation.

"On top of that, I had to wait a long time to talk to Betsy. The minute I walked in the door, she tossed me the keys to the shop and asked me to lock up, then wait in her office."

"Why did she do that? That doesn't sound like Betsy. Normally she's got time to chat unless the shop is full of people."

"Nobody was there," Randy answered brusquely as he took the porch stairs two at a time into the house. "Except for Laurie's grandma. And this is the weird part— Oma was just sitting on the chair by the counter, crying her eyes out. I've never seen her cry before."

Spence couldn't hide his alarm. "I never have, either, and I've known her for thirty-eight years. Did you ask what was the matter?"

"I couldn't, with Betsy shooing me off like that. But I was scared that something had happened to Laurie, and so once Betsy got Oma calmed down, I asked her about it right off."

"And she said?"

"She said, 'Laurie's fine, and now that you're a man I know I can count on you to guard Oma's privacy and not talk about anything you might have seen today at this shop.'" Spence swallowed another grin as Randy's chest swelled with pride. "Of course, she didn't mean I couldn't tell *you*, Dad. I mean, Betsy tells you everything." He grinned mischievously, then tacked on, "She said to give you her love."

"Mmm," Spence replied, wondering whether it was Betsy's original tone or Randy's rendition of the message that made it sound as though she were sending greetings to a maiden aunt.

As if he sensed his father's disappointment, Randy corrected himself melodramatically. "I mean, she said to tell you she can't live without you another day, and she's counting the minutes till Friday night."

This time it was Spence who battled a blush. "I doubt that was how she worded it, Randy. Betsy is nothing if not discreet."

"Come on, Dad!" Randy burst out with a laugh. "It doesn't matter what Betsy says. *I* know what she means. She's crazy about you. Any fool can see it."

Spence avoided his son's piercing gaze. "We're...close, Betsy and I," he cautiously admitted.

"Close?" Randy guffawed. "Dad, who are you kidding? You're head over heels in love with her! You remind me of the way I was acting when I first fell for Laurie. All moony-eyed and—"

"Sit down and eat your supper, Son," Spence ordered, deciding it was time to pull rank. "Tell me about your plans for the dance after the homecoming game."

It was an effective ploy, one that had always worked in the past, and it did divert Randy's interest from the sub-

ject of Betsy for at least another hour. But later that evening, when he came to say good-night before he went to
bed, Randy stood in the living room doorway, hair
slicked down from a bath in a way that reminded Spence
of the way his son had looked as a little boy, and brought
the subject up again.

"Dad?"

"Mmm?"

"Are you going to marry Betsy?"

Spence's eyes widened at the blunt probe. If Randy had
still been teasing him, he would have said no and playfully ordered him to bed. But the boy looked very serious, so he answered, "Would you like me to?"

Randy shrugged. "I think it's up to you, Dad. I mean,
I won't be here forever."

Spence met his eyes, man-to-man. "Let me put it another way. Would it trouble you to learn that I was
thinking along those lines?"

He shrugged again. "No, Dad. I like Betsy just fine.
The only thing that bothers me—"

"Yes?"

"Is why... well, why you've never talked about getting married again. Before Betsy came to town there
wasn't anybody you were really interested in, but it's been
different with her right from the start. At first you
wouldn't even admit she was special to you. You
wouldn't even admit you were dying to see her every
Monday night! And I—well, to tell you the truth, I sort
of expected her to move in here while I was at Mom's this
summer, but you never even brought her to the house.
And since I've been home, you've hardly seen her at all,
even though I can tell you miss her a lot. At first I
thought you two had had a fight or something, but you

seem so happy when you're together that...well, I just don't know what to think."

When the long rush of words came to an end, Randy awkwardly stared at his father, and Spence, unable to meet that ingenuous gaze, studied a crack above the mantel. But Spence had always taught Randy to tell the truth, especially to loved ones, so somehow he managed to share his own uncertain feelings with his maturing son. "Sometimes I don't know, either, Randy," he confessed thoughtfully. "I'll tell you straight—I care for that woman a great deal. And I'm pretty sure she cares for me, too. But marriage is so—" he struggled for an appropriate word and ended up saying "—dangerous. I just don't know if I'm brave enough to take the risk."

Randy stared at him in silence for a moment. "You're thinking of Mom," he concluded sagely.

Slowly Spence nodded. "I guess I am."

"You don't really think Betsy would tear up your life like that, do you? I mean, it's not like she has any kids."

"Neither did your mother when I married her."

"But Mom is...so different from Betsy. Betsy's so strong, so independent." And then, though he blushed at his confession, Randy admitted, "She's also awfully sweet."

"So was your mother," Spence had to emphasize. "She was once every bit as delightful as Betsy is right now. That's what scares me, Son. I sure don't think Betsy's cut from the same piece of cloth as your mom, but there just aren't any guarantees."

Randy sighed, contemplating his father's message. "Most of your problems with Mom were because of me, Dad. You and Betsy don't have to have any more children."

Thinking back to his last conversation with Betsy, Spence realized it was very likely they'd want more little ones, in spite of their business obligations. "It's possible we might not," he conceded. "But if we did, and things turned sour at some point down the road, I'd be looking at exactly the same kind of heartache I went through with you." By now he was thinking out loud, grateful that he could share his muddle of feelings with somebody who loved him. "And then there's the business. If it were just mine, maybe I wouldn't fight so hard to save it. But to me Black Gold Supply means your grandpa and your great-grandpa and your uncle Bill. And someday, it means *you*, Randy. It's all I've got to leave you except for this old house."

"No, Dad," Randy corrected him as he strolled across the room. He stood just inches from his father and waited until Spence's eyes were on his face. "The business is just...money. And maybe family history. I might like to run it someday, but, then again, I might not. I don't really know what I want to do with my life. I don't even know if I want to live in Ohio." He knelt down next to Spence as though he were the man and Spence the child. "What you've got to leave me—what you've already given me, Dad—is so much more than Black Gold Supply! You've let me know that you were willing to sacrifice everything that matters to you for the privilege of having me be a part of your life. Nothing that I stumble across in some old will half a century from now will ever be worth more to me than that."

As though the grave confession embarrassed the boy, he stood up quickly, gangly elbows swinging, and scampered back toward his room. Spence was still pondering his son's words—so tender, so truthful—when Randy stopped in the hallway and asked again, "So, Dad, are you *really* thinking about marrying Betsy?"

And though Spence knew there were myriad questions about that possibility he had yet to answer, he heard himself confess out loud, "Maybe, Son. Someday." And after Randy had gone to bed, he said to the wall upon which the family pictures hung, "If she can bring herself to sign that agreement—yes."

CHAPTER FIFTEEN

AS IT TURNED OUT, Randy came down with the flu and missed the homecoming game, so Spence didn't get to join Betsy on Friday night after all. The following weekend there was a last-minute calamity in the booths that comprised Witches' Row, and Spence was so busy he barely managed to give Betsy a call. By the week before the Renaissance faire, Betsy was beginning to think she'd forgotten what he looked like. It had been nearly a month since they'd been alone.

In desperation, she'd called him to set up a lunch date at Charley's for Friday, which he'd accepted with alacrity. But when she arrived at the shop at nine o'clock in the morning, Oma—who'd beaten her there every day since their misunderstanding so she could preview the condition of the shop—informed her that Spence had called to cancel.

"Oh, no!" Betsy wailed, making no effort to hide her frustration. "We won't have a minute this weekend with the faire going on. Did he say why he couldn't make it?"

"He said that something had come up that just wouldn't wait."

"Business?"

Oma shrugged. "I got the impression it was personal. He said he was going to Columbus and he'd check in with you as soon as he got back."

"Columbus?" Betsy echoed. "On a weekday? He never takes a weekday off!"

"Maybe Janet needs something for the faire."

"Maybe." But she remained unconvinced. Along with her disappointment there remained a ghost of worry as the day progressed. What did Spence need in Columbus that was personal? A doctor? A bank? Muskingum had both, but they were both pretty limited in the services they provided. If something were wrong with Randy, she was sure he would have mentioned it.

Her tension broke around two o'clock when the front door to the shop burst open and Spence, grinning from ear to ear, grandly marched inside.

"Spence?" she asked, all but forgetting she had a customer waiting for her to cut three and a half yards of gold braid to trim a costume. "What is it? You look like the cat that swallowed the canary!"

His grin grew even wider, and he rocked back and forth on the balls of his booted feet. "Take care of Mrs. Hayworth and then meet me in your office."

He was halfway to the back when Oma materialized from the other side of the room and said, "*I'll* take care of Mrs. Hayworth. For heaven's sake, Betsy, don't keep the man waiting at a time like this!"

It was the first friendly gesture Oma had made in several weeks, and although her scolding tone was not appreciably warm, Betsy thanked her quickly and hustled to the back of the store. When she poked her head into the office, she found Spence pacing in front of her tiny couch. Without preamble he pulled her inside, locking the door before he took her in his arms for a very long and very satisfying kiss.

It wasn't the kind of kiss Spence generally reserved for the bedroom, but it wasn't the quick buss he offered her for a public hello or goodbye, either. There was something terribly intimate, terribly gentle, about the way he took her in his arms, and Betsy felt the knot of tension within her unfurl in the cocoon of his warmth.

"I'm going stark raving loony without you, Betsy," he confessed when he finally released her. "I miss you so much I can't see straight."

"So why did you cancel lunch today?" she demanded to know, her curiosity growing by leaps and bounds. "What on earth was so important that you had to take off to Columbus on a Friday morning?"

"Well, it's all really quite simple." His smile shone like a sunbeam. "I didn't decide to ask you to marry me until just last night."

Betsy opened her mouth to reply, but no sound came out. Over the past six months they'd only talked about marriage a few times, always framing the hypothetical concept with "maybes" and "only ifs" and "probably nots." Every time Spence had brought the subject up he'd bludgeoned Betsy with his unwavering insistence on a premarital pact, and ever since the Sunday afternoon they'd seriously talked about having children, Spence hadn't mentioned marriage at all.

"Spence?" she asked again, eyes shining with rapturous, newfound hope. "What are you saying?"

Soberly he laid one palm on her cheek. The gesture was so simple, yet so compelling, it caused a lump to rise in Betsy's throat. "I *love* you, lady," he declared with a sense of earnestness she'd never heard in his voice before. "I'm tired of hurried lunches and ten minute phone calls and monthly Friday night dates. I want you at my breakfast table every morning. I want you cuddling up beside me while I read in bed at night. And on Saturdays, I want you to pick flowers from my garden while I pull the weeds." Spence kissed her again, slowly this time, with a tenderness that asked not for sensual pleasure but for a deep, abiding kind of love. "Betsy," he confessed as he slipped his fingers through her loose blond curls, "I just can't be happy living without you anymore. I want you to be my wife."

Betsy tried to reply, but there were no words grand enough to capture the depth of her joy. All she could do was slip her arms around Spence and press her face against his throat. His arms came around her then, hard and strong and sure, and he rocked her back and forth while she clung to him, still struggling for words.

"Are you sure? Are you really, truly, finally sure?" she whispered.

"I'm sure," he replied, his deep voice cracking with feeling. Once more he kissed her, lips warm and firm, as if to underline his conviction. "I'm so sure that I decided to zip into Columbus so I could do this right. As I recall—" he pulled a tiny box out of his shirt pocket with great fanfare "—this is the one that's supposed to be a tribute to a gracious wife."

Betsy's eyes met his uncertainly as she took the box, then blinked in disbelief when she opened it. The miracle inside wasn't an ordinary engagement ring—it was the sixteenth century wedding ring with the cluster of rubies set like a flower that she'd admired so much at the artifact shop! It had been exquisite then, and it was at least a hundred times more beautiful now that it was a gift from Spence.

"I want you to know that I did read the words engraved inside, Bets," he admitted, repeating the pristine, timeless words. "'A faythfulle wyffe, my wealthe in lyffe.'"

Betsy rarely cried when she was happy, but now the threat of tears constricted her throat. "Oh, Spence," she managed to exclaim, even more awed by the giver than by the gift. "I never believed that this would happen! I never really thought I'd ever be able to marry you!"

"Well, I haven't heard you accept the job offer yet," he reminded her with a smile that deepened the laugh lines around his kind gray eyes. "It's a lifetime position, you know. Twenty-four hours a day. No vacations, no wages, no time off. But you do get sick leave, and room and board are free."

"Oh, Spence!" Betsy bubbled again, knowing she was starting to sound like a parrot but unable to articulate her feelings more clearly.

"Should I take that for an affirmative answer?" he teased her with a wink. "I've got a ton of deliveries to make this afternoon, and I'd hate to leave here without being sure that our future is all sewed up."

Betsy touched his lips with a trembling hand, still shaking her head with awe. She stood on tiptoe to give him one very slow "yes, I will marry you" kiss, and he laid both hands on her face as he kissed her back, as if to solemnize the exchange of vows. For a moment they just stood there, sharing a huge smile, joy wrapping around them.

Then Betsy hugged him tightly and burst out, "Spence, I'll be useless for the rest of the day, not to mention the weekend! And I've got so much to do behind the scenes at the faire!"

"Do it with this on your finger," Spence suggested, grinning as he slipped the ruby-studded ring on her hand. "I'm not sure whether this is supposed to be an engagement ring or a wedding band, but I'd like you to wear it while John Percy's back in town."

"Spence! You've got to get over this jealousy of John Percy!" she chided him in jest, too happy to waste a moment's thought on the other man. "I don't even *like* John!"

"I know. Really, I know," Spence said, then hugged her again as he laughed. "But something about that man just makes my hackles rise. I think I'd feel that way even if he didn't make such a point of ogling you."

"It's just a game for him, Spence. He isn't really particularly attracted to me. Or to Janet, either, for that matter. He fusses over both of us equally, you know."

"That's another black mark against him. Fie!" he cried out, suddenly switching to Elizabethan English as he waved an imaginary sword in the air. "He hath no more brain than earwax, nor more wit than a sleeping sow!"

"Practicing for your next duel, I see," Betsy ribbed him, feeling ridiculously lighthearted.

"Oh, yes, I've really been working on my list. Randy's been coaching me so I'll be ready to defend your honor again, if need be. But if Percy's still sniffing around Janet's skirts, I guess I'll have to defend her honor, too. Do you suppose I can use the same insult twice?"

"I don't know why not. John always repeats himself, just like that stupid Falstaff in *The Merry Wives of Windsor*," Betsy pointed out. "But don't worry about Janet, Spence. I think she's made it very clear to him where she stands."

"Good. And speaking of Janet—" Spence gave her one more lingering goodbye kiss, then took a step toward the door "—I'm going to ask her to draw up our prenuptial agreement on Monday just as soon as the faire is over." Without drawing a breath he continued, "Then

I'd like to call Mr. Egleston, the reverend, to set up the wedding within a week or two unless you've got a yen for something fancy. In this town you don't invite a single friend unless you're planning to invite them all, so I think we'd be better off with a quick private ceremony. You don't have a great flock of relatives that will be offended if we just get married in my living room, do you?''

While Spence kept talking, Betsy stood perfectly still in the center of her office, struggling for breath. She felt as though somebody had just kicked her in the chest. How could he possibly bring her this sentimental, costly ring, shower her with happiness, convince her that he'd given himself to her forever, then knock her flat with such an obvious sucker's punch?

"Betsy?" he questioned, his tone growing strained. "I said, do you really feel the need of a formal wedding? It's not my first choice, but I could live through it if it would make you happy. Randy would get a real kick out of standing up for me in a tux."

Slowly Betsy lowered herself to the couch, clutching the armrest for support. Vaguely she realized that Spence was still talking, but after a few more determined sallies, he gave up the effort of casual speech. He didn't join her on the sofa, though, or ask her what was wrong. He kept his position by the door, as though he were afraid to come any closer.

"I can't believe you did this to me," Betsy murmured when she finally found her voice. Her eyes were dark, accusing, and the fiery rage of betrayal burned in her heart. "Did you honestly think I'd be so bowled over by the ring that I wouldn't notice the contract? Did you think I'd be so elated that you finally asked me to marry you that I'd forget about everything else?"

A shadow of hurt darkened Spence's face, but Betsy read no hint of shame. "I thought *we* mattered," he said quietly. "You and me. Everything else comes after that." More insistently, he stated, "In my eyes, that ring is an extravagant romantic gesture, but I bought it to make you happy, Bets. For you, a premarital contract is equally absurd, but I thought you'd sign it as a gift to me. Not because you think it's necessary or even very smart. Just because I need it so desperately to put my mind at ease."

Betsy leaned forward and covered her eyes, suddenly overcome with grief. "I love you, Spence," she managed to tell him, amazed she could still say the words when he was being so cruel. "I want to be your wife. I swear to you that I will never tear up our children in a divorce. I promise never to damage Black Gold Oil Supply or sell off your part of the Spencer family land." Slowly she met his level gaze, tears now washing her anguished face. "Doesn't *that* put your mind at ease?"

"Of course it does." For the first time his tone held a hint of self-reproach. "If I had any doubts about it I wouldn't be here begging you on bended knee, Bets. All I'm asking you to do is put that down on paper and add your John Hancock at the bottom." He crossed the room to kneel beside her, lifting her chin with a gentle hand. "Is that really so much to ask?"

"Oh, Spence!" Betsy wailed, pressing her cheek against his palm as she battled fresh tears of indignation. "I'm asking you to believe in me. To believe in *us*! Is *that* really so much to ask?"

He exhaled heavily, then stood up and jammed both hands deep inside his pockets. His face was gray now, and his eyes were as bleak as Betsy's. Still, his voice was stern and steady as he declared, "Betsy, this issue is not negotiable. Your tears won't wear me down." She watched his loving face darken with shadowy memories of another woman, another time. It was as though Tiffany had just entered the room with them and was sitting beside Betsy on the couch. "You have to sign the contract or you can't wear the ring. I'm sorry, sweetheart, but that's the bottom line." His whole body was rigid now; his biceps bulged with tension. There was no trace of her passionate lover in the man who now said coolly, "Now do you want me to call the pastor, or take that gold box back to Columbus?"

In all her life Betsy had never hurt more than she hurt at that moment. Never had she been so torn. "Don't do this to me, Spence! Don't do this to *us*," she begged him, rubbing the perfect rubies with her thumb, wondering why the words engraved inside meant so much more to her than to the sad-eyed man who stood before her. "That contract is an act of *hate*, not an act of love! If you can't marry me without it, then maybe you're not ready to marry me at all!"

For a long, terrible moment Spence stared at Betsy, rage radiating from his wounded features. She could see his hands ball into fists in his jeans pockets, and when his mouth set in a hard, uncompromising line, she knew she'd gone too far.

An endless moment of silence stretched between them before Spence admitted, "Betsy, I hate to say this, but—" he swallowed hard and took a great breath "—I think you may be right."

Betsy's pulse started to hammer. Something in his tone was chilling. For a man who was about to relent, he didn't sound very conciliatory. Cautiously she asked, "Are you saying I'm right about the contract?"

Slowly—too slowly—he nodded. He no longer looked angry; he looked bereft. Sorrow laced his tone. "I'm

saying you're right that I shouldn't have to ask you to
sign it. It shouldn't matter to me." He stopped, staring
at her with miserable eyes, as though something precious to him had vanished in the night. "I should have
complete faith in the woman I'm going to take as my
wife."

Spence was saying what Betsy had begged him to believe all along, but his lips were stiff, fighting the words,
and Betsy knew that whatever pain was choking his heart
eclipsed the joy they'd shared just moments earlier. She
started to tremble as she prodded, "Does that mean
you're ready to marry me without the contract, Spence?"

For the space of a dozen heartbeats, he met her eyes
before he slowly shook his head. He could not conceal
the grief in his manly voice as he confessed, "No, Bets.
The long and short of it is, I think that maybe—" he
traced her jaw with one callused fingertip, as though he
were doing so for the very last time "—I'm not quite
ready to get married, after all."

FORTY-EIGHT HOURS LATER, Spence was ready to run his
foil through John Percy's black heart or strangle him
with his own bare hands. The man seemed determined to
spoil his weekend. On the first morning of the faire, John
had challenged Spence to a duel as soon as a crowd had
gathered, and this time he'd pulled no punches, humiliating him with his superior swordsmanship and crowing
about it in front of Randy. Worse yet, Sonny Barnes had
dropped by with his new bride in time to witness the de-
bacle and spent another ten minutes badgering Spence
about his purple tights. In addition to the duel, John had
aggravated Spence by grilling Randy in great detail about
how his birthday cartwheel had come into his posses-
sion. When Randy mentioned that it had been a gift from

Betsy and his dad, Percy had pointed out darkly that one just like it had turned up missing—along with the rest of the monarch collection—on the night Betsy had stayed in Gaffer Paul's house. John never came right out and said he thought the two events might be linked by more than coincidence, but even the subtle implication made Spence's spine tingle.

Get a grip on yourself, old boy, he ordered sternly. *It's not really Percy you're mad at on Betsy's behalf. It's this damn fool inside your skin named Geoffrey Spencer.*

He'd only seen Betsy in passing since Friday, a day neither one of them was ever likely to forget. In the end they had agreed to shelve his proposal until the faire was over and they'd both had some more time to think about it. But when Betsy had taken off the ring, whispering hoarsely, "I guess a faithful wife isn't enough wealth for you, after all," Spence had realized that nothing he could say to her on Monday would ever make up for what he'd said to her before he'd tucked that ruby ring back in its golden box.

So far the faire had been a great success. Janet estimated their profits at seventeen thousand dollars, more than enough to justify all their efforts and renovate the park. They'd had visitors from as far away as Kentucky and Maine—though admittedly the ones from Maine had just happened to be passing through—and most of the guests had come in costume and really gotten into the Renaissance mood.

Mrs. MacGillicuddy had been in her glory since the morning the faire began, hustling about in the imperial lady-in-waiting outfit she'd chosen to emphasize her authority. Randy, dressed in gold-and-green slops and a glittery doublet, was playing his part with panache. He loved dishing out Elizabethan insults and handing out foils. In between duels he'd sneaked off to Mongers Crossing to practice his romantic quotes on Barbara Peterson, who seemed interested in Randy for many more reasons other than his admitted weakness in math. Every time Randy mentioned Barbara, a gigantic grin split his face; Spence had noticed with relief that his son hadn't referred to Laurie Potter once in the past four or five days.

Spence himself had grown more glum with each passing hour, and Betsy, whenever she hurried past him, tried but usually failed to smile. It was almost six o'clock, an hour before the close of the faire, when he spotted her rushing in his direction. She lifted one hand in greeting, but she wouldn't have stopped to speak if he hadn't stepped out into her path.

"Bets?" he asked softly. "Is everything all right?"

"All right?" she repeated, her eyes cool and wounded. "Are you talking about the faire?"

He tugged on the ridiculous padded doublet where it made his neck itch. "Well, you seemed to be in quite a hurry."

"I just got a message that there's a costume alert over at the arena."

"A costume alert?" he asked, struggling to find humor in the phrase. "Is something so torn that it can't be mended?"

To his dismay, Betsy's face clouded over, and before she pushed on past him, she murmured almost inaudibly, "Only my heart, Spence."

Instinctively he reached out to stop her, but she shrugged away from his hand.

"Betsy," he begged her. "Betsy, please..."

"Betsy, please *what*?" she demanded, angry with him again. "Please marry me? Please forget I ever asked?

Please wrap up your own feelings in a tiny box and bring them out or put them away whenever it suits Spence Spencer?''

He knew he'd asked for that, but after two days in an emotional vacuum, even her fury was better than her studied silence. "Betsy, we said we'd let it sit till after the faire. We didn't decide anything.''

"*You* didn't decide anything. Or rather, you made up your mind and changed it again. But I've decided where *I* stand.''

Slowly, uncertainly, he reached out for her hand again, and this time she let him take it. Around them the noises of the faire were bubbling, and the smell of hot buttered cinnamon buns filled the air. Somebody at the horse arena was shouting, "Betsy! Where the hell is Betsy?'' but Spence clung to her fingers, kneading them with lonely desperation, and his eyes begged for her forgiveness.

"Where *do* you stand, Betsy?'' he asked in a low, hoarse voice.

For a moment she did not move, did not answer. And then she suddenly gripped his fingers, as though to underline the intensity of her words. "I've decided that I just can't keep treading water, Spence. You're tearing me apart.''

"Betsy, that's the last thing I want to do to you! Surely you know that—''

"What I know is that I can't force you to trust me, but I *can* take responsibility for my own happiness and my own life. And that's exactly what I'm going to do.''

Spence's chest suddenly felt too small to accommodate his heart and his breathing grew harsh and labored. "What are you trying to say?'' he asked, certain that whatever she had in mind was going to hurt him.

Betsy couldn't meet his eyes as she took a deep breath, and she flicked away a single tear before she found the words to say, "If it were up to me, Spence, I'd marry you tomorrow. But the time has come for me to accept the fact that you're never going to give yourself to me, so I've...made other plans."

"Other plans?" he gasped, suddenly feeling as though he were bouncing along in a roller coaster without a safety belt. "What kind of other plans?"

"I've got enough capital to expand, Spence," she blurted out quickly, as though she were afraid she'd change her mind. "I'm thinking of starting another store in Atlanta. One of my brothers is moving there."

Spence was stunned. There were a thousand reasons he didn't want her to move to Atlanta, but he only found the words for one. "You can't leave Muskingum! You told me yourself that Oma wasn't experienced enough to take over the store. And ever since she left it in a mess that day—"

"It doesn't matter, Spence," she answered in a crisp tone he'd never heard her use before. "I'm a businesswoman. If Oma can't cut the muster, I'll hire someone else."

"And what about me?" he demanded, fear making him angry. "If I can't live up to your ideals about love and marriage, will you find a replacement for me, too?"

The arrow of pain that darted across her lovely face wounded Spence as though it had lodged in his own heart. "There's a place in my heart that will always belong to you, Spence," she whispered in a voice so low and broken he could hardly make out her words. A fresh tear took the place of the one she'd just wiped away, and this time Betsy didn't try to banish it. Her eyes were huge and haunted as she stared at him. "The last thing I want to do is give you up, but we just can't go on like this!"

"Okay, maybe we can't," he conceded, "but there's got to be a better solution than having you pull up stakes!"

Betsy swallowed hard as red blotches framed her eyes and anguish marked her lovely face. "If you think of one, come tell me, Spence," she begged, giving his hand one last squeeze before she let him go. "I'll be in the bus garage packing costumes for an hour or two after the faire."

A voice from the arena was calling her name again, and Betsy rushed off toward the thunder of horses' hooves. She'd taken only three quick steps before she whipped around to face him, her eyes dark with ill-concealed pain. Hoarsely she pleaded, "Don't misunderstand me, Spence. It's going to kill me to leave Muskingum. If there's any way at all you can bring yourself to waive that damned agreement, I'd still be terribly proud to be your wife."

"LOOK AT MY BODICE!" Laurie Potter whined when she spotted Betsy on the outskirts of the horse arena moments after her heart-wrenching scene with Spence. "I was leaning over the fence to give water to one of the noblemen and I caught got on a nail! Look at me! I'm a mess!"

While Laurie was hardly a disaster, her bodice was in pretty bad condition—partly because it had been so tight to begin with that the fabric had had no give—and Betsy soothed the girl with the promise of finding something to cover her for the duration. Hurriedly she led her past the football stadium to the bus garage in hopes of finding a spare woman's bodice in one of her packing boxes.

The sheet-metal building was a bleak barn of a place that suited Betsy's mood at the moment. Her last encounter with Spence had been just as dismal as their farewell on Friday afternoon. It was obvious that nothing had changed. He loved her, but not enough. He trusted her, but not enough. He wanted to marry her, but not enough to relinquish his obsession with that damned legal pact.

"Laurie, you've only got an hour or so to go," Betsy suggested, finding it hard to think about the faire at the moment. "Couldn't I just stitch up this rip or pin it?"

"No!" the girl wailed. "I'm an abigail, not a peasant! Besides, I want to look pretty for Troy."

"Troy?" Betsy muttered.

"Yes, the knight on the black horse who Janet Spencer hired. Isn't he the cutest guy you ever saw?"

Betsy smiled as pleasantly as her own misery would allow. "He's a nice-looking man," she agreed. "But I thought you had your heart set on Howard Walsh."

Laurie had the grace to giggle. "Well, he's nice, but he's away at college now."

"Which means he's probably too old for you, and I'm sure this Troy person is, too." It was really none of Betsy's business, but her own agony was so akin to the pain she'd seen in Randy's face a few weeks before that she couldn't help but mention, "There's nothing wrong with dating a nice boy your own age, you know."

Laurie flushed. "You're talking about Randy. You think it was awful the way I left him for Howard!"

Betsy shrugged and kept her eyes on the pile of men's cloaks she was sorting through as a last resort. Since Oma had been keeping them at home, it had been a long time since she'd examined them closely, and she was hopeful that a jerkin could pass for a woman's vest in a pinch. "I think when you've been going steady, or whatever you call it these days, you owe it to the boy to tell him yourself when you're no longer interested in going out with him.''

To Betsy's surprise, Laurie began to cry. "Oh, Betsy, I couldn't! I just couldn't break his heart! I like Randy so much.''

Betsy stared at the girl, marveling at the inconsistencies of youth. "Then why did you break up with him?''

"I didn't want to! I didn't mean to! I just got bored over the summer. I wanted to do things, and he was gone. So I finally decided to go out with somebody else.''

"Laurie," she suggested gently, "did it ever occur to you to tell Randy that? He's convinced that you think he's a total jerk.''

Laurie wailed even louder. "I hate myself!''

"Come on, let's not be unreasonable here," Betsy suggested pragmatically. "If you're still interested in Randy—"

"Well, I'm not exactly," Laurie declared, abruptly reversing herself again as she untied her breast-flattening red bodice and slipped it off. "I mean, I still want to do things with him, but I don't want to be tied down to just one guy. Besides, he's got a crush on Barbara now.''

Betsy felt at least a thousand years old as she offered, "I think if you and Randy just talked all this out, you could enjoy dating anybody you wanted and still be very good friends.''

"You think so?" Laurie asked, a rainbow of relief brightening her pretty young face. "Is that what you and Spence do?''

"Not exactly," Betsy snapped, cutting off any further questions along that line. At the moment every mention of Spence's name was enough to gouge another deep hole in her heart. The past two days had been an absolute nightmare, but now that she'd shared her plans with Spence she knew that the torment of her own indecision was about to come to an end. Either he'd come rushing to her side after the faire to slip that ruby ring back on her finger, or he'd never mention marriage again. Either way, Betsy's path would be clear to her by sundown.

"How about this?" Laurie suddenly asked her, tugging out a hanger with a pair of chaps and a leather-fringed vest. "I know it would sort of make me look like a cowgirl, but at least it's made of something they had back then."

"I don't know," Betsy answered, viewing the long fringe skeptically. "It's so terribly western. Maybe you could wear it inside out."

Laurie giggled as she pulled the vest off the hanger. "I love men in western clothes. Wouldn't Troy look great in these chaps?" As the chaps inadvertently slid off the hanger and hit the concrete floor, the dull sound of cushioned metal echoed through the bus garage. "Now that's weird," Laurie muttered as she picked them up again.

"What's weird?" Betsy asked, reversing the vest to see if the other side might be less jarring wrapped around a Renaissance chemise.

"I thought I heard conchos. You know, those silver things some cowboys wear on the sides of their chaps? But these aren't real silver. They're just big buttons." As she toyed with one playfully, the thread broke and it came off in her lap. Absentmindedly she glanced at it and said, "Oh, I guess there's silver inside. But why is it all wrapped up?"

"Wrapped up?"

"Yeah, wrapped up," Laurie repeated as Betsy slipped the rearranged vest over her thin shoulders and tucked the fringe inside. "It's got a little cardboard holder with some clear cellophane inside. Maybe not cellophane exactly, but—"

Suddenly Betsy snatched the button and turned it over. To her amazement, she discovered that Laurie hadn't imagined the cardboard or the cellophane . . . or the dull bronze coin inside. Breathlessly she dug the wrapped coin out of the leather-covered button. It had letters on it that appeared to be English, but the coin bore no resemblance to the American money that had been crossing palms at Muskingum's Chipping-under-Oakwood for the past two days.

A sudden heart-thudding excitement seized Betsy. She felt like an archaeologist who'd just made an earthshaking discovery at a dig! "Gaffer Paul is missing a bunch of coins that are terribly valuable, Laurie!" she burst out. "I always thought this outfit had been sent with the costumes by mistake. But if there are more coins hidden inside these other buttons, I—" She stopped, stunned and breathless, as Laurie tugged off another button and checked what was inside. This one had three coins, much smaller than the first, and every button they opened after that held more secrets. Secrets that were worth a fortune to whoever had sewn the coins inside!

An instant later she realized who that someone had to be. Somebody who had access to the coins and to the chaps in Pittsburgh and had expected to recover them in Muskingum...perhaps today. Somebody who might have already have prowled through her house and her shop in search of them! *And to think I accused Oma of lying to me when she insisted that she'd left the shop clean!* A sudden cold fury seized Betsy, a fury that bore John

Percy's name. Betsy and Janet had laughed at his seduction games, finding humor in his clumsiness, never once suspecting that he, like Falstaff, had had an ulterior motive.

"Wow!" Laurie gushed, ripping off button after button with abandon. "I feel like Nancy Drew! What are we going to do with them?"

"We're going to tuck them in the bottom of my purse until the faire is over and I can call Gaffer Paul," Betsy decided quickly. "In the meantime, I want you to go see if you can find Marvin Oates for me, and if you can't, go tell Spence I need to see him right away."

"Sheriff Oates! Boy, is this exciting!" Laurie was beside herself now. "Do you think somebody might try to steal these coins before you can give them back to that old man?"

A vision of John Percy's smiling face suddenly caused Betsy's throat to fill with bile. How he'd cozened that sweet, doddering fellow! How blatantly he'd used their little Renaissance faire for his own purposes, and done his best to manipulate Janet and her! "Oh, I imagine the thief will try to retrieve them," Betsy said grimly, and then she vowed with a vengeance, "but he'll take them over my dead body."

WHEN LAURIE CAME BOUNDING toward the dueling greensward a half an hour after Betsy had dropped her bombshell about leaving Muskingum, Spence assumed she was coming to see Randy. But to his amazement, she just grinned at his son and headed straight for Spence.

He was surprised to see her wearing a leather cowboy vest instead of the chest-flattening red thing she'd had on that morning. He had a vague memory of seeing the fringed vest before and a certain sensation that it was somehow out of place as a sixteenth century garment.

John Percy's roving gaze also came to rest on young Laurie's bosom when she was still a dozen yards away, and the intensity of his stare forced Spence to add one more black mark to the man's name. Even if Laurie wasn't Randy's girlfriend anymore, she was still a good Muskingum kid and far too young for a rogue like John.

"For God's sake, Percy, she's only fifteen!" he growled at the other man.

Eyes still on Laurie's chest, John glanced up with more surprise than umbrage. "Who's fifteen?"

"That sweet young thing you're ogling. Isn't it bad enough that you have to chase every grown woman you meet in Muskingum? Do you have to leer at our children, too?"

Percy continued to gawk at him as though he'd lost his mind. "I assure you, Spencer, I have no designs on that young girl."

"You'd better not. And it would serve you well to forget any other female you've met here when you leave the faire tonight."

Percy laughed, an ugly, triumphant sound. "Don't blame me if you can't hold on to your woman, Spencer. And as to your brother's grass widow—"

Spence raised one hand in warning. "Don't finish that line, pal. One more word about Betsy or Janet and I'm likely to ram this foil right down your throat." It was the first time he'd ever spoken to Percy with the raw hostility that had gripped him since the day they'd met, and now he made no effort to veil his true feelings.

Percy, who normally treated everything as a joke, responded in a vicious tone that Spence had never heard him use before. "I don't have to put up with this," he snarled. "I'm here to do you hick-town people a favor, and have you ever shown one iota of gratitude to me?"

Spence knew he spoke the truth, but he still couldn't find it in his heart to thank the man. He'd always wondered why Percy had been so helpful in the first place. Granted, he was a fencing buff, but how could he find so much free time? Before Spence could think up a proper reply, the other man grumbled, "I'm taking a break. You think you can manage here without me, Spencer?" he challenged, tossing his practice foil to Spence as he gripped the hilt of his silver saber, which lurked in its jewel-encrusted sheath. "Just give it a try."

Spence was still steaming when Percy disappeared from view in the general vicinity of the bus garage. *What do you want there except for Betsy?* the green-eyed demon in his heart demanded. *What do you want except for my wife?*

That last word rolled on his tongue as though it had always belonged there, and he discovered, to his shock, that the word "wife" coupled with "Betsy" had a wholly different ring to it than the same word paired with Tiffany's name. For the first time since he'd known Betsy, Spence felt no fear whatsoever of what would happen when John went out of his way to flirt with her, even though she had every reason in the world to be furious with the man she loved. In the quiet of his heart, Spence realized that Betsy was his woman—heart and soul—and she could never be unfaithful to him.

He desperately hoped she could never leave him to start a store in Atlanta, either. But he knew that was a risk he just couldn't take. *I've got to find the courage to let the old fear go,* he told himself, suddenly more frightened of losing Betsy right now than of losing anything else somewhere down the road.

Before Spence could find a way to triumph over the scars of his past, Laurie leaned over the roped greensward fence and gestured him to join her. It took him a few minutes to satisfy the dueler who'd arrived just as Percy was leaving, but once the "victor" had taken off with a smile on his face, Spence strolled on over to the girl.

"Hi, Laurie," he greeted her as cheerfully as he was able. "What's up?"

She leaned toward him furtively and whispered, "I've got a secret message for you. From Betsy."

Spence was surprised and actually a little disappointed. Betsy had said what she'd had to say and she'd left the ball in his court. It wasn't like her to play juvenile games such as sending messages with children. Apprehensively he said, "Go ahead. I'm listening."

Laurie grinned with unabashed delight. "We found a bunch of money, Spence! Kings' and queens' coins, Betsy said. Worth a fortune to Gaffer Paul."

"You're kidding!" It was great news, but surprising, if not bizarre. "Where did she find them?"

Her young bust lifted proudly. "She didn't. *I* did. In the chaps that go with this vest. Somebody had sewn them inside these giant leather buttons. Ingenious, huh?"

"Ingenious," he agreed. But he didn't share Laurie's enthusiasm, because he suddenly realized that the monarch collection hadn't gotten mixed up with Betsy's costumes by mistake. Somebody had willfully stolen those coins from Gaffer Paul, somebody ruthless and cunning...who wasn't likely to let them go without a fight.

"Betsy said to tell you that you were right all along, but when I asked her to explain what she meant she said there wasn't time and I should just hurry over and tell you about the coins and you'd know what to do. I was supposed to go find Marvin Oates first, but he was at the horse arena when I left with Betsy and now I don't know where he is, so I guess I ought to call the sheriff's office, don't you think?'' She took a long breath after the endless explanation, then tacked on, ''Betsy said you'd know just what to do with the thief!''

With sudden panic and perfect hindsight, Spence realized why John Percy had set off for the bus garage in such a hurry. He must have realized that if Laurie was wearing the cowboy vest, the chaps must be somewhere nearby, most likely in the wardrobe closet in the back of the bus garage...where Betsy was waiting for Marvin Oates. Waiting all alone.

Despite the eager new would-be dueler who Randy had just armed with a mask and foil, Spence bolted over the rope fence and broke into a dead run across the track that circled the football field. He'd covered this very ground a thousand times as a boy but had never made such incredible time; not even the floppy hat or the sheathed foil that scraped the dirt every few yards slowed him down.

Damn right I know what to do with that bastard! Spence growled to himself, goaded by panic for the woman he loved. *I should have killed John Percy the first day we met. And if he's done anything to Betsy*—the fear made him break out in a cold sweat as he saw the side door to the garage slam closed—*I swear to God I'll kill him yet.*

CHAPTER SIXTEEN

WHEN BETSY HEARD a man's footsteps at the bus garage door, she called out, "Marvin?" but he didn't hear her. At least he didn't reply. A moment later she heard a sword sheath scrape the wall as somebody stepped around the pile of giant tires near the door. Assuming it was Spence, who must have felt the need to come see her the instant he got Laurie's message, Betsy rushed to greet him with relief.

"Spence, I can't believe this!" she burst out breathlessly. "All this time I knew John was playing a game with us, but I never—"

She stopped cold as she focused on the tall form before her. Despite the uncertain light, she could see an ugly snarl on John Percy's face, and she knew in an instant that he wasn't going to waste another moment playing games.

"Where are they?" he demanded brutally. "Just hand them over and you won't get hurt."

Betsy's whole body shivered, but she stood her ground. "If you think I'm going to let you rob that sweet old man, John, you're mistaken. Those monarch coins mean everything to him!"

"Ha! What does he care? Half the time he doesn't even know they're gone! He's so rich he can't even count his fortune, and he's so old he can't live for too much longer. Do you know what he's going to do with all that wealth?

All those priceless coins and artifacts?'' His low tone was nearly feral. "Give them to a *museum*."

"It's the right place for them, John. They represent a piece of our heritage—"

"Heritage! What about *my* heritage? Don't I have a right to some money, some comfort in my old age?"

"You've got a long way to go till then. Why don't you earn your own wealth?"

"Why should I? My father left me a fortune, but I've been struggling to make ends meet for two years. Is it my fault that the damn horse lost the race? My bookie swore it was a sure thing. I figured I could get my nest egg back with just a few sales from Paul's collection and he'd never even know the difference. So who was I hurting? I smuggled the coins and that stupid cowboy outfit out of his mansion in my fencing bag one night and returned the jerkin the next. The coins hung there innocently for two weeks before he shipped the costumes to Muskingum, and I helped him pack, just to make sure he didn't leave the outfit behind. I knew you wouldn't use it because it wasn't right for a Renaissance costume, and I figured I could 'liberate' it from your house or shop and you'd never notice it was gone. I figured once you let me be a participant it'd be easy. But I never found the damn thing—not at your house, not at your shop, not even in this damned garage on the day of the practice faire!" His tone grew grim with frustration. "But you can be damn well certain I won't leave here without those coins today!"

Slowly he edged closer, his eyes deadly with intent. "Now you've got two choices, Lady Elizabeth," he threatened Betsy, hissing like a serpent. "If you give me the coins without any trouble, I won't have to hurt you. Just remember that if you try to report me, I've carefully laid the groundwork so the blame will fall on you."

"On me?" she croaked. "How could it possibly?"

"Don't you remember? Paul noticed the coins were missing the night you stayed at his house. And where did they finally show up? Among your costumes in Muskingum a month after you gave a George III cartwheel to your boyfriend's son!" His laugh was evil. "Paul's known me for fifteen years. He's known you for less than six months. Whom do you think he'd believe? Especially since I've gone out of my way to get him thinking along those lines as a precautionary measure...."

"What?" Betsy gasped, remembering how cool Gaffer Paul had sounded the last time she'd talked to him on the phone.

"He knows you stayed with him the night he discovered the coins were gone, but he no longer remembers whether they disappeared before or after you arrived. And I called him yesterday to report on the faire, and just happened to mention the fascinating coincidence of Randy's birthday present. He was especially interested, since he remembered that Spence had waxed poetic over the monarch collection when he was in his home."

Betsy was too incensed to be frightened. "Forget it, John! I won't let you get away with this. I'll tell Paul the truth and he'll believe me!"

In a few brief strides, John crossed the room and closed both long-fingered hands around her throat. "Then let's move on to option two, Betsy! Tell me where the damn coins are or I'll make sure you can't utter a sound while I search for them myself!"

Betsy's haughty pride evaporated in the hideous fear that gripped her as his bony fingers tightened and his hot breath whipped her face. She realized in an instant that she had grossly underestimated the idle playboy. He was a killer, not a fool. He'd found an easy meal ticket for the rest of his life, and he wasn't about to let her get in his way. They were in such an isolated part of the school grounds that no one would hear her if she screamed, and with the milling crowds in the other buildings, he could saunter right through the gates and be miles away before anybody even noticed she was missing.

"Dammit, Betsy, this is your last chance!" he snarled, loosening his grip long enough to slap her in the face just as Spence bolted in the door.

The guttural sound that escaped from Spence's throat would have done a samurai warrior proud, and John took it as a genuine death threat. He didn't wait to see what might happen next; in the blink of an eye he whipped his silver saber out of its jewel-covered sheath and lunged straight for Spence.

It was clearly the last form of attack Spence had been expecting, and he had to duck before he could draw his own sword. But Spence was carrying only a lightweight, safety-tipped practice foil, and Betsy knew that even if the two men's fencing skills were evenly matched, their weaponry was not. Against Percy's heavy saber, Spence didn't stand a chance.

When she had watched the two men fight over her before it had been a splendid joke and had made for a great story. But now they were dueling in earnest, and Betsy quaked in terror as she realized that the man who'd once promised her in jest to "bare his chest to another man's sword" might end up doing precisely that.

She reeled in the suffocating heat of the bus garage as John lunged at Spence again and Spence made a defensive parry. The clash of swords made a terrible din that echoed in the sheet metal building, and the decades of dust that coated the cement floor made her gag and clouded her sight. She wanted to cry, to run for help, but the furious male bodies blocked her exit. They'd only exchanged a few angry parries and thrusts, when John drew blood, piercing Spence's right arm near the wrist. Instinctively Betsy screamed as Spence's foil clattered to the floor, and she screamed again a moment later when he lowered his head like a raging bull and charged at John Percy's chest.

SPENCE TOOK A FEW MINUTES to explain everything to Marvin Oates before Betsy insisted that he get some medical help. Actually, hours passed before he'd cooled down enough to realize he was pretty badly cut. He'd already been bleeding before he tackled John, and the silver saber had also sliced his shoulder just an inch from his neck before the other man had gone down.

"Old football ploy," he told Betsy, who wept silently beside him the whole time the doctor dressed his wounds. "Good thing I never lost the knack. Feint for the chest, drop to the knees. I always told you I was a lousy fencer, but I was one hell of a defensive tackle."

A white-faced Randy asked him a dozen times, "You are going to be all right, aren't you, Dad?"

To which he replied, "Of course I am, Son. I just don't get the chance to be a hero very often and I'm milking it for all it's worth."

Randy relaxed a little bit after that, but Betsy started to cry again. Not knowing which of his loved ones was really in worse shape, he ordered, "I want you two to go home together and keep each other company tonight. I'll give you a call in the morning."

Spence wouldn't have let Randy spend the night alone under any circumstances, but he could tell that Betsy was immensely pleased he'd chosen her to be his boy's temporary guardian. Despite the searing pain in his wrist and shoulder, he took comfort from the fact that Betsy would be warming his cold bed tonight...not to mention the fact that before long, he'd be sharing it with her full-time.

Spence knew he wouldn't be well enough to make love to her for a week or two, but the first thing he wanted to do when he got home was cuddle up under the covers with Betsy and just hold her for a good long while.

He had irrevocably decided to marry her, and he wasn't going to waste any more time fussing over technical details. In the first instant he'd realized she was in peril—even before Percy had drawn his sword—his priorities had clicked into place with a resounding snap. Black Gold Supply had meant less than nothing to him, and his pride had simply vanished. He hadn't even been able to recall Tiffany's name. Even the children he hoped one day to share with Betsy had taken their rightful places in the order of things—part of a loving family that belonged together for a lifetime, not pawns in an impending divorce.

Spence was determined to make up for all the misery he'd caused her, but after a friendly nurse gave him Demerol for the pain, he was too drowsy to map out any strategy beyond giving up the premarital contract he'd so cruelly insisted upon. In the morning, he vowed he'd think of something truly spectacular to make Betsy smile again.

He was just drifting off to sleep, when she slipped back into his room, alone, and quietly took his hand. "Spence, can you hear me?" he heard her murmur. When he groggily opened his eyes and squeezed her fingers, she leaned over to kiss his cheek. Her breath was sweet and her scent was soapy-clean Betsy, and he longed to draw her down on the pillow. "They won't let me stay with you very long, Spence, but there's something I want to tell you before I go."

"Mmm?" he mumbled, fighting the pull of drugged sleep.

"Something happened when I saw you bleeding, Spence," Betsy confessed in a raw, aching tone. "Something just ripped inside me."

His eyes fluttered open once more. Despite the twilight of the hospital room, he could see her beautiful blue eyes shining brightly, shining with tears of love for him.

"I still wish you had more faith in me, and I hope someday you will," she murmured gently. "But in the meantime, if the only thing blocking our marriage is that prenuptial agreement—" her voice cracked with emotion "—then I'll sign the damn thing for you."

AFTER A QUIET NIGHT of shared fears and confidences, Betsy and Randy had an early breakfast before Randy took off for school in the Chevy—with his father's permission—and Betsy called Oma to apologize for her earlier accusations and to ask her to take over Ye Olde Fabric Shoppe for a week or more. She had planned to go back to the hospital to pick up Spence, but when they'd talked on the phone in the morning he'd insisted that Janet could drive him home since she'd have to come out to the house with some paperwork anyhow. Before Betsy had been able to dwell too much on the unsavory notion of signing the prenuptial contract, Spence had told her, "There is something special you could do for me, sweetheart, that nobody else can do."

"Name it," she'd promised.

"Go open the nightstand by my bed and dig out that golden box. I'd like to see that ring on your finger when I get home."

It was the easiest favor Betsy had ever done for a man; just the sight of those rubies made her feel as though Spence had really claimed her. He'd already talked to Reverend Egleston about their wedding when the pastor had come to see him in the hospital, and she had even begun to feel welcome in Spence's house, especially since Randy had given her the history of every single person whose photo graced the family picture wall.

Spence and Janet arrived at about ten o'clock, and despite the cheery grin and tender, healing kiss with which Spence greeted Betsy, it was obvious that he was still in pain. Still, he slipped his good arm lovingly around her as Janet trailed them into the house.

"I know you two can keep each other busy while Randy's gone, so I'll be brief," Janet declared, grinning ear to ear as she plucked some papers out of her briefcase. "Spence has already signed these, Betsy, so if you'll just read them over and put your name next to the X on each page, the rest is up to Reverend Egleston."

"I don't think I want to read them," Betsy replied stiffly. "Signing them is bad enough. If what you've written is okay with Spence, then it's okay with me." It wasn't a very warm response, but it was the best Betsy could come up with. Even though Spence had risked his life for her, given her the Renaissance ring and already made wedding plans, she still felt that he'd somehow let her down by insisting she sign the hateful contract. Was it really so much to ask for him to trust her as utterly as she trusted him?

A flash of concern crossed Janet's sweet face. "Betsy, I think you'd feel a lot better if you'd just take a look at these. I went over everything with great care, and I—"

"I'm sure you did, Janet, and I don't mean to sound ungrateful for your time and expertise." She couldn't quite bring herself to meet Spence's eyes as she finished softly, "It's just that if it were up to me, none of this would be necessary."

This time Janet took the documents and pressed them firmly into Betsy's hand. With the determination that she displayed only in emergencies, Spence's sister-in-law declared, "If you'd just read the fine print, Betsy, I think you'd realize that all your dreams have just come true."

Puzzled, Betsy met Janet's eyes and realized that her friend seemed to be laughing at her. Then she sneaked a glance at Spence, who wasn't laughing, but was wearing such a broad smile that she had a sudden vision of him on Christmas morning waiting for a loved one to open a very special gift. He walked around the kitchen table until he was just a few inches away from Betsy, then reached out tenderly to touch her face.

The expression in his kind gray eyes was infinitely loving as he whispered, "Sweetheart, I don't need a premarital contract anymore. All I need is you." He leaned down to kiss her, just once, before he straightened and confessed, "The only thing I still want to negotiate is where we're going to spend our honeymoon."

Betsy stared at him in disbelief. Joy bubbled up from deep in her throat as she burst out, "You're going to take me on trust?"

"I am."

"You believe in me? You don't think I'll destroy your life?"

"Yes, to the first. No, to the second." His happiness eclipsed all other emotions she'd ever seen on his rugged face. "All I'd ask of you is to find a way to forgive me for botching things up so badly the first time I asked you to marry me."

"Oh, Spence!" Betsy was about to throw her arms around his neck, when she realized that she was still holding some very legal-looking documents in her hands and Janet was still waiting by her side. "If you're not making me sign a prenuptial agreement, then what is this?" she questioned, a ghost of suspicion still lurking in her voice.

"It's a gift," Janet informed her, happiness trilling through her voice. "A gift I never imagined I'd see a Spencer man give to *any* woman. Bill never even offered it to me."

This time Betsy had to look at the papers, and when she did her eyes opened wide with shock. *Change of ownership...Black Gold Supply...Betsy Hanover... sole owner...*

"Spence?" His name came out in a hushed, reverent breath because Betsy was too stunned to find her voice. From a financial point of view, she suspected that Black Gold Supply was less of an asset than a liability, but as a statement of faith in the woman Geoffrey Spencer loved, it was worth solid gold. "You're *giving* me your business as a wedding gift?"

Gently he brushed a golden curl away from her cheek with the back of his big, gentle hand. "Not as a wedding gift, sweetheart. Just a gift of love." Tenderness roughened his low tone. "I'm giving you Black Gold Supply whether you marry me or not."

"Oh, Spence!" Betsy cried again, then lost control of her voice altogether as her blue eyes filled with tears. "I can't believe...I never thought..." She tried to find some coherent words to thank him, but her voice trailed off as fresh tears flowed down her cheeks and over his hand.

"It's really quite simple, Bets," Spence said gently, still caressing her wet face. "I wanted to let you know that I would give anything—*anything at all*—for the privilege of having you in my life. And the only thing that means more to me than the business is my precious son. And he's not mine to give."

Still weeping too hard to speak, Betsy dropped the legal papers on the table as she buried her face in Spence's sturdy neck. Silently he drew her closer, rocking her gently as her tears washed away all the pain that had

haunted the two of them for so many months. Betsy had
no idea how long they stood there or how long she cried,
let alone what she promised Spence and what sweet words
he said to her, but when she finally stopped weeping, he
claimed her lips once more before he slowly led her
through his old farmhouse, room by room, asking for her
advice on the ancient furnishings. The place desperately
needed a woman's loving renovation.

It wasn't until he mentioned that Janet had always
wanted to rewallpaper the kitchen that Betsy realized they
hadn't seen hide nor hair of Janet in half an hour. A
quick glance out the window revealed that her red Datsun was no longer parked in front of the house. "Oh,
Spence, we forgot all about her!" Betsy lamented.

But Spence didn't share her consternation. "Oh, I
wouldn't worry about it, Bets," he consoled her as they
reached his old room. Gingerly he eased himself onto the
bed, then pulled Betsy down beside him with his unin-
jured arm. "I suspect that Janet is happy as a clam at the
way things turned out. Besides," he added tenderly as he
drew her closer yet, "I don't think we need a lawyer anymore, do you?"

A sunbeam smile was Betsy's only answer.

Harlequin Superromance

COMING NEXT MONTH

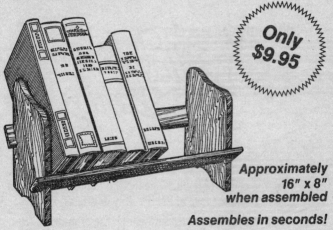

Lynda Ward's

LEAP THE MOON

...the continuing saga of *The Welles Family*

You've already met Elaine Welles, the oldest daughter of powerful tycoon Burton Welles, in Superromance #317, *Race the Sun*. You cheered her on as she threw off the shackles of her heritage and won the love of her life, Ruy de Areias.

Now it's her sister's turn. Jennie Welles is the drop-dead-gorgeous, most rebellious Welles sister, and she's determined to live life her way—and flaunt it in her father's face.

When she meets Griffin Stark, however, she learns there's more to life than glamour and independence. She learns about kindness, compassion and sharing. One nagging question remains: is she good enough for a man like Griffin? Her father certainly doesn't think so....

Leap the Moon...a Harlequin Superromance coming to you in August. Don't miss it!